Royally Abandoned

To Aunt Bunny.

DEDICATION

Kelsey and I have a motto, "A book is better when you have someone to share it with." We believe this is true whether you're an author sharing your work with readers or a reader sharing it with other readers. But now, we've taken this motto a step further. We're sharing this book not only with all of you, but with each other. We're long distance best friends who don't get to see each other all the time. One of the things that keeps us together, other than our obsession with reality tv, is a good book. We read the other's work, we share recommendations when we find a five star read, and we share our thoughts on life. With this book, we'll forever be tied. It's the newest friendship bracelet with the permanence of matching tattoos. So this book is dedicated to Tule Publishing for helping to take our friendship to the next level, and to the readers who finish a great book and can't wait to recommend it to a friend.

CHAPTER ONE

G REYSON CHARLES RUDOLF Leopold Montgomery
climbed nimbly from the Mansard roof, careful not to
disturb the cedar shingles. When his boot-clad feet were back
on solid ground, he wiped his hands on the towel he pulled
from his back pocket. He glanced up at the roof he'd spent
the afternoon repairing and smiled. It would definitely hold
up for the winter, but it would need to be properly rein-
forced before it started raining in spring. Though Greyson
didn't intend to be around that long. He made a note in his
phone to ensure someone came by around March to see
everything right.

"Thank you, Your Highness," the homeowner said, bowing before Greyson, one hand on his cane. "I wasn't sure
what we were going to do. My back just isn't what it used to
be."

"No," Greyson insisted, reaching out to shake the man's
hand. "It is my honor. You have been a resident of my
kingdom for many years, and we are grateful for your loyalty
to us and Aldora. If anything happens to the roof before
February, give this number a call." Greyson released the
man's hand to pull out his wallet. Finding what he was
searching for, he extended a business card with his valet's

phone number. "I trust you won't pass this around?"

The old man gazed at the embossed gold seal—the royal seal—with obvious adoration. "O-of course not, Your Highness. I will take this number to the grave."

"Perfect. Please, don't hesitate to ring if anything comes up, and have a good day."

"Thank you, Your Highness," the man said once again, pocketing the card.

Greyson crossed the yard to the narrow drive, then swung a leg over his motorcycle. Taking one last look at the roof, he slipped his helmet on before pulling the clutch lever and flipping the kill switch. When he turned the key in the ignition, the Brough Superior roared to life.

He took the long way home, surveying the countryside he grew up riding in. Of course, he grew up riding horses, not motorcycles. The hills he sped past now were covered in the last of the fall wildflowers. The vibrant oranges and deep purples created an amazing backdrop when the sun set. He always loved stopping and watching the magic touch the land, but it would be several hours until evening, and he didn't have that kind of time.

Soon, the turrets came into view, the red and gold flags on the peaks whipping with the wind. But instead of approaching the main gates, the one normally crowded with tourists, he rounded the high stone walls until he reached the private family entrance. The guards who flanked the gates bowed as Greyson approached, and the wrought iron swung open to allow him inside the castle grounds.

After he pulled into the open garage, he climbed off his

motorcycle, giving it a pat on its sculpted leather seat. He loved the bike and hated to leave it behind to sit unused and unappreciated in one of the garages. He'd bought it in the marketplace when he snuck out of the castle to avoid another boring Parliament meeting one afternoon. Greyson had worn a disguise—and had definitely been overcharged—but that almost made it better. It was the first purchase he'd made while pretending to be an average man, and it felt good. If he wanted to, Greyson could've just commandeered it and taken it for his own or ordered a top-of-the-line bike be delivered right to him, but that was his family's style, not his.

"Goodbye, old friend." He slid his fingers wistfully over the seat of the bike before heading inside with his head held high. The motorcycle was only the first on his list of farewells.

"Greyson!" His mother's call was high pitched with annoyance, making him cringe as he walked through the foyer. "Where have you been? You were due at the Parliament luncheon *three hours* ago, and your lack of attendance was duly noted."

When he rounded the corner, the toe of her nude Louboutin tapped loudly on the marble floor as she awaited his response. People always remarked on their similarity— tan skin, sculpted cheekbones, and gray eyes—but while he was quick to smile, she always had a perfectly sculpted expression of polite aloofness, which only cracked when she was particularly pleased or angry. At the moment, it was the latter.

"I told you, Mother, I needed to fix the roof I spoke to you about. Remember the man who came before the throne yesterday to submit a complaint about the state a builder left his roof in? Temperatures are dropping, and I couldn't leave his family in that sort of predicament."

"A noble pursuit, but it's not your responsibility," she said, straightening the hem of her purple velvet jacket. "If you felt that strongly, you could have sent someone over there to handle it. I don't understand your obsession with working with your hands and building things. Your palms are going to get blistered and rough, then you'll be forced to wear gloves at all the holiday events."

Greyson rolled his eyes at his mother's dramatics, as he doubted anyone would care what his palms felt like. But he still stuck his hands in his pockets almost automatically. He wasn't ashamed, but he also didn't need his mother to be proven right.

"Mother, I have something I would like to discuss with you and Father. Do you mind accompanying me to his study? He should be done with the luncheon by now, correct?"

"Are you referring to the luncheon you decided to brush off?"

"Yes, that one. Please, the study?" Placing his hand on the middle of his mother's back, Greyson gently pushed her forward.

"Greyson, remove your hand. I am perfectly capable of walking. More so, I do not appreciate your nonchalance about missing such an important event and then demanding an audience."

He tried to brush off the irritation that crept over his skin, making him itch. The feeling was always the same—the hot annoyance building in his chest, overflowing to make him clench his teeth. That was just how it was with his parents. They lived in this enclosed bubble, which left them distant from the world, from people with real problems and feelings. Everything was just protocol, parties, pointless meetings with no resolutions, and the same parade of upper-class patrons. Their life was just…fake.

He dropped his hand, leading the way up the stairs to a set of mahogany doors. Greyson knocked loudly. Howard, his father's butler, opened the door wide enough to slip out before closing it behind himself. "Prince Greyson, Queen Philipa, how may I assist you?"

"Howard, I need to speak with my father immediately."

The butler's gaze slid toward the queen, who remained stonily silent. "Master Greyson, you are aware of how busy your father is at this time. It would have been prudent for you to make an appointment. Unless there is a dire situation, I would be pleased to relay a message to him, if you would like?"

"Yes, actually," Greyson said, taking a deep breath. He'd practiced his words carefully for weeks, repeating them before a mirror until all trace of unease had been washed away. "I'm going to officially abdicate the throne and move to the United States. I have already purchased a plane ticket, and I intend to leave in a matter of hours."

Squawking, his mother crumpled to the floor in a pile of

designer clothes. Howard went to her aid, then began fanning her madly with one gloved hand. He then spoke into the microphone on his headset, "We need medical assistance in the East Wing, outside His Majesty's office. Her Majesty has fainted."

Greyson had to avert his gaze. His mother tended to air on the side of the dramatic. The last time she "fainted" had been when the prime minister's wife suggested they have the summer garden party in an actual garden instead of the summer palace in the ballroom. Screaming and falling over was his mother's go-to move when she didn't want to handle something or wanted additional time to think.

"What's going on here?" Greyson's father asked loudly, emerging from his office. "Oh, Philipa…" He crouched beside her, then gave Greyson a hard glare. His father's steel eyes lost their warmth. It was as if he knew exactly whom to blame for the queen's outburst. "What is the meaning of this?"

"I was trying to have a discussion with you and Mother. Howard stated you were busy, so I decided to relay a message with him in your stead. Mother, as you can tell, did not handle it well."

"Please explain to me what horrible thing you said to upset her."

"I informed her I would be abdicating my throne and leaving for America in a few hours."

The king laughed, a dry sound that certainly didn't have any humor behind it. "You're having a go at us, surely? You cannot mean it?"

"No, this is not the life I imagined for myself. It's not something I ever wanted. Now with you considering stepping down, my timeline is quickly dwindling. I need to make a move before I'm trapped here."

His father's lips formed a tight line, his brow lowering. "Yes, I can see what a horrid life you have here, what with an unending bank account, all your wishes granted with a snap of your entitled fingers, and your perfectly planned life wrapped in a pretty bow. And let's not discuss the pain something like this would cause your family, leaving in such a manner. Look at your mother." His voice rose. The volume jarred the queen, who began to stir.

"You have another son. The family name won't be ending with me."

"You are correct. It will *not* be...because you will *not* be leaving. What would you do? It's not as if you can put princely duties on a resume. And if you think I'm going to allow you to continue to use funds that rightfully belong in this kingdom, then you are mistaken. You will be penniless and alone on your little adventure," his mother snapped.

Greyson straightened his shoulders, trying to hide the sadness flitting through his chest at her words. She thought him incapable of anything more than being a pampered prince. While he wanted to go to America for himself, he also longed to prove to everyone he wasn't a useless figurehead or a soft-handed boy. Even if his parents fought him on it, Greyson needed to prove, at least to himself, there was more to him than the silver spoon in his mouth and the crown on his head. If he didn't, and he just accepted the crown he'd done nothing to earn besides grace the world with his presence, then he'd be another portrait in the throne room as opposed to someone who actually lived. And he wanted nothing more than to feel alive.

"And I will find my way. I've plans, Mother."

It was then the castle medical team arrived, consisting of an emergency medic flanked by two nurses pushing a gurney. But as soon as they appeared beside her, his mother waved them off and allowed Howard to help her up. Gaze flitting from her husband to her son, she leaned heavily against the footman.

"But Greyson, darling," she began, her voice timid and wet. "You cannot leave us. What will…I mean, will you not miss us?"

"I'm not leaving forever. I just am eager to find my own life. The family business is not for me."

"*The family business*, as you call it," his father spat, "has been in this family for seven generations. You have a duty to your ancestors to—"

"No, that is the point, Father. I do *not* have this duty. You placed it upon my shoulders, and I'm now placing it upon Harrison's very capable ones. I *am* leaving." Before Greyson could lose the rest of his carefully curated courage, he turned and began striding toward his chambers.

He heard the hurried sound of heels before his mother grabbed his arm and pulled him to face her. Then she stared pleadingly into his eyes. "Greyson, I cannot allow you to do this. To abandon your country, your duties…your family. No, you shan't."

Her voice cracked, and the unfamiliar sound made his heart lurch. He'd expected some resistance, but not raw emotion. He loved his parents. True, they weren't going to be featured on a magazine for parenting advice, but they'd given him the absolute best of everything. He never thought of it in that way—like he was abandoning them. But seeing how hurt she appeared now, he couldn't help but reconsider. Even is only for a few seconds. He'd be leaving his family for the first time since returning from boarding school. And his mother begging him—it wasn't a queen commanding her subject. Instead, it was a mother imploring her son. Greyson took a ragged breath. Yes, he did love them… and he knew they loved him, so they'd understand eventually.

"If you love me like I know you do, you will want me to be happy. You have to let me leave. I love Aldora, but I want to do well in the world, learn a proper trade, and meet a woman who isn't just after the crown. I need that, Mother."

She opened her mouth and closed it again multiple times, then dropped her arms to her side. "Greyson, such a decision should never be made lightly. What if you…what if you merely leave for now without the finality of abdication? Go on this trip, then we can talk again at Christmas when we've all had time to think. You will be home for the holidays, yes?"

"Yes, Mother, but this is not an instant decision. I have wanted to do this for—"

She lifted her hand, stopping him mid-speech like she often did to courtiers. "Greyson, if you love me like I think you do, you will do this for me. If you are ready to make this decision now, waiting one month should not make a difference. I assure you that your father is not going to step down within that time, so there is no need to worry. Who knows, perhaps you'll find America is not the fabled land of milk and honey you dreamed."

Greyson slowly nodded. He had wanted to make his leaving as easy on his family as possible, but he couldn't ignore the obvious pain marring her face. She was right. One month's time wouldn't sway him, but it might give his family time to adjust to reality. "All right, I will do it for you. But over Christmas, when I don't change my mind, I need you to accept my decision. Is that the deal?"

Her tense shoulders softened slightly. "I appreciate it. But I can't talk to your father about your accounts. He means it when he says he will block your funds."

"I don't need the money. That's the point. I want to live like a normal person."

"But why?"

"Because I want to make my own way, and I need to experience a normal life to make that happen. In the United States, people don't know our family or who I am. I can be invisible."

"Does this have to do with Arielle?" she asked carefully. "Really, I think she would have made a lovely bride. I still cannot believe you ended it. Although, she would certainly take you back if you asked."

Hearing Arielle's name pained him a little, but only because he grieved the time he'd wasted, not her as a person. "I did love her. But she wanted the title of *princess* more than *wife*. If I am to find love, I cannot have the title attached. It weighs me down."

"Will you keep in touch?"

"Of course, Mother."

After he hugged her, he turned and went to his room before he lost his nerve entirely.

AFTER SEVERAL ROUNDS of long goodbyes, Scarlett Calhoun left the Georgia Peach charity luncheon. It was a beautifully organized event, which managed to raise around seventy thousand dollars for relief efforts after the hurricanes. She felt a sense of accomplishment as she climbed into her car to head home, then checked her hair in the rearview mirror. It was still full of body, her recently highlighted strands shining in the sun.

"Scarlett," someone shouted before she stuck her key in the ignition.

Twisting in her seat, she automatically plastered a smile on her face. Mandy, whom Scarlett had known most her life, was headed straight toward her car. "Hey, Mandy. I'm sorry, but I'm about to go. I'm seeing my parents for dinner, and you know how my mama is about tardiness." Scarlett faked a laugh that sounded hollow, even to herself. She'd spent the entire event avoiding Mandy, but now she was trapped.

"Oh, this will only take a moment, sugar." Mandy placed her hands on her hips, then gave Scarlett the same forced smile in return, the one they'd both been taught during debutante classes.

"What can I do for you, Mandy?"

"I just wanted to make sure there were no hard feelings about Reginald," she said, twirling the princess-cut ring with a four-carat diamond on her pale, freckled finger. It kept sending sparks of reflective rainbows into the black leather interior of Scarlett's car. "I didn't mean to do anything or for you to get hurt. The heart just wants what the heart wants, you understand?"

"Of course. You two were clearly meant to be. Now, I need to get going. Have a nice afternoon," Scarlett replied hurriedly, putting her large black sunglasses on. She could feel the ridiculous tears getting ready to fall, and she couldn't give Mandy the satisfaction of seeing how much pain she was in.

"Right, well, we'll talk. I will definitely need your advice on wedding planning."

"Sounds good!" Scarlett threw the car into reverse and peeled out of the parking lot, leaving rubber and her pride behind her.

As she started along the main road, she hit the voice-control button on her steering wheel and said, "Call Betsy." The radio shifted into phone mode, then began dialing.

Scarlett's best friend answered after the second ring. "Miss me already? We just saw each other maybe ten minutes ago."

"You'll never guess what just happened." Scarlett explained about her encounter with Mandy, her throat growing tighter with emotion by the moment.

"Wow, seriously? You know that ring was meant for you,

but that man sure as heck wasn't."

"I know, but I'm glad I don't have to worry about him anymore. He wasn't right for me, and I think I always knew deep down. Really, Mandy did me a favor by taking him off my hands. But if she thinks I'm going to help plan this wedding, then she's delusional."

"We can worry about that later. It's possible she just wanted to see your reaction. It would be a huge scandal if she had you plan it, and no one would respect her for putting you in such a position."

"I hope you're right."

"I always am."

"And one more thing...she called me *sugar*."

"That's the worst! When I first moved here from Pennsylvania and heard that word, I thought it was just a cute little nickname. Now I know better. Mandy is such a witch sometimes."

"She'll get her just desserts with Reginald as a husband."

"You got that right, *sugar*."

By the time Scarlett pulled up the long drive leading to her parent's house, she was feeling much better. Betsy had the ability to always tell it like it was and pull laughter out of even the direst of situations. And what better time to try out Betsy's best friend's skills than when Scarlett's ex-fiancé's *new* fiancée flashed a massive ring in her face? She also understood it wasn't the man she was grieving—it was what could have been that had her stomach tied in knots.

The sun was just beginning to set behind the colonial mansion, painting the white building with streaks of reds and yellows. The tips of the leaves on the trees that lined the drives were dipped in orange, still clinging to their branches. Fall was just beginning to truly settle upon her little piece of Georgia heaven, and there was never a more beautiful place to spend the season's change than the house she grew up in.

She pulled her car beside her mama's white Range Rover, then checked her makeup in the rearview mirror before getting out. If so much as one eyelash were out of place, her mama would know something was amiss and demand a full replay of everything that happened at the luncheon. While unloading drama to her mother was often therapeutic and comforting, Scarlett knew her old-fashioned parent might have some hefty words of wisdom to lay upon her only child…and a terse phone call to bestow upon Reginald's mother.

Scarlett climbed the steps, then opened the front door without bothering to knock. She could smell the sweet scent of the late fall honeysuckles, for which the Honeysuckle Manor was named, wafting toward her from somewhere beyond the front porch, so she paused just a moment before going inside. Hearing her parents chatting, she followed their voices before finding them in the casual sitting room, sitting on an overstuffed green couch her father swore Abraham Lincoln once owned.

It was comforting to know her parents would almost always be there, like they lived in a magic painting, ensuring they'd never change. Her mama was still the lithe, golden-haired debutante she'd been in her youth, a necklace of pearls her constant accessory. Her father had changed a bit over the years, but only to grow rounder as he'd retired and had more time for home cooking and pie for dessert. Still, as far back as Scarlett could remember, he was red-cheeked with bright green eyes and an easy smile beneath a gray mustache.

"Hello, Mama, Daddy," Scarlett greeted them, kissing each on the cheek.

"How was the luncheon, darlin'?" her father asked as he picked up his newspaper.

Scarlett took a seat opposite them, thankful to rest her feet. "Very successful. This contribution will be the Ladies of Savannah's biggest donation this year. I hope we can keep it up for the summer party at the club."

"I'm sure you'll do marvelously, Scarlett," her mama said, rising gracefully. "Come help me in the kitchen? There are just a few things left to do before we eat."

Trying to ignore the way the high heels pinched her toes, Scarlett followed her mama out of the room, down the long hall, and into the massive chef's kitchen. The scent of honeyed ham came from one of the two ovens while the other smelled of biscuits. On the stove were pots of green beans and mashed potatoes while a fresh apple pie sat waiting to be cut for dessert on the marble countertop.

"What can I do?" she asked, taking in the nearly finished meal.

Her mother passed over a pair of oven mitts. "Just help me plate. Start with the rolls, please."

Scarlett slipped the mitts on before slowly opening the oven door. She carefully slid the tray from its rack, then turned off the appliance. The flakey golden-brown biscuits were done to perfection, and she wondered how her mother always managed to time things exactly right without ever using a timer.

When the bowls and plates were filled, they transported everything through the double wooden doors to the dining room. The many inserts had been taken out of the cherry-wood table, leaving it small enough to comfortably sit their family of three. Her father was already at his place at the head, a glass of sweet tea by his side.

Scarlett sat and waited silently as her mother carved the ham. After serving Scarlett's father a bit of everything, her mother filled her own plate before motioning for Scarlett to begin. She had eaten so much at the luncheon, enough to be polite but not gluttonous, but if she didn't take a healthy helping of everything before her, she would be given a stern talking to about rudeness before a hostess.

While eating, they carried on a polite and steady conversation consisting of all the safe and proper topics. They spoke of the upcoming harvest festival and what baked goods the Ladies of Savannah would donate. Then they listed all the families that would receive the official Calhoun Christmas card. By the time they began to discuss white or cream linins for their annual Christmas cookie baking party over plates of apple pie, Scarlett just wanted to go home and sleep off all the food.

She adored her parents beyond measure, but all she longed to do was return to her cozy apartment, wash off her makeup, get into her favorite pajamas, and cuddle up with her dog, Blitzen. Being at dinner with her family meant she was constantly at attention. Normally, she wouldn't mind a few hours of sitting straight and keeping her bites small and tidy, but after an afternoon running away from Mandy and rubbing elbows with the other women who were just like Scarlett's tight-laced mama, she was bone tired.

"Are we boring you, Scarlett?" her mama asked, breaking her from her reverie.

She blinked and took her napkin from her lap, placing it on the table beside her plate. "No, I'm sorry. I'm just feeling a bit worn out from this afternoon."

"Do you need to lie down, darlin'?" Her father looked to her with concern as her mother poured more sweet tea into his crystal decanter.

"I think I should just head home."

Her mother frowned. "Now, if you're feeling ill, you shouldn't drive. I'll have the maid change the sheets in your bedroom."

"Now, now, Delia," her father began, patting her hand. "I'm sure it's not all bad."

"Well, all right. Call us when you get home so we know you've arrived safely. Although you wouldn't have to worry us to death if you just stayed home with us."

Her mother had said that last part in a whisper. They hadn't liked the idea of Scarlett living on her own after college, but when she had her own inheritance to pay her bills, there was little they could do to keep her in the nest. Still, it was a sore spot for her mother in particular, who firmly believed children should stay at home until they were married, not live by themselves a disastrously long ten-minute drive away.

The night was cool when Scarlett stepped outside, and she basked in the sounds of the evening. All was silent on her parent's estate, save the gentle rustle of leaves in the wind and the ever-present concert of crickets. If she could, she would have stood there forever, soaking in the scent of the honeysuckles and reveling in the light from the moon. But she needed to get away from the old manor home and back to her own world, where no one cared if her hair was out of place.

CHAPTER TWO

G REYSON STRETCHED, TWISTING his back from side to side to loosen out the kinks. He had a long day, and his muscles would remind him of it for hours to come. He wiped the sawdust from his safety glasses as the workers slowly trickled from the lot. The shift had just ended, but Greyson hated to leave. Although his muscles ached, it was nice to be useful…and to be able to pay his bills.

In the week since landing at the Savannah-Hilton Head Airport, things had gone surprisingly according to plan. Using the last of his pocket money, which most would classify as a month's wages, he had purchased a beat-up Ford pickup truck and put a deposit on a tiny, fully furnished flat over a bakery. While there wasn't much left after that, there had been a flyer asking for construction workers taped to the window in the bakery and he'd thanked his lucky stars.

He took it as a sign he'd made the right move, and he'd had a job within moments of stepping into the foreman's trailer at the building site. The nice thing about the construction job was the foreman apparently never did background checks or cared if prospective employees had a work permit. As long as a person could hold a hammer and didn't fall off the roofs, they were good to go.

Part of Greyson wished he could call his mother to tell her he'd made it safe and sound with a job and a flat all his own. She thought he had moved without a single plan in his educated brain to make sure he survived, but she was unaware of the meticulous organization that had gone in to his smooth transition from prince to construction worker. He'd sorted a work visa—using diplomatic ties to keep the royal seal from being affixed—and had an international driver's license. He wasn't stupid and soon, when he could formally say he had made a life for himself, he would show his family. There was just one thing missing from his American dream.

Although he could've worked for hours still, the light was fading and a recipe he wanted to try called his name. One thing he hadn't anticipated about living on his own was the amount of cooking that needed to be done. Without a staff to prepare him the elaborate dinners and the simplest cups of tea, he was lost and alone with nothing but a secondhand cookbook to show him the way. So far, it had been a week of burnt chicken and overcooked vegetables.

Greyson waved at the foreman as he passed him on the way to the dirt lot he'd parked his truck in. He climbed inside, then slammed the door shut before turning the key. It was no royal Rolls Royce, but it was all his.

To get home, he had to travel a long country road that skirted the city and almost reminded him of Aldora. The green hills and black starry sky lacked the rugged, untouched nature of his kingdom—well, his brother's future kingdom—but it was still beautiful. Greyson could drive the whole way with the radio on and the windows rolled down to let the fresh air wash off the scent of gasoline, tar, and wood from the build site.

He was rounding a sharp corner when he saw headlights coming straight at him in his lane. Greyson slammed his foot on the brakes, one hand groping for the emergency stopper that didn't exist in a truck as old as his. But just as he braced for the vehicles to collide, he managed to pull his to an abrupt halt just as the other driver did the same.

The car—a topless, red convertible—sat half off the road. When he couldn't see any movement within, he almost feared the worst. If the airbags hadn't deployed, the driver certainly could have seriously hurt themselves. He had to see if they were okay.

He hopped out of the truck, half wanting to yell at the person for driving in his lane, when he realized something. Instead of being in the right lane, the way Americans drove, he had been in the left, like in his country. He'd been so wrapped up in thinking about home, he had reverted to his old way of driving on the left-hand side. Not believing he could have been so stupid, he prayed the driver wasn't hurt.

As he reached the car, he spotted a lone woman within, lit by his headlights. Her gently curled blond hair was swept messily over her eyes, her red-lipped mouth forming a perfect O of shock. She squeezed the steering wheel so tightly her knuckles were white.

"Miss, are you all right? Are you injured?" he asked when he reached the driver's side door.

The woman pushed her hair from her pale face, her blue eyes large and luminous. "I-I'm okay. Are you?"

He paused a moment before replying. She was beautiful, and her gaze nearly took the breath from his lungs. It felt as if she had robbed him of the power of speech. "Perfectly," he rasped, clearing his throat.

"I hope the car's all right," she said as she opened the door. She stepped onto the grass in her bare feet, then carefully picked her way to the hood. "Thank goodness, not a scratch. How's yours?"

"It doesn't matter. I must apologize for my driving. I'm actually an incredibly good driver, but it seems the habit of being in the left lane hasn't formally left me yet."

A slow smile curved her full lips. "Wow, what an amazing accent. Where are you from? I can't place it."

"Near Liverpool in the United Kingdom."

Greyson's answer wasn't a lie, exactly, as the small island nation of Aldora *was* close to Liverpool. In fact, it was a mere three hours away by boat. He had told everyone he encountered the same thing, and no one asked for more specifics than that. Apparently, no one he knew in America cared where he was from as long as he was a good construction worker and tenant.

"How long have you been in Savannah?"

"A week. I'm Greyson." He held out a hand, hoping she didn't press for a last name.

She warmly accepted the gesture. "Scarlett. Will you be in town long, Greyson?"

"I will as long as I don't run anyone else off the road."

Scarlett laughed. It was a tinkling, musical sound that immediately put him at ease. "You should try to keep from doing that. If you're okay, I should get going."

"I am, so continue with your evening. I again offer my sincere apologies for my negligence."

"Don't worry about. Just be careful, especially in these hairpin turns. They can be dangerous, even when you're on the right side of the road."

He watched as she climbed behind the wheel of her car and gave him a cheery wave. As she sped off, he returned to his truck, finding he couldn't get his mind off the barefoot blonde.

THE MORNING AFTER the near miss, Scarlett dressed in her workout clothes and prepared to take Blitzen for a nice trip to their favorite dog park. There was nothing Blitzen liked more than exercise, and Scarlett did her best thinking while strolling the streets of her historic hometown. She took the same route as when she'd found him two years before on a bitter Christmas Eve night. Every time she passed the street where the tiny puppy shivered in the cold, she still checked it, just in case.

She had a lot on her mind lately, most centering on the loss of the life she'd almost had. When Reginald dumped her the year before, she'd been devastated. But when she thought about their relationship, she couldn't help but feel she'd been in love with the idea of love instead of Reggie. True, he'd seemed like the doting boyfriend, but there was never the inexplicable connection or the chemistry the movies and books portrayed. Maybe he'd felt the same—hence the

Mandy situation. Still, it stung. Time did heal all wounds, and with that chapter of Scarlett's life seemingly closed, she felt like she was ready to rebuild her life into one she would love to live. Without the pressure to hold a grand wedding and be a prim and proper hostess for one of the South's most prestigious families hanging over her like a storm cloud, she had somehow become free. But with the loss of her pre-determined identity, she felt a little adrift.

Her life to that point had been just as her parents planned. Scarlett had grown up with horseback riding lessons and debutante balls. She'd dined with old-money million-aires while spending her weekends at the club. Once she'd graduated high school, she'd attended Duke like her parents had, and majored in English literature with a minor in art, which was the perfect combination for a young lady.

But she could feel the change in the air. It was like the sight of the heirloom ring on Mandy's finger had severed Scarlett's last ties to the past, giving her the strength to wash her hands and move on. She was only twenty-four with the world at her fingertips. If she wanted, she could open the bed and breakfast she'd dreamed of, travel to Africa with a nonprofit and dig wells, or return to school for something like accounting or physical therapy.

Scarlett was still considering her options, daydreaming about where her life could go, when they got to the dog park. It was busy, with a handful of dogs tearing around the fenced-in area. Blitz began pulling at his leash to be set free. She bent to unhook it, letting him loose. But just as she did, she accidentally unfastened his tag from his collar. It fell to the ground as he ran toward his playmates.

She was so preoccupied with searching for the small metal loop that anchored the tag, she hadn't realized she'd forgotten to close the gate behind her. She only noticed when Blitz dashed past her in a flash of golden fur. He leapt joyfully down the sidewalk, apparently thrilled with the scenery and freedom.

"Blitz, come back here!" she called, beginning to hurry in his direction. He was usually so good with commands, but not that day. He just peeked at her before continuing his frolicking at a much faster rate.

Feeling felt her stomach drop, Scarlett broke into a run. Savannah wasn't some small sleepy town. The roads were busy, and she didn't trust the dog would stay out of harm's way. "Blitz, come back. Here, boy!"

She followed him down the street as fast as she could manage, but she was no match for the dog. He led her down alleyways, through private yards, and then lost her after she sprinted around the corner of a brick building and couldn't spot him. The road was devoid of cars, for which she was thankful, but it was also empty of a certain dog.

"Blitzen," she yelled, using his full name to show she was no longer playing games. She meant business. Scarlett continued to run as she searched, holding a hand against the stich in her side. "Blitzen, you get back here right now!"

Passing a small deli, she scanned a messy construction site across the street. She spied Blitz, slowing to change her direction to the dog's. He was sitting obediently beside a man in a hardhat and orange safety vest. She was going to call out to the dog, but she feared he'd run again. So instead, she settled into a walk and tried to catch her breath as she approached.

"Blitz, you can't do that," Scarlett chastised as she bent to hug the dog. While he was preoccupied with happily greeting her, she securely clipped the leash on and looped it round her wrist so he couldn't escape. Scarlett took a few relieved inhales, trying to catch her breath. Apparently, the occasional yoga class was not enough exercise to keep up with Blitz.

"He probably just smelled the bakery's biscuits. You can't blame the dog," the construction worker said, his British accent rolling over the words. "I had a few this morning myself."

Scarlett focused on the man's face. When the brim of his hat lifted, she let out an audible gasp. The man from the near-crash stood before her, dark hair hidden by a yellow construction helmet. He wore a plain white t-shirt and jeans with a tool belt around his hips. She hadn't thought she'd ever see him again, but there he was. If possible, he was even handsomer in the daylight. Blitz wasn't just a good couch companion, but he was also great at finding men as well. She made a mental note to get the dog a biscuit—well, after they had a long talk about running away.

"Oh, Greyson, right? I'm so sorry. I hope Blitz wasn't bothering you. He's usually such a good boy. I don't know what came over him."

"Well, maybe I should buy him some biscuits to thank him for allowing me the honor of crossing paths with you again."

Smiling with one brow raised, Scarlett flipped her ponytail. "That was a nice line, I must admit. But not quite enough to make me swoon."

"Ah, then I must try again. How about you let me buy you dinner? I'm afraid I don't know any good places in this area and my cooking skills…well, let's just say I wouldn't even feed my meals to your dog."

Scarlett gazed at her dog, resisting the urge to inform the man Blitz ate a strictly organic diet she made herself every Sunday night using the best ingredients from the farmer's market. Resisting, she focused on Greyson, impressed by his deep gray eyes, the slight scruff on his chin, and the warmth in his smile. She'd never dated outside of her family's circle. But where had that left her? None of her relationships had worked out, and maybe it meant she needed to expand her dating pool.

"Did you say his name was Blitz?" Greyson asked.

"Blitzen."

"What a unique name for a dog."

"Unique one for a reindeer, too. But I found him a few Christmases ago, so he needed a name to fit the holiday."

"Perhaps you should've named him Dasher or Comet, seeing how fast he is."

Giggling, she shook her head. "Nope, not my Blitz. Those names are too ordinary, and he's anything but." He laughed, too, and she liked the sound. It was honest and full of heart. "Do you like barbeque?"

He grinned, one dimple showing on his work-tanned

face. "Can't say I've had the pleasure of having real American barbeque yet."

"*Hartman's* has some of the best barbeque in the area, and it's just down the street."

"So now there's a place, but will there be company?"

"I guess you'll have to show up around seven to find out." Scarlett winked, then gave him a small wave as she swiveled, holding the leash tightly. Leaning down at bit as she walked to ruffle her dog's fur, she whispered, "Good dog."

SCARLETT STOOD IN her walk-in closet, skimming her fingers across the rows of color-coordinated outfits. Her cell phone was wedged between her shoulder and ear as she spoke with Betsy, careful not to muss the hot rollers in her hair.

"The construction worker who almost ran you off the road? While I think it's great you want to expand your horizons, you should consider wearing a helmet and knee pads," Betsy joked.

"Hey, I'm ready to mix it up here. Why not? Besides, we're going to Hartman's. The owners have known me since I was, like, three. If he turns out to be Jack the Ripper's great-great-great grandson, then they'll be there to take care of me."

"Yeah, and as soon as you show up with a man, Mrs. Hartman is going to call your mama and tattle about you dating outside the fold."

Scarlett's stomach dropped, and she collapsed on the seat

of her dressing table. "Oh, no. I didn't even think about that."

"Just call him and change the location."

"I would if I had his number."

"Why didn't you ask for it?"

"I was trying to be mysterious. You know… like, he'll show up to see if I'm there, then have to wait and wonder whether I'm coming. I'll stroll up ten minutes late—make this grand entrance with the wind blowing my hair perfectly around I saunter gracefully in dressed in the flowy pink dress I wore to the Spring Fling last year."

"Yeah, that's a good dress, but it's time to return to the real world. If I were you, I would be careful tonight. Your parents are going to want to know all about this man."

Scarlett took a deep breath, squaring her shoulders. "You know what, who cares? I live alone, my inheritance came from my grandmama so they can't threaten to cut me off anymore, and I have my own functions to attend they have no hand in. I don't need to follow their rules all the time. And you know what else? The construction worker is gorgeous, he has a British accent, and Blitz likes him."

"Well, Blitz has always been a good judge of character. Didn't he growl at Reggie that one time you ran into him during a walk?"

"Yes, he did. Thinking about it now, the whole thing was fantastic. But it's time I take control of my life, and this date with Greyson is the first step. Tonight's going to be amazing."

GREYSON WASN'T EXACTLY starting over with nothing like he said he would. He'd packed brought some of his finer clothes carefully in his three monogrammed suitcases. As he slid his Prada leather belt into his Armani trousers, he stood in front of the mirror to see the effect. But he couldn't focus on his clothes when all he saw was his old life.

He appeared as if he were planning to traipse through the halls of his castle instead of getting a casual bite to eat with a girl. Greyson wanted Scarlett to see he'd put effort into his appearance, but wouldn't she be suspicious how a construction worker could afford designer clothes? Her high-end convertible and genuine pearl necklace suggested she was used to the finer things in life, so she would definitely notice his brand-name accessories. And he didn't want a girl who wanted him for money or status. He'd made that mistake once before, and he didn't want to do it again.

Greyson checked the time on his mobile, making his decision. He left his flat and locked the door behind him, spinning his truck keys around his finger as he took the stairs to the street two at a time. He would go to the secondhand shop beside the grocery store to buy a full outfit from shirt to shoes, then change in his car before heading to the restaurant garbed as a perfectly average man. If Scarlett didn't like him for the man he was trying to become, then hopefully he'd at least get some good barbeque out of the ordeal.

Once at the store, he quickly realized he had no idea how to shop on his own. The stores he'd frequented in his old life, someone waited on him, giving him perfectly tailored options he'd rarely needed to try on. Flipping through the pants, he realized he didn't even know what size he wore. He grabbed several pairs in varying shades of blue, three white shirts, and four belts to try.

After leaving the dressing room, he took another trip to the racks to grab a few in his newly discovered size. He grabbed three colors he liked and two pairs of shoes, but then he noted the prices. He'd been paid from his construction job the day before, but he needed to make it and his remaining pocket money last. The fancy dinner would probably cost the same as the clothing total. So Greyson returned the surplus to the rack and bought only what he needed, figuring if he required additional items, he could get more on future trips. Luckily, no one at the construction site cared where he got his jeans or even noticed the Burberry tags.

When Greyson got to the restaurant and checked the clock on his dash, he grimaced. He was fifteen minutes late. Muttering under his breath, he quickly parked, half-running to the front doors. Scarlett was sitting on the bench just inside the restaurant. From the expression on her face—the scowl, the pursed lips, the knitted brow—it was apparent she was not happy, nor impressed. Maybe he just should've worn the nice clothes.

"Scarlett, I'm so sorry," he began, trying to flash his most charming smile. "I got held up. I'm hardly ever tardy anywhere. Really, would you like me to show you my school certificates? You'll see, zero tardies."

The corners of her mouth lifted slightly. "Well, what now? Are they going to take your certificates away if I tell them you've been late?"

"They might. Please allow me to show you a charming night to make it up to you. If you're still feeling slighted after dessert, then I will dial the number to the proper authorities and turn myself in."

"I guess that's fair. I reserved us a table, but they won't seat you until your full party is here. So, we're good now."

As they walked to the hostess stand, Greyson took a moment to truly study Scarlett. The pink dress she wore played up her feminine side. It matched her tanned skin perfectly, her curled hair bouncing delicately on her shoulders the perfect complement. She was beautiful. And she'd given him a chance, despite his poor behavior. He made a promise then and there to make sure she didn't regret it.

SCARLETT WAS MIFFED, although she tried not to show it. She'd shown up fashionably late—a full ten minutes—and Greyson had been nowhere to be found. True, if something important had delayed him, he'd had no way to reach her, but that wasn't the point. He'd missed her grand entrance. And instead of a perfect hair flip, she'd had to wait on him on a bench. But she figured what was good for the goose was good for the gander, so she couldn't truly be angry when she had been late on purpose.

But sitting across from him in the restaurant, watching him talk about woodworking and how it was his passion, Scarlett couldn't keep the frustration in her heart. Instead, something else was beginning to take over. She couldn't quite place the feeling, but she knew it to be a mix of admiration and a warmth she couldn't ignore.

"So, construction is just a way to pay the bills right now?" she asked as the waiter delivered their first course of the house salad.

"You could say that. In my flat, I have a spare room I hope to use as my workshop whenever I have free time."

"What are you going to build?"

"Back home, I made bureaus, bookshelves, tables… Made a rocking chair once, although it's much harder than it looks. When my cousin was pregnant, I even made her a crib."

"A crib, wow." Scarlett's insides melted. Flashes of a homemade crib and matching rocking chair came into her mind as she imagined herself in the scene soothing her own baby. *Their* baby—with his gray eyes, her curly blonde hair, his dimple, and her button nose. Then her brows shot sky high. *Whoa.* Talk about a big jump. She needed to get a hold of herself before she started picking out china patterns just because a guy with dreamy gray eyes showed his soft side. "Um, could you excuse me for a moment? I need to visit the powder room."

Scarlett didn't wait for his answer. She grabbed her purse, jumped up, and hurried to the bathroom. When the door was locked behind her, she stared at her reflection in the mirror. "Get a grip. You just met this guy." Scarlett retrieved her compact from her purse, then lightly dabbed her nose with the pad. "Remember, this is just a regular guy. Go back out there and act normal. This is only the third time you've seen him. Yes, his good looks belong on a runway, his hands show his passion for woodwork isn't just fluff, and his eyes shine in the candlelight like in cheesy movies, but that's no reason to get all crazy." She nodded her head, fluffed her hair, then snapped her compact closed. "Let's do this."

Scarlett smiled when she saw Greyson. Unlike other men she'd dated, he hadn't jumped on his phone the moment she left. Chin in hand, he gazed out the window nearest to their table. He seemed content to just be, to enjoy what was before him. Her bathroom pep talk flew out of her head. True, she wasn't planning a June wedding, but she couldn't keep herself from feeling a little giddy in his presence. All those finishing classes and debutante training pushed to the wayside, Scarlett was just a regular girl out with a regular guy she was beginning to like.

"So, I've told you my passions," he said a little later as he pushed his half-finished salad away. "What's yours?"

"It probably sounds silly to you. I mean, I haven't done anything to try to make it come true…it's just a dream I have. I don't even know if it's going to happen."

"Well, out with it. What is it?"

"I want to open my own bed and breakfast," she admitted. "I just love the idea of making a cozy place for people to stay at while enjoying Savannah. And I don't want to just buy one—I want to manage it and work to make it my own. Like, take away all the coldness of the chain hotels to create an environment I build from scratch. Just a beautiful place filled with hospitality and warmth." She peeked from under her lashes to see if he was laughing. Instead, he was smiling. "What?"

"To be honest, I'm impressed."

"How so?"

"You strike me as a…uh, what's the term people around here use? Ah, yes…*Southern belle*. You clearly have means to do whatever you wish, yet you want to spend your time catering to people?"

"Southern belles spend most of their time catering to people," she said, trying to contain her laughter. "But I see your point. I was raised with a silver spoon. But I think it's what would make me a great inn owner. I know how to set a beautiful table, twenty ways to fold napkins, how to make up the most beautiful bed you've ever seen, and how to be sweet and polite when someone is upset. I was raised to do this. And I love the idea of owning my own business. I don't have to listen to anyone or follow anyone's instructions. That's the downside to Southern belles. We are made to play by someone else's rules from birth."

"I can't tell you how much I relate. I turned down the family business to follow my dreams for the same reasons. I just want to make my own way. I love that you do, too."

"What's your family's business?"

"Politics," he answered after a short pause, a knit appearing in his brow. "My family works in Parliament. They wanted me to go into it as well, but it's not who I am. So I left and came here to start fresh." He shrugged, lowering his head, and she thought she saw something flit across his face. But as quick as it flashed, it was gone just as fast. He straightened, flashing a weak smile Scarlett puzzled over. There was something bothering him there, but she didn't want to pry.

"I'm glad you did." Scarlett took a sip of her water. The more she got to know him, the more she liked him. He seemed to understand her on this instant level she hadn't thought possible. "You're the first person I've told about my dream of owning a bed and breakfast. Well, besides my best friend Betsy. But that doesn't count. I tell her everything."

"Why did you tell me, then?"

"It felt right… I don't know."

"No, I get it. It does feel right," Greyson said. When he reached his hand out to take hers, the spark from his touch was like fireworks. The fuse started to burn at the tips of her red nails and seared up her arm to explode in a glorious display in her chest.

The rest of the meal passed seamlessly with her growing more comfortable by the moment. Greyson had an openness about him. It made her want to tell him all her hidden secrets. There was something about his gray gaze that invited her to keep talking. As they finished their main meals of pulled pork sandwich for him and brisket for her, she felt a bit melancholy knowing their date was nearing an end.

"I can't believe I've been here for weeks and haven't had real BBQ yet."

"Does that mean you liked it?" she asked, hoping he would say yes. If he didn't, she'd have to reevaluate a second date, which would be a real shame. She wanted to see him again, but rejecting the very food that ran through her family's veins might just be a deal breaker for another date. If he asked her, anyway.

"Liked it? It was awesome. Did I say it right? You Americans sure like to say 'awesome.'"

"We do. And yes, you said it right." She had to bite her tongue to stop herself from adding *'you've said everything right'*. That'd be creepy. No, she was not chasing this man off. Again, she reminded herself to keep it together.

When it came time for dessert, Scarlett ordered for them both. Hartman's peach crumble was to die for, and since it was Greyson's first time having real Southern barbeque, she couldn't let him miss out on the last Georgia peaches of the season.

But instead of the waitress delivering it, Mrs. Hartman appeared beside their table, plates in hand. Her small eyes scanned Scarlett and Greyson in the casual way only a Southern woman could, taking meticulous mental notes for gossip fodder.

"Hello, Scarlett." Mrs. Hartman pronounced Scarlett's name the traditional way—*Scah*-lett—in her polished drawl as she placed the crumble before them. "Who is your...*friend?*"

"Mrs. Hartman, this is Greyson. Greyson, this is Mrs. Hartman, the owner of this restaurant." Scarlett was careful to keep her voice smooth and neutral to hide her horror at her earlier fears coming true.

Greyson stood and shook Mrs. Hartman's hand. "Lovely to meet you. I'm so pleased my introduction to Southern culinary hospitality was in your restaurant."

"The pleasure is mine." Mrs. Hartman turned to Scarlett. "And how's your mama, darlin'?"

"Very well, thank you. She hopes she'll see you at the Jackson's anniversary party next week," Scarlett politely answered.

"Tell her I'll be there, and I'll return her Bundt pan." Mrs. Hartman's gaze shot to Greyson again, who had sat and was respectfully paying attention. "Have a lovely evenin', darlin'. Enjoy the crumble."

Scarlett held her breath until Mrs. Hartman disappeared into the rear of the restaurant. The old gossip was probably already on the phone with Scarlett's mama, and she sent up a thankful prayer she'd remembered to put her cell on silent. As soon as her mother heard Scarlett was having dinner with a man, the frantic calls and never-ending questions would begin.

Scarlett tried to ignore the annoying little voice in the back of her mind that kept reminding her the date was almost at an end. Instead, she decided to focus on the last few moments together. She listened as he raved about the peach crumble, reached for her purse when the check came, then thanked him as he paid the bill. His wallet had the familiar Burberry print, and she thought it almost odd someone wearing an off-brand button-down would own such a high-end accessory.

"I had a nice time," she said after they exited. He insisted on walking her around the building to the lot, saying no woman should be out alone late at night. But she had the sneaking suspicion he didn't want the date to end either, since he lingered even after they stopped at his car.

"So did I. Perhaps we could do it again some time?"

"I'd like that."

"Could I have your number? I could ring you."

She reached into her purse, unclasped her holder, and pulled out a beautifully scripted card. It had her full name, email address, and phone number printed on it. While she didn't have an actual business, she always carried the cards with her. They were more of a calling card—so her contact details were ready whenever she met a potential donor to one of the charities she helped, or when handsome British construction workers asked her for a second date.

He glanced at the card before slipping it into his back pocket. "Goodnight, Scarlett."

"Goodnight, Greyson."

She wondered if he would kiss her then, or if he would leave her to drive off and wonder when his call would come. But to her surprise and immense pleasure, he lifted her hand and pressed his lips to her knuckles like a Disney prince. Then he opened her car door and helped her inside, leaving her with a simple, "Drive safely."

She kept her exterior a carefully polished veneer until she waved him to his own vehicle. Then she allowed herself a moment of pure, blissful excitement that felt like a thousand bubbles all floating to the surface of her skin. She hadn't felt that kind of spark before. When she'd met her ex and he'd shown interest in her, it'd been her mission to impress him and win his affections. Almost like a challenge. But with Greyson, it was different. *He* was different. Her hand still tingled from his kiss, and her heart was beginning to soar. She wasn't hopeful of a good match to set up her future, only for another date with a man who didn't care about their societal obligations.

Greyson actually listened, but he didn't care about her resume. He didn't ask which of her grandparents came over on the Mayflower or what her thoughts on the current stock market was, although if he had, she had quite a few on the rise of gold. He was happy to let her go on about her passions. Her real passions. Not the ones she told at dinner parties to further polite conversations. This kind of connection—in a world where bloodlines and family connections were held higher than love—wasn't just rare but almost unheard of. And that was what set her heart on fire.

After she shook her hands to refocus her energy, she turned on the car and headed out of the parking lot. It wasn't too late, so she used voice commands to call Betsy. Scarlett needed to tell her all about her first real date.

CHAPTER THREE

T HE NEXT MORNING, Greyson knew he had dodged his mother's calls long enough. He wanted to be a bit more settled before contacting her, but the voice mails she left were growing increasingly more frantic. Even though he didn't feel ready to share everything that had happened in the two weeks since he'd left Aldora, he didn't want to hurt her.

"Goodness, Greyson, where on earth have you been?" she cried when he answered.

"I'm sorry. I didn't want to call at an inopportune time and disturb you. The time difference…"

"And that's why you decided to ignore my calls?"

Sighing, he sprawled on the couch in a pose sure to have caused his mother to reprimand him for being improper and far too common for a prince had he been home. "You're right I apologize. How are things at home?"

"Your father's still in a state, Harrison has been attending all functions in your place—and making a mess of things, I might add—and I've been beside myself wondering what's become of my eldest son."

"I've settled into Savannah, Georgia quite nicely," he began, trying to keep things light. "I have a job doing construction for a reputable company."

"Construction?" She said the word like it was something filthy.

"Yes, Mother, construction."

"And you enjoy this?" she asked in a tone that made it sound as if she'd just enquired if he enjoyed eating slugs.

"I do. It's nice to feel needed and useful."

"You're needed here. Have you given any more thought to...to returning home and taking your rightful place as crowned prince?"

He groaned, dropping his head to the back of the couch to stare at the ceiling. "Must we discuss this? I thought we agreed to wait to speak at length about it at Christmas."

"You're right, you're right. Then tell me more about your life."

"I've rented my own flat, and I even went on a date last night." He waited for her to respond, but the other end was silent. "Hello? Are you there?"

"I'm here," she murmured. "You've met a girl there in America?"

A smile crept over Greyson's face. Just thinking about Scarlett was enough to send him into that delicious flurry he always experienced when her name came to mind. "Yes, I have. Her name's Scarlett, and we went out to dinner."

"And you'll be seeing her again?"

"I hope so."

"And you're...you're happy?" His mother's voice had grown weepy, and she sniffed a bit. "You're happy now...away from us?"

"It isn't like that. And I won't be away forever. You'll see me for Christmas."

"Do you promise?"

"Of course. I'll be there. I'll even let you choose what I wear to the Christmas ball. We can sit as a family to have a proper holiday."

"I'd like that." She cleared her throat, seeming to compose herself. "But I must go. The minister of health's wife is coming for tea, and the staff has just informed me that we're out of clotted cream."

And just like that, his mother had made the transformation from worried parent to composed queen. "Go tend to your emergency. I'll ring you soon," he quickly said.

"Ta, Greyson."

The mobile clicked, and he heaved a sigh of relief. He hated feeling as if his parents were disappointed in him, although it couldn't be avoided. But since the first difficult activity of the day was finished, he could prepare for the hardest—the call he would soon make to Scarlett.

SCARLETT HAD BEEN dodging her mother's call all day. Wanting to get the inevitable conversation over with, Scarlett settled on the couch with a cup of coffee and answered on the third ring.

"Hey, Mama."

"Hello, Scarlett. How's your Saturday?"

"It's nice and quiet. Yours?"

"Well, I just had the nicest conversation with Mrs.

Hartman."

Scarlett stifled a groan of annoyance. "Oh, I saw her last night. She told me to tell you she'll bring your Bundt pan to the Jackson's."

"Yes, so she said. And did you have a nice dinner there?"

"I know what you're calling about."

"Whatever do you mean?"

Rolling her eyes, Scarlett sipped her coffee before she answered. "I know you called to talk about my date. He's a very nice man named Greyson."

"And what's his last name?"

Scarlett opened her mouth, but then snapped it shut. That was a good question. "Well, you know, it was only our first date, so there's no need to start considering his pedigree and monogramming towels." Yes, she had three possible names for their future children, but she wouldn't be sharing those just yet. Maybe she should wait for a phone call or something from Greyson first.

"Greyson…Greyson…what do his parents do? Don't the Thompsons have a son named Greyson? Tall boy with glasses who works at a startup in California?"

"He's not from around here, so don't start playing Sherlock Holmes. He just moved to Savannah from England."

Her mother gasped, and Scarlett could almost hear her clutch her pearls. "*England*? You mean he's not a *Southerner*?"

"No, he's not."

"Then what does he do for a living?"

Scarlett bit her lip. While working a physical job was

nothing to be ashamed of, she didn't feel like listening to her mother rip him apart. "That doesn't matter right now. I only just met him."

"Doesn't matter? Scarlett, really, what a thing to say. Surely you'll bring him by soon so your daddy and I can meet him?"

"I hardly know him, and I can't just spring my parents on him first thing." Scarlett had never actually brought a man home to *meet* her parents. All her former boyfriends knew them, so the family dinner was more of a formality. Greyson would be introduced to them for the first time, and the thought terrified her.

"But what better time to introduce us than when you've just met? We can certainly weed him out of the bunch if he turns out to be a less-than-agreeable man."

"We'll see."

"Perhaps you could bring him to the Jackson's anniversary party? Introduce him to all your friends so he can start to make some ties in Savannah."

Scarlett bit her lip, setting her coffee on the side table. Greyson had the manners and grace to rival anyone she had ever met, but to toss him to the proverbial wolves seemed like an easy way to scare him off. Her parents could be abrasive and condescending. He seemed too sweet to survive in the cutthroat world of debutantes and polo clubs. But more than that, what if her family chased him away? Scarlett wasn't ready to take the risk. And more than that, an anniversary party wasn't the place for a second date. It was too much.

"It's not my place to extend an invitation to someone else's party. If I remember correctly, you always said one should never go anywhere one wasn't invited."

"Martha and George won't mind a bit. They've known you since before you were even born. I'll just call them up, and—"

"No, don't do that," Scarlett pleaded, twisting a strand of hair nervously around her finger.

"Don't worry, I'll see to everything. See you soon for dinner."

"No, Mama, you won't. Please, I've only just met him. Give me a few dates before I introduce him to everyone."

"You wouldn't have to worry so much if you just dated a man we already know."

After taking several measured breaths in order to mask her annoyance, Scarlett kept her tone level. "Well, Mama, I did, and he left me after three years to propose to someone else. I just don't want to bring someone into the circle, in front of Reggie, until I'm officially in a relationship."

Her mother was silent for a few beats. Scarlett knew Reggie's decision to leave her had hurt her mother more than Scarlett herself. Mama had been planning a spring wedding, and she'd probably been considering colors for the nursery she would set up in her house for when the grandkids slept over. Now the fantasy was gone, so she tended to cave when that card was played. "All right. I guess you're being prudent. But just remember, darlin', we *will* have to meet him eventually."

"I know, just let me find out if he is even worth you

meeting," Scarlett pleaded.

She said goodbye and hung up, thankful her mother actually listened to her. But as Scarlett thought about her date, she couldn't help but think he probably *was* worth meeting. At least, she was glad she had.

She was about to call Betsy to tell her about the date, since she hadn't answered the night before, when Scarlett's cell rang again. The caller ID flashed an unknown number. Other people might have ignored the phone, but Scarlett never knew when a potential charity donor might call so was always careful to be available.

"Hello, Scarlett Calhoun speaking," she greeted in her carefully poised debutante voice.

"Scarlett? It's Greyson. How are you?"

Her stomach did a little flip. "Hi! I'm good. Yourself?"

"Fine, fine. I know the usual rule is to wait two days before ringing someone, but I find those old rules rather outdated, don't you?"

"Well, I am an old-fashioned kind of girl," she teased.

"Then I could always hang up and try again in a few days?"

Scarlett could almost hear the smile in his voice. She enjoyed their back-and-forth banter. It sent warm—and yes, even fuzzy—feelings into the pit of her stomach. She didn't want him to wait a few days. Frankly, she'd wanted him to call first thing this morning to beg her for another date. "No, don't worry about it. You've already broken the rules, so you might as well continue."

"Now you've given me permission to continue, I'd like

to begin by saying I enjoyed dinner last night."

"As did I."

"And I was hoping you'd like to do something next weekend?"

"I have an event on Saturday. A family friend is having an engagement party, but I'm free on Sunday. Would that work?"

"Perfectly."

"What did you have in mind?"

"To be honest, I'm not sure yet. I just knew I wanted to see you again. Sunday gives me plenty of time to plan something spectacular to wow you."

Her cheeks flamed, her lips rising into a smile. Scarlett liked his honesty. She was also strangely please to learn he was taking his time to plan an outing she would enjoy. He was just so refreshing. "I like the sound of that."

"Good, I was worried there for a moment. You were a little quiet."

"Mysterious. I was being mysterious…" she stated, jokingly drawing out the last syllable in a *woo-woo* fashion.

"Then I'll look forward to trying to figure you out. Wait, was that cheesy?"

Scarlett giggled. "Yes, but I kinda like it."

"I'll ring you Saturday afternoon with more details, and I'll pick you up Sunday."

"Great. See you then."

∽

SCARLETT SAT IN the uncomfortable mahogany seat, doodling flowers in the corner of her Lily Pulitzer planner. The Ladies of Savannah's event board was meeting to discuss which charity they would support at the masquerade ball in May. However, it had quickly veered off course and had turned into #weddingpalooza with Mandy as the main act.

Mandy wanted to have people donate to a charity in lieu of wedding presents since—*wouldn't you know it, sugar*—they already had everything they needed in Reginald's brownstone. The one Scarlett had painstakingly decorated when she'd believed it would be hers and Reginald's starter home after their wedding. But that wasn't the point. No, the point was Mandy was now Reginald's fiancée and she hadn't yet decided which charity they were going to donate to. Never mind the invitations for the masquerade ball needed to be printed and sent by the end of the next week, the wedding apparently took priority. But seeing as Mandy was the chairwoman, she had the veto power and she had a lot to say about her wedding whether everyone wanted to hear it or not.

Scarlett slid her eyes toward Betsy, who, though not a full member yet, was at least there, trying to send positive vibes. Betsy grinned, dimples appearing in her heart-shaped face, but it wasn't helping. Scarlett couldn't take much more of listening to Mandy go on and on about her dream wedding and how much money her guests could raise for charity. Giving in, Scarlett stood to go to the bathroom.

"Excuse me, Scarlett, what're you doin', sugar? We're still meeting," Mandy said, pausing to let someone else talk for the first time in fifteen minutes. Hand to heart in a dramatic fashion, Mandy's sickly sweet words didn't match the gleeful malice in her eyes when she loudly asked, "Is this too hard for you, honey? Me talking about Reggie and all that? Oh my word, where *are* my manners?"

"No," Scarlett replied, waving her off. "I just need to use the restroom. It was my mistake. I had a double caramel latte before the meeting, and—"

"She must realize we still have a lot to talk about when you're done going over what color table runners you're having for cocktail hour," Betsy cut in, giving Mandy a saccharine smile before flipping her dark hair and rising to her feet. "I think I'll visit the little girl's room, too."

"Well," Mandy started, clicking her pen. "I would've expected you both to have handled your situations ahead of time, but we wouldn't want a scandal, so do hurry along now."

"Right, Mandy, we wouldn't want a scandal," Scarlett said, sarcasm unintentionally leaking through as she continued to the bathroom, Betsy behind her.

"The anniversary party tonight should be fun," Betsy said when they entered the bathroom. "The Jacksons always throws the best parties."

"She called me *sugar* again." Scarlett took her lipstick out of her purse, then forcibly applied it. The color was darker than she normally wore, but she found the shade fit well with her current mood.

"Well, I guess we're going straight into trash-talking Mandy…" Betsy's eyebrow rose sternly as she reprimanded Scarlett. "Your mama didn't raise you that way." But then

Betsy ruined it with a giggle that came out half snort, slapping a hand to her heart to mimic Mandy. "*Honey…*

Scarlett grinned, returned her lipstick to her purse, and leaned heavily against the counter. Her temporary amusement faded to aggravation. "We've just spent two hours talking about Mandy's wedding without accomplishing anything we met here to do. I don't know how she became chairwoman in the first place. Who would give that woman power?"

"Her daddy does have more money than everyone else," Betsy pointed out.

"Not the point." Tears sprang to Scarlett's eyes. She didn't want to be there. Of course, her heart *was* into the charity aspect, but she felt Mandy was being intentionally cruel. While in retrospect, Reggie was no prize, he'd still been Scarlett's once, the man she'd expected to marry and raise a family with. Mandy had won, taken away the future Scarlett had thought was set in stone. She didn't understand why Mandy felt the need to continuously pour salt in the still-healing wound. "I just—"

"I know, Scarlett." Betsy pulled Scarlett into a hug, holding her tight. "Don't cry. Your face will get all blotchy, then Mandy will know she got to you."

"I just don't get why she tries so hard to rub this in my face. Mandy won. She has the ring, the date is set, and Reggie and I broke up almost a year ago. She's even living in the house I designed. What more does she want from me?"

"I don't know. But I do know we should go out there because, right now, we know those ladies are definitely talking about us. So, put a smile on your face and start laughing like we just have the most fun times."

Scarlett took a deep breath, then forced a giggle. It sounded fake in her ears, but Betsy was making such a ridiculous face, trying to force her own laughter, so it wasn't too long before Scarlett and Betsy were laughing hysterically for real.

Their friendship wasn't out of obligation or a solid connection involving pilgrims and founder's rights. It was one of sheer affection. Unlike the "friendship" Scarlett had with Mandy, which was forced on them. This made her think of Greyson and Reginald—and the differences between them. How she'd felt about Reginald, that affection born from obligation, compared to the butterflies and sparks she had just looking at Greyson. It was an interesting thought.

Still, Scarlett's and Betsy's now-real laughter rang out until they stepped into the dining room to discover everyone was gone. Their show had been for naught. The sounds of car doors slamming came from outside.

Mandy appeared in the hall beside them. "Well, we're all finished for the day, which I guess is just as well for you two, since you didn't seem very interested. As the chairwoman, I'm going to have to ask you both to pay attention next time and be fully present in the meeting. We're trying to do some good in the world."

Scarlett bit the inside of her cheek to keep from grinning. Mandy's ridiculously stern expression was so opposite of the authoritative one she was probably aiming for that it was almost like watching a little kid pout. "Understood."

"And you." Mandy crossed her arms, whirling on Betsy. "You're still on probation as a member. Remember, it takes a unanimous vote for someone to get a permanent seat at *my* table."

"Mmm, I'll keep that in mind," Betsy said, linking her arm with Scarlett's. "See you later."

"Figures," Scarlett mumbled as they stepped into the bright afternoon sunlight. "I guess we were gone for too long. We'll have to read the minutes to find out if anything important happened."

"True, but at least we don't have to listen to any more from the Bridezilla today."

About to say something her mama would definitely disapprove of, Scarlett jumped when her cell started to ring. She quickly went through her bag, wishing she would just remember to put it in the designated pocket so she didn't lose it all the time. But it wasn't there. That was when Scarlett realized it was in the back pocket of her white skinny jeans, vibrating away. Crazy how when flustered, even the most obvious things escaped attention.

Greyson's name flashed across the screen. Scarlett took a deep breath and answered, trying to keep her awful afternoon out of her voice. "Hello?"

"Scarlett, it's Greyson. Is this a good time?"

"A great time," she said as Betsy leaned into her, trying to hear, but Scarlett brushed her off.

"Perfect. So, about our date tomorrow—"

"Yes, I'm definitely looking forward to it."

"Right. I am, too. How do you feel about a picnic? I've

checked the weather, and it should be a very temperate day."

"I love that. I haven't been on a picnic in a long time." Actually, as she thought about it, she realized she'd never been on a picnic. Well, unless her Girl Scout troop's fully catered luncheon in Central Park during a weekend trip to New York City counted. As for her adult life, Reggie wasn't one for the outdoors, and her other boyfriends had tried so hard to impress her with fancy dinners, concerts, and anything to show they had tons of money.

"Good. If you message me your address, I can pick you up around one. Does that work for you?"

"Yes, definitely. I can't wait."

"Me neither."

GREYSON HUNG UP the phone with a sigh. "It worked."

He ran a hand through his hair, then flopped on his bed. He'd just received his paycheck the day before. Despite his overtime, he just didn't have the money to take Scarlett out to a fancy dinner...or even to the movies, really. He needed to save money for his upcoming rent payment, and his truck was beginning to make a sound that made him a little nervous. Being a normal non-royal was definitely not as easy as it seemed.

But still, Scarlett had said yes. Now, he just needed to figure out how to do the picnic right, but also how to do it within his budget. He had read dozens of classic novels where the man wooed the woman during an outdoor date beside a picturesque pond. Had seen happy couples in movies bond over sandwiches and wine on a beach. It seemed anyone could figure out how to have a proper picnic, so how hard could it be?

He grabbed his keys to head to the closest grocery store. Cooking something was obviously out of the question, since cereal was the only meal he managed to make without setting off the smoke detectors in his flat. While he was certainly a fan of sugary cereals, they were hardly appropriate.

He hopped in his truck and ignored the odd thumping sound, choosing instead to simply turn the radio up a little higher. On the way, he was trying to think of items he could get to make his picnic work. He definitely needed wine—that was certain. During their dinner, Scarlett, though she'd admitted she wasn't much of a drinker, had stated she liked a glass every now and then with her food. So that was first on his list.

Then he thought about dessert. His mind was always on chocolate. The last time he'd been in the store, he noticed they sold premade truffles and caramel-filled confections, but they were pretty expensive. He would just have to wing it. See what was there and within his budget.

After parking the truck, he headed in, determined to make the best of the date. After grabbing a trolley, he began aimlessly walking up and down the aisles. He saw a box of biscuits that had a huge dent in the side. It had a *half off, damaged goods* sticker, so he put them straight into the basket. While some were probably crushed, he figured he could find the best-looking ones inside and just put them in a bag. He could eat the remainder for lunch since he didn't care if they were a little smashed.

"Perfect," he murmured as he headed down another aisle displaying wine bottles. He didn't know much about wine, since it had always just appeared in his glass at the proper moments. And, if he were being honest with himself, he preferred a good ale. Shrugging, he grabbed the one featuring a label with delicate script. It wasn't from a winery he was familiar with, but the bottle seemed lovely.

When he finished scavenging the supplies he hoped would make his meal amazing, Greyson felt pretty proud of himself. He did wish he'd had enough for the fancy picnic basket to put his finds in, but the actual food had taken up almost his entire budget. What was the point of the basket if he didn't have any food to put in it?

An idea came to him, and he felt ridiculous he hadn't thought of it before. Why didn't he just make a basket? He'd used the last of his pocket money to buy some tools and wood last week, obviously before meeting Scarlett, and he couldn't think of a better use for it.

Feeling even more excited than before, Greyson went home, not even the slightest bit discouraged by the sounds his truck still made.

SCARLETT STOOD NEXT to Betsy at the party, scanning the guests for a friendly face. The Jacksons had been married for fifty years, and Scarlett couldn't help but be a little jealous. She wanted a love like that.

As she watched the Jacksons, her heart started to ache

even more for the life she desired. Their motions were so automatic, and they seemed to be in tune with each other. When he finished his drink, she was by his side with another. When she told a joke, he laughed loudly, even if it wasn't really funny. When they were close by, his hand always rested on her knee, her back, her hand…it was as if they were magnetic. After all those years, they still seemed so in love.

"Cheer up, buttercup. You look like you're going to cry," Betsy said under her breath. "Is everything all right?"

"Yes, I just want that. I want to be as happily married as they are."

"I know. I do, too. One day."

They stared a little longer than was socially appropriate before gravitating to the appetizer table to see what they could snack on. But before they reached the salad selection, Mandy stepped before them, a cat-like grin on her face.

"Scarlett, Betsy," Mandy greeted, blowing them air kisses.

Scarlett twisted her lips into a smile, but she found it hard to make it feel genuine. She was sure it appeared closer to a grimace, but she kept it on her face, hoping it would improve. But seeing Mandy's arm linked with Reggie's, the diamond of the ring sparkling, Scarlett couldn't help but wish she could click her heels three times and return to her apartment. Blitz was excellent company, and her list of recorded shows called her name.

"Scarlett, you're looking well," Reggie greeted robotically.

"And you," she managed.

"Well, I know I'm a little peckish," Betsy said. "Scarlett, help me get some food before I pass out in this room full of doctors and cause a scene." Betsy steered her out of the partygoers' earshot and on to the patio. "All right, enough is enough. You need to get over this Mandy-and-Reggie thing. It's been a year since you and Reggie broke up, and you still get that puppy-dog look in your eyes like he just dumped you yesterday."

"I know, but they *just* got engaged and she's always trying to pick on me." Sighing, Scarlett glanced toward the party, knowing her friend was right. "It sounds stupid, but it's like a fresh stab wound. You know she's wearing his grandmother's ring, the one he took from his mama's jewelry box when he and I were still a thing."

"And are you mourning the loss of Reggie the Veggie or a princess-cut diamond?"

A giggle escaped Scarlett's lips. "Reggie the Veggie?"

"He has all the charm and finesse of a potato, but that's not the point. The point is you didn't love him. You wanted to, but you didn't. Stop acting like he was the love of your life."

"You're right, but she now has what I could've had, and it makes me wonder if it's not something I still want. He would've provided for me, given me a good life, and before he dumped me for her, he was a good man. I don't know. Sometimes, I think I screwed everything up." That last sentence had rolled around in her mind for months since the breakup, but it was the first time she said it out loud. Maybe she was the problem—the one who didn't try hard enough, who couldn't make it work.

"And what about Greyson?" Mandy asked gently.

"What about him?"

"You're going on a second date with a man you described as gorgeous with manners, class, and a way with Blitz."

"I'm just getting to know him, but I think I could like him. I mean, I do like him. I don't know. What if I can't make it work with anyone?"

"Oh, Scarlett." Betsy reached out her arm, then wrapped it around her friend. "No, you are one of the kindest and giving people I've ever met. If it doesn't work with Greyson, then it's him…not you."

"I just don't know…"

"Well, I do. You trust me, don't you? I'd never sugarcoat or lie to you, right?"

"Of course not, that's why I love you."

"Then believe me now. Greyson could be your future, so let's focus on him and let the Reggie dream, though I consider it more of a nightmare, go. Maybe start to think about other things like…should we sneak into the kitchen and see if we can convince the caterers to give us a piece of cake early?"

"I could definitely go for cake right now."

"See? If you were planning a wedding, you never could've gone for cake now because you'd feel the need to diet to fit into some ridiculously puffy dress your mama chose."

"Good point." And just like that, Scarlett was laughing.

A minute ago, she was tearing up at a beautiful engagement party, imagining she'd end up an old spinster with eight dogs all named after reindeer. But after just a few words from Betsy, Scarlett was giggling and very much looking forward to seeing Greyson. Yes, the fear was still there. But this fear, it was something she would handle. She had to.

Scarlett followed Betsy back into the house, feeling much better and craving chocolate. It didn't take long to convince the caterers to part with two pieces of rich cheesecake that sadly wasn't topped with chocolate. And after they demolished their slices, Scarlett and Betsy returned to the party. But just as they began to discuss how to sneak out early, Scarlett's parents waved her over.

"Duty calls." Scarlett said goodbye to Betsy before walking over to the window where they stood talking with the Jacksons. There was someone with them, but he had his back to her, so she wasn't sure who it was. But he definitely seemed familiar, so she put on her debutante smile.

"Scarlett," her mother said, her Southern drawl coming in thick. "You remember William Birmingham the third? Reginald's elder cousin."

The man turned to Scarlett and smiled, revealing a series of perfect white teeth.

"Right, I think we met a couple of times over the years." Scarlett extended her hand to shake his. "So good to see you again, William."

"It's my pleasure, Scarlett. When your parents told me you were here, I have to admit I was excited. It's hard to forget a beautiful face like yours, and I couldn't wait to see you again."

"Thank you, that's a very kind thing to say."

"Scarlett, William was just telling your father and me that he's been made partner in a law firm down here. He's been away at a series of rather prestigious conferences, but now he's back and ready to settle down. Isn't that nice?"

"Congratulations," Scarlett said carefully. She was beginning to get a bad feeling she knew where the conversation was going.

"Darlin'," her mother started. "Why don't you two get together sometime? I'm sure William could use a tour of the town."

"Oh, he probably doesn't," Scarlett countered, laughing lightly to take the edge off her words. "He grew up here. He must remember it well."

He laughed, a warm, rich sound. "I do remember it. But if you'd be willing to accompany me to dinner, I'd still appreciate that. One can never have bad company. Are you available tomorrow, perhaps?"

She opened her eyes wide at her mother, hoping she'd get the hint. Scarlett was not going to go out with her ex-boyfriend's cousin. If they ended up together, she'd have to see Reggie and Mandy at every holiday, Scarlett would be reminded she was second best, and Mandy would consistently rub it in her face. No, not going to happen. Scarlett wasn't desperate, and she did *not* need her mother setting her up. She'd found a man she was excited to see again, and his last name was not Birmingham.

"I'm sorry, William, but I'm currently seeing someone. If

you excuse me, I'd like another cider." Scarlett took a deep breath as she headed toward the refreshments table. She had just ordered another drink at the bar when a hand clamped on her upper arm.

"Scarlett Anna-Beth Calhoun," Mama whispered harshly in her ear. "How *dare* you be rude to William? And in front of the Jacksons? I could simply die of shame."

"How could you try to set me up with Reggie's cousin? Did he even remember me, or did you point me out in the crowd and *strongly* comment I haven't been out with anyone in a while?" Scarlett hissed, ripping her arm from her mother's grasp. Scarlett wasn't sure if the heat on her face was born from embarrassment or anger.

Her mother's light eyes softened slightly, and her jaw worked in the way it tended to do when she was cornered or faced with facts. Pausing a moment, she rearranged one of Scarlett's already immaculately layered curls. "Well, you haven't been out with anyone in a while."

Scarlett shook her head, hoping she mussed the style her mother had been going for. "I have. I *told* you I've been seeing someone. And I didn't lie. We are going out again tomorrow."

"Are you official? Because if not, there is no harm in going out with two men. People play the field all the time to see their options."

"I am not interested in William. He's Reggie's cousin, and I don't want to date in the family. It's too weird."

"Scarlett, you can't be so dismissive. You don't even know the man. What if you just gave him a chance? What harm would that cause? You could have a nice meal, good conversation, and who knows, maybe even find someone you enjoy spending time with who just happens to have a good standing in our world. Besides, then the box of mono-grammed towels in the attic from last year would see the light of day."

"Mama, I already met a man whom I'm seeing him to-morrow. Please respect my wishes. I don't want to begin anything with William. I'm not going to change my opinion on that."

"Oh, Scarlett, sometimes I wish you weren't so difficult." Her mother pursed her lips, then took a deep breath through her nose, nostrils flaring. Then, before either could say anything else, she turned on her heel and strode away.

Scarlett watched her go, hoping the conversation made it to her mother's subconscious. If not, there was a good chance Scarlett would be having it again at Mandy and Reggie's engagement party. Luckily, the party wasn't until January, giving Scarlett plenty of time to sort out what was going on between her and Greyson. In the meantime, she needed more cake.

CHAPTER FOUR

G REYSON HAD DEFINITELY gone overboard with the basket, but he was excited. When he'd finished it last night, he'd suddenly gotten the urge to do a little carving. Before he knew it, the basket had frills and loops on the handle and around the mouth. It even sported an intricate heart on the front. Basically, it was cheesy and over the top. But then again, Scarlett had said she liked cheesy. As he packed it for the date, he couldn't help but think it would be perfect for her.

Once the basket was ready, he went to get dressed. But as he stood before his wardrobe, he realized he didn't have another not-too-nice shirt to put on. He'd forgotten to return to the discount store and grab more clothes. Well, even if he'd had the time, he certainly didn't have the money.

"It'll be fine." Greyson grabbed one of his oldest button-down shirts and a pair of jeans where the designer label was hidden. That outfit would just have to do. Maybe he could tell her the discount store had a sale on designers? No, he didn't want to come out and lie. So far, he'd told her the truth, just left out the prince part. He wouldn't mention the clothes unless she did.

Greyson grabbed the basket and put it in his truck, then headed over to Scarlett's. She'd texted him earlier, and he'd spent ten minutes trying to think of a good response. Back home, he'd been so smooth with women. Or so he'd thought. Now with Scarlett, he was beginning to think the women he'd dated hadn't actually found him that charming. Maybe it had all been the title. Were his jokes even funny? He certainly thought so, but that wasn't saying much. Most people laughed at their own jokes, right?

Well, it was now or never. He strode up to the building's door, then told the doorman he was picking up Scarlett. The man in the flashy red suit allowed Greyson in, stating Miss Calhoun was expecting him. Greyson continued into the building, entered the lift, and exited on the third floor where Scarlett was hopefully still waiting and as excited as he.

When she opened the door, Greyson momentarily forgot how to speak. His motor functions shut down, and he just froze.

"Greyson?"

Hearing his name, he shook it off and smiled. She was wearing a flowy strapless top with billowing sleeves starting just below her shoulders. The white fabric was streaked with black diagonal stripes. Her tight black trousers accentuated her long and slender legs, giving the illusion they went on forever. Everything about her was stunning, but it was her smile that distracted him. It went into her eyes. The way they shone, it made him want to know what else he could do to keep the sparkle there forever.

"Are you ready for the picnic?" Greyson managed to ask

after another beat or two.

"Yes, just let me put my shoes on. You can come in for a few minutes while I grab them."

Her apartment seemed to be a perfect reflection of her. The white furniture, gold accent tables, and watercolor prints on the pale blue walls of the living room were perfectly feminine, just like she was. There were also several large windows overlooking the tops of the buildings beyond and let in streams of bright sunlight.

As soon as he stepped in the door, Blitz bounded over from his spot on the couch and sat in front of him expectantly.

"Hello there, mate," Greyson said, petting the dog on his oversized head. "Some attack dog you have here," he teased as Blitz laid down, showing his stomach.

"I know." Scarlett groaned from what Greyson assumed was her bedroom. "He doesn't even freak out when someone knocks on the door. It's weird. But he's just so cute. I'm hoping if a murderer came to the door, he'd kill them with kindness."

"Yes, I can see how that would happen," he said, laughing. Blitz had weaseled his way in between Greyson's legs, circling him like a giant furry fish. "Do you want to bring him? To the picnic, I mean."

Scarlett reappeared from her room. She grinned, her red flats clicking on the hardwood floor. "Yeah, actually, I would. But he's terrible with listening when there's food involved. There's a good chance he would eat all of it, then run after a bird and get lost. Maybe afterward, we could take him to the dog park or something?"

"Brilliant idea. I hate the idea of leaving the little chap all cooped up." He actually thought the dog probably got plenty of exercise, but anything that prolonged his date with her was a brilliant idea.

Scarlett grabbed a jumper and her purse from off the counter. "Ready," she told him, shouldering her bag.

They headed down the lift and to Greyson's truck. He opened the door for her, satisfied with the wash job he'd managed to give the truck before coming over. While the vehicle was old and a bit battered, at least it was clean.

"Any preference on music?" he asked as he pulled out of the parking lot. "I don't know a lot about the music scene here."

"Well, I don't know much about it, either. I'm a fan of country music, but outside of that, I don't know any other bands or things."

"Then country music it is. Besides, I think that's what the truck is set to anyway."

Greyson turned the music up a bit as they drove. He kept thinking he should say something, but nothing immediately sprang to mind. They'd done the basic *get to know you* things, had even gotten into the *hopes and dreams* part, which normally came later. Now, he was back to thinking that everything, including the apparently false idea he was a great conversationalist, was just palace façade.

Nerves were soaring through him, almost more than when they'd shared their first date. He liked her a lot, and he wanted things to go well. It was like, if this went well, he was proving to himself he could make it in the real world and not everything in his life was hopeless. But then he shook his head, trying to calm down. That was way too much pressure to put on a second date. He needed to get it together.

"Are you ready for the picnic?" he asked, pulling the truck into one of the many empty parking spots.

"Yes."

"Great, then wait there." Greyson got out of the car and went to her side, opening the door and offering his hand to help her down. Then he slid the seat up to remove his handmade basket from the storage area.

"Oh my gosh. What is that?"

"It's our basket. Remember I told you I like to work with wood? I had some extra around my flat, so I thought, why not use it now?"

Her blue eyes widened, reminding him of the way she'd appeared when he had almost run her off the road. He assumed it was her "surprised" face, although he hoped it was a pleasant one and not one where she had just seen her life flash before her. "You made this for our picnic today?"

"Yes."

Scarlett's hand shook a little as she reached out and touched the carvings, running her finger over them, almost examining them. Greyson's heart pounded. Was she judging his work? He'd painstakingly smoothed out each carving, so he knew none should give her a splinter. But still, with each stroke, he found it harder and harder to breathe.

"What do you think?" he dared to ask.

Scarlett finished tracing the carving and then lifted her

head, a glisten in her eyes Greyson thought may have been the slightest bit of tears. "I think it's the most beautiful basket I've ever seen."

A smile spread across his face as pride quickly overtook the panic. She liked it. "Let's go, then. I hope you like what's inside more."

Greyson offered her his hand, and she took it quickly. He felt a spark when her fingers touched his, and he savored the feeling. They walked hand in hand to the park. But unlike in the truck, their conversation started to flow smoothly like it had at dinner the other night.

SCARLETT PICKED A place in the grass, out of the sun in the shade of a giant tree. They were a little way off from the kids playing soccer, the teenagers up to no good, and the mothers pushing their children on swings while simultaneously texting or talking on phones. Scarlett and Greyson had their own little corner of the world.

Greyson pulled a red-and-black plaid blanket out of the basket, then spread it on the grass. Scarlett sat, taking her shoes off and placing them beside it. Then Greyson opened the basket and pulled out a bottle of wine. He handed it to her with the flourish of a restaurant connoisseur.

"I don't know much about wine," he said as she took it. "I know you said you liked to have some with dinner, so I wanted to make sure I had a bottle."

Scarlett glanced at the label, fighting back a little laugh. It was cooking wine. While she hated to burst his bubble, she knew she had to tell him. "Um, Greyson? This isn't for drinking."

He blinked, his gave shooting to the bottle. "What?"

"Yeah, this is the type of wine you use when you're cooking. I like to put it in clam sauce. Sometimes, I use the red version when I'm seasoning meat."

His mouth flattened into a tight line, and she could almost see the gears turning in his head. "So you don't drink it?"

"Uh, no, you don't."

"Darn, what a terrible oversight." He ran his hand through his dark hair. "I should've brought a water or something else as a backup."

Scarlett placed a hand on his arm as he sat heavily beside her. His concern with making things perfect warmed her heart. "It's all right. Let's lay the rest of the food out, maybe eat a little, and then we could take a walk. There's this nice British pub down the street. Maybe you want to go in there? I'm sure it'll make you feel at home"

Greyson adamantly shook his head. "No, this was the plan. Uh, let's just continue."

He continued unpacking the food from the basket, carefully placing it on the blanket, and Scarlett tried to hide her smile. There was chicken salad in a container but no bread, along with cookies, apples, and a big bag of nondescript chips.

"I hope you like chicken salad. I've discovered it lately, and I have to admit I've become a bit obsessed."

She peered into the basket's open mouth. "Did you bring

any silverware? Or maybe some bread for us to eat it with?"

Greyson's face fell, and he slowly shook his head. "No. Truthfully, I have never planned a picnic before. And it appears I've failed at this endeavor."

Scarlett hated to see him so distraught. Before he could get more upset, she grabbed one of the apples and took a big bite. "I don't know," she said when she finished chewing. "The basket is remarkable, so you definitely scored some major brownie points there. These are pretty good, too. Granny Smith apples are actually my favorite. And don't get me started on chocolate chip cookies. Also a huge staple of my diet. Actually, it looks like you did pretty well to me."

His shoulders relaxed, and she felt a stream of pride flow through her with the knowledge she had been able to put him at ease.

"I have the worst sweet tooth. For my birthdays, we always used to eat these double chocolate cakes with chocolate chips spread on the top," Greyson offered.

"That sounds amazing. Did your mom make them? Maybe you could ask her for the recipe for me, and I could make it for you."

He busied himself with polishing one of the apples on the bottom of his button down, even though the green skin was flawless. "Oh, uh, my mother never made them."

"Who did, your father?"

"Mother always had them made, honestly."

"By who? A family friend or someone?"

"Yeah, or someone. I can ring Mom to see if she can track down the recipe if you'd like."

"Sounds amazing," Scarlett said as she bit into the hard chocolate chip cookie. It was definitely stale, but like a champ, she continued to eat it and even grabbed a second one.

"So you like to bake?" Greyson asked, rolling the apple around in his hands.

Scarlett started to talk about how she loved to lose herself in the kitchen, to try recipes, and even cook fresh food for Blitz, all the while finishing her apple. They talked for a bit longer, abandoning the failed picnic food. But it was beginning to be hard to ignore the thirst in her throat. She needed something to drink. "Hey, Greyson, I have an idea. Why don't we go back to my apartment and try dinner instead? I can make you a home-cooked meal. Maybe show you a thing or two about cooking. We can even sit on the balcony and pretend we're in the park."

"Oh no, I can't ask you to do that. Really. I have utensils at my flat. I can eat the chicken salad there."

She scrunched her nose at the container. The contents smelled anything but fresh. "Right, so, that's not chicken salad. At least, it's not *good* chicken salad. Let me do this. I want to. You're new here, so consider it a *welcome to America* meal."

"I hope I'm not impeding on your plans for the evening. I wanted this lunch to do well, but the whole thing's gone to seed." His face turned downward as he began to put the cooking wine and rejected food back into the basket. His ears were pink, and he didn't make eye contact as he cleaned up.

When he reached for one of the apples that had rolled to

her side of the blanket, Scarlett took his hand and gently stroked the back of it with her thumb. "It *did* go well. I know how much trouble you went through with the basket. I mean, no one has ever gone through that kind of trouble for me. So the food wasn't perfect. Who cares? I happen to be incredible at cooking, if I do say so myself. With your basket and my food, we could make a pretty perfect picnic. Besides, if you did everything right, then I'd feel like I have nothing to contribute to the date. Now, we can make it our date. It's almost better than way, don't you think?"

Greyson smiled. "Is that what you want?"

Scarlett thought his smile the most wonderful she had seen. She adored he had been so worried about pleasing her. Reggie had certainly never made the effort. Rather, he'd have just paid someone to set it up. And yet, Greyson was here. He regarded her with such joy and effervescence, apparently overjoyed just to spend more time with her. Scarlett had to look away. It was all so intense and meaningful. She didn't know what to do with her emotions, or even how to label them. But there was one thing she did know. She wanted the perfect picnic with him.

"Of course it's what I want.

"As you wish."

BLITZ HOPPED AROUND excitedly when Scarlett unlocked the door and let them inside her apartment. She patted him on the head as she tried to squeeze around him, but Greyson fell to his knees and lavished the excited dog with attention.

The fact Blitz thought so highly of him was certainly a point in his direction.

She went to her kitchen, then laid her purse and sweater on a chair. Since she'd recently gone to the grocery store, she had many options. While she wished she could wow him with a four-course meal, she had promised to teach him a thing or two about cooking. As she opened her refrigerator and took note of the contents, she had an idea.

"Greyson, how does salad and pasta sound?" she asked as he rounded the corner to the kitchen and stopped in the entryway.

"Wonderful. Just tell me how I can be of assistance." He rolled up his sleeves as he spoke.

Scarlett washed her hands thoroughly. "After we're all clean, we'll start by prepping the ingredients. I'll get everything set out."

Reaching into the fridge, she began pulling things out. She placed garlic and Parmesan cheese on the granite countertop. Then she moved to the cabinets. Soon, walnuts, olive oil, and a food processor joined the collection. Greyson was eying it with unveiled interest as he dried his hands.

"Can you go over to the windowsill and pick a bunch of basil leaves?" She pointed across the room to the bay window, which was filled with a dozen potted plants in varying stages of growth. "We'll need a lot for the sauce."

After she set a large pot of salted water on the stove to boil, she went to a hook by the table and retrieved her pink apron to tie around her waist. Then she set out her cutting board and a freshly sharpened chopping knife. She was so busy readying things for her lesson, she hardly realized Greyson was having trouble already.

"Is this enough?" he asked, holding out a handful of leaves.

"That's mint."

He frowned at the pile in his palm. "Like the flavor?"

Scarlett pursed her lips, trying not to laugh. "Sort of. No matter, I'll whip us up some lemonade to drink while we cook and put those mints to good use."

"Then which one was I to pick?"

"Come on, I'll show you." She took him to the window, then began pointing at the pots. "See this one? This is mint. Beside it is the parsley plant. This one in the red pot will soon grow tomatoes, while this one is thyme. The larger, more curved leaves are the basil." She plucked one leaf, then rubbed it slowly between her fingers and held it out to him. "Here, smell it."

"Oh, I thought these smelled wrong." He glowered at the mint leaves he still held, and Scarlett took them.

"Let's start this lesson. It looks like you have a lot to learn."

Scarlett went through the basics as they made their pesto sauce and mixed a fresh batch of minty lemonade. To her surprise, Greyson had no idea how to chop a vegetable or that water would bubble over the top of a pot if not carefully watched. She wondered how he had survived for so long without being able to accomplish such basic tasks. He wasn't lying when he'd told her he wasn't a good cook.

But at the same time, he was a fast learner and so much

fun to be around. As they made their late lunch, he acted like a contestant on a cooking show. Every stage was greeted by him calling out the remaining time left in the round and every ingredient was given a lengthy backstory, as were they. He was a traveling pineapple salesman who had culinary talent in his blood while she was a successful food truck owner in the Arctic circle.

While she had been on dates catered by international chefs and dined with the rich and famous, that afternoon was so different. As they sat on the blanket spread out on her balcony, overlooking the Savannah skyline, eating their pasta and sharing an actual bottle of wine, Scarlett couldn't imagine a more perfect date.

CHAPTER FIVE

G REYSON TAPPED HIS newly minted library card on the counter as the elderly librarian swiped his books. After his night with Scarlett, he knew he needed to familiarize himself with the inner workings of a kitchen. While they got along fantastically, his cooking skills left much to be desired. He could hardly manage to boil water without creating a piping hot mess on the tiled floors, and the old cookbook he had found in the kitchen at his flat was missing more pages than it had.

He had thought over everything that had gone wrong into the wee hours of the night, then been exhausted when he'd left for work that morning. The fact he couldn't manage a simple picnic was mortifying, and he vowed to never embarrass himself like that again. If he could at least prepare a few dishes, then he would be able to hold his own in the kitchen with Scarlett.

When he got home, he brought his books into his small living room and kicked off his boots. With a little planning and some time to prepare, he would be able to take Scarlett on a proper picnic. Or maybe he would take her to the zoo he had passed on the way to his latest worksite and make their date last all day.

Even though things were messy, he loved the way Scarlett managed to just make light of everything he screwed up. No matter what came her way, she was able to handle it with the poise and grace of, well, a royal. He even thought she would make a better royal than he himself ever did, and he wondered if there was a duchess or king somewhere in the Calhoun family tree.

Greyson shut his cookbook, then rubbed at his tired eyes. His lineage was one he needed to sort out if he and Scarlett continued in the direction they were heading. It was soon in their courtship, but he felt so at home and at peace when he was with her, like he had known her for years. If they carried on, he would need to come clean. There was some danger to be noted in that regard. True, he'd wanted to meet a woman, to find love, but he'd never thought about what would happen regarding his true identity. Yes, he'd have to tell her. But how, and when he did, what would she say?

The inevitable conversation could go many ways. She could be positively delighted to hear where he came from and understand why he lied, and everything would be perfect. Or she could push him to take the crown, falling prey to the princess curse, and beg him to be a royal again. Or she could hate him for lying and never speak to him again.

There were a number of ways she could take the news, and only a few that would work in his favor. But before he worried too much about how she would react, he needed to ensure his feelings for her were true. He needed to just stay in the moment and see where life took him.

And in the meantime, he was finding it hard to keep his mind off Scarlett. It had been three days since he heard her voice. He couldn't wait any longer, so he picked up the phone.

She answered on the second ring. "Hey, Greyson!"

"Hello, how are you?"

"Pretty good. I was just thinking of taking Blitz for a walk. What about you?"

"I visited a library after work today," he said proudly. "Will you be going to the dog park?"

"Maybe. Why? Would you like to come with?"

Greyson glanced out the window. He had finished work early when the architect announced the size of the windows were off, so there was still at least an hour of daylight left. "Certainly."

"Perfect. I'll start walking toward Main Street, and we can just meet in the middle somewhere."

When the hung up, Greyson took a quick shower and changed into a clean shirt and jeans. Then he pocketed the keys for his flat as he hurried down the stairs to the road. He was glad he had chosen that moment to call her. If he hadn't, he wouldn't have had the chance to see her.

He had only made it maybe two blocks before he saw her coming toward him, her blond ponytail bouncing. Blitz pulled at his leash as they drew closer, and Greyson couldn't help but smile at the sight. "Hello, you two," he said as they came together. "Ready to go to the dog park?"

"I was thinking we might make a little detour, if that's

okay?"

"Certainly. Where did you have in mind?"

She bit her lip, furrowing her brow slightly. "I think it'll be easier to explain when we get there."

"Sounds very mysterious."

"Hardly, but it is something I want to show you."

"Good. I haven't explored Savannah too much."

"Then it's lucky for you I'm a fantastic tour guide."

He took the leash from her, then held her hand in his free one. As they strolled deeper into the heart of the city, she pointed out the historic landmarks and the mom-and-pop locations—like which had the best ice cream and the place she'd once found a four-leaf clover she still kept in her wallet for luck. She spoke animatedly about her hometown in a way that made Greyson want to make it his home as well.

Soon, they stopped before an overgrown lot rimmed by a black wrought-iron fence. He took in the long grass and faded and battered house that stood several yards from the sidewalk. A *Condemned* sign was staked beside the gate, but the words and number below were worn like it had been there a while. While it might have once been a striking Victorian manor home, it was quite obviously abandoned and left to the elements. Without the care of people, nature had firmly taken over.

"This is it!" She motioned toward the house with a swooping arc of her arm.

"It's…" He searched for the right words to say. The building seemed so far gone he couldn't imagine why she was so excited. He thought perhaps it had some sort of significance to the people of Savannah, so he tried to keep his confusion hidden. He had looked like an idiot before her one time too many already. "It's very big."

"It's my favorite house in all of Savannah."

She said her words with such feeling Greyson was taken aback. Out of all the multimillion-dollar homes and historic mansions lining the street, she loved the dilapidated Victorian with the willow tree out front? There had to have been something about it he was missing.

Gazing at it adoringly, she squeezed his fingers. "If I could, I'd buy it and fix it up in a heartbeat."

"Would you?"

"I think it would make the most perfect bed and breakfast. Just picture it with a bit of landscaping with that wraparound porch filled with flowers and rocking chairs for guests. I would paint the entire exterior gray, then have the lattice trim a pale violet and the shutters the same blue as a robin's egg. You know, those were the original colors back when this house was built in the 1880's. I dug up the originals with the city."

He couldn't help but smile as he watched her out of the corner of his eye. "You've done your research."

"You probably think it's dumb, but I just love this house. I hate it's gotten to the point where it'll be knocked down, but…well, it's a real mess, so I just have to settle for admiring it from afar and mourning when it's gone."

"Will it be gone soon?"

"Probably knocked down in the spring."

Greyson squinted at the sad building, his eyes drawn to

the stained glass that framed many of the windows. He tried to picture it as she described, with the lawn a vibrant green instead of the washed-out brown and the fully alive willow tree gently swaying in the wind. She would be standing on the steps to the front door, which would be wide open for company, and the inside of the house would be alive with colors from the stained glass when the last of the day's light hit it just right. The house would again be in its glory for all to admire, and not just her.

"You think it's silly," she said in a small voice, turning away from the house.

"What? No, of course not. Some fresh paint, a roof…why, I bet the hardwood floors in there are original. It would be a lovely house. So, it may be the carpenter in me, but all I see is potential. Frankly, I can see why you like it. I'm surprised no one else has sorted out the gem it could be."

A ghost of a smile touched her lips. It was just a small movement—one he probably wouldn't have noticed had he not been studying her so intently. It was beautiful. "I had a feeling you would understand."

And with that one sentence, she could've asked him for the world and he'd have found a way to give it to her. *"I had a feeling you would understand."* She was thinking of him, considering how he saw the world, how he saw her, and she trusted him to see what she did. It meant she understood him as well. While that was what he'd always wanted in a partner, it terrified him as well. How could he be falling so fast for this woman? He stole a quick glance at her, the wind slightly blowing her hair, the sun shining on her porcelain skin. How could he not?

"Trust me, Scarlett, if there is one thing I truly understand in this world, it's the importance of following your dreams."

SCARLETT INSPECTED THE ribbons on the latest wrapped present before setting it on the pile. She and Betsy collected gifts every year for the needy children of the city, and Scarlett loved getting a head start on shopping. That way, even the last-minute additions to her list would get something special under the tree.

"Nineteen," Betsy declared, making another line on her clipboard. "Only…thirty-six left to go."

They sat on the floor of Betsy's parents' living room. Scarlett always liked Betsy's house. The massive colonial sat in the heart of the city, and it held a warmth Scarlett always wished she felt at home. It was always full of laughing people, freshly baked goods, and no one ever cared if someone wore yoga pants at the dinner table and not strictly at the gym.

"That's pretty good. With Christmas only two weeks away, I'll have time to finish these up. I still have some shopping to do. Are you still free to come with me tomorrow?"

"Sure am," Betsy replied as she tried to wrap an oddly shaped box without crumpling the paper too badly. "My sister's coming home from college for winter break soon, and I want to get her something good. Last year, she gave me a great handheld anemometer for when I go sailing and that cute captain's hat. Maybe you can help me look?"

Betsy had been a sailor since she was old enough to walk. Even in her college days on the coast, she had been on the sailing team. Scarlett didn't even know there *was* such a thing as a sailing team, but Betsy's love of boats and interest in the latest gadgets always made her the easiest person to shop for.

"No problem. I'll take a look at some stuff online and get a few ideas ready before we go out, so you have some options if you don't see something that speaks to you."

"Ah, thanks. You're a lifesaver. I'm quite the worst at getting presents for my family. If you didn't help me, I'm pretty sure I'd have been disowned."

"Yes, trying to buy your mom a fertility statue so she'd feel confident she'd get grandchildren one day was not your best idea," Scarlett reminisced, laughing at how seriously Betsy had insisted the trinket was the perfect gift.

"I maintain she'd have liked it. Though, the canvas print you got that artist to paint for her was better."

"Speaking of gifts, what do you want?"

"Besides better boating weather this spring?"

"I can wish upon a star for you, but how about something I can actually handle?" Scarlett said with a laugh. "What about a pair of those fancy binoculars? Didn't you say you lost yours?"

Betsy grinned, flashing her dimples. "If a pair of Fukinon Techno-Stabis ended up under my Christmas tree, I wouldn't argue. In fact, I may name my firstborn after the gifter. Speaking of future babies, are you getting your new man something?"

Scarlett's face heated, and she busied herself with cleaning up the bits and pieces of paper. "He's not my man."

"Isn't he though?"

"Well, we haven't put a label on it. But on Sunday, we went for a picnic and then cooked at my apartment."

"Ooh, he cooks, too?"

Scarlett giggled. "Hardly. I don't think he's used to feeding himself, so we just made pesto pasta so he could learn."

"Well, the way to a man's heart is through his stomach, so I think that was a very good move."

"But I didn't tell you the best part."

"What is it?"

"So you know how I told you he likes to work with wood in his spare time? He made this perfectly adorable basket, just for our picnic."

Betsy grinned. "How cute is that? I bet it was amazing."

"It was. I'll have to show you next time you come over."

"You kept it and didn't bring it over?"

Scarlett shrugged. "A lady never picnics and tells."

"You're ridiculous. When can I meet him?"

"I don't know…do you want to?"

"Of course I do. He sounds so much better than any of the men all the ladies at the club are trying to hook me up with. Does he have any brothers—male cousins, maybe? A best friend who broods in the background I can charm?"

Scarlett dug through her memories, trying to recall something of Greyson's past. All she knew was his family was involved in politics and his mother didn't bake her own cookies. That rang strange, considering how she had told him the ins and outs of her mama's gardening hobby and her daddy's interest in architecture history. "Hmm...I never actually asked anything about his family. But if it means we could be related, it seems like I should."

"Content to just make goo-goo eyes over a plate of pasta instead?"

Scarlett threw a handful of ribbon at her, laughing. "You shut your mouth, Elizabeth!"

Betsy scowled. "Don't call me that."

"But it's your name."

"No, it's my aunt's name and my grandma's name and my mom's middle name. They can all be Elizabeth. I'm just Betsy."

"Well, *just Betsy*, I even took Greyson to see the house."

"Planning your future already? Maybe you should find out a little more about him before you call a hall and put a deposit down."

Scarlett's cheeks filled with heat. Truth be told, she had done her fair share of daydreaming about Greyson. She could imagine him building a rocking horse for their child. Maybe making her a porch swing where they would sit in the evenings and sip sweet tea, listening to the cicadas chirp in the summertime. She even had a flash of him replacing the shutters on the old house in preparation for their moving day.

"I'll take that as a *yes*," Betsy said dryly. "What's his last name? Have you written it in your dream notebook yet? You know, with your first and his last, all surrounded by pink hearts?"

"I have not had a dream notebook since I was in middle school, and I don't even know his last name."

Betsy's mouth fell open with Scarlett's confession. "Are you kidding me? How can you search for him online if you don't know his last name?"

"I haven't."

"Seriously? That would've been the first thing I'd have done. What if he's a wanted criminal from England who came here to escape the hangin' rope?"

"Well, they probably don't use the *hangin' rope* anymore. But I'm just getting to know him the old-fashioned way. If he turns out to be a criminal from England, then I'll end it before I become the Bonnie to his Clyde."

"I guess that's fair. Just keep in mind, at some point, everyone's going to have to meet him. You can't hide him forever."

"I'm not hiding him."

"Then let me meet him. I'm not your mama. I don't care one bit if he works in construction and his family didn't come over on the Mayflower, not as long as he treats you right. So, what do you say? Let me meet him? You insisted on meeting my last boyfriend to be sure he was good enough for me. As it turns out, he wasn't, but you helped me see that. Now, I'm invoking the same right."

Sighing, Scarlett began searching under the couch for any trash she had missed. "Mama is already starting to text me about meeting him, so I don't know how much longer I can keep her away. Besides, she may be crazy, but I don't like keeping things from her. I think maybe I'll invite him to the cookie party. There will be so much going on and so many people there she won't be able to grill him as if it were just the four of us for dinner."

"You don't think that's going to scare him off? The cookie party is sort of a big deal in your house."

Scarlett pondered her point. On the one hand, bringing Greyson to a family party would be making a statement. Whether they established their relationship or not, her family would consider it a done deal. How did she feel about that? Was she ready for such a big step? He wasn't her usual type, but that endeared her to him a bit.

Greyson smiled at waiters and acknowledged their presences. Unlike Reggie, who saw everyone as beneath him. Greyson also walked with an air and a grace that screamed private finishing school. Something about Greyson didn't quite make sense. The more she got to know him, the more she wanted to figure him out. So far, she liked everything she'd uncovered. But then, a vastly different thought crossed her mind…how would Greyson feel about meeting her family? Would it be too much, too fast? Would he be comfortable in her lavish world? Would he judge her for her family's behavior?

"You're coming to the cookie party, right?" she asked Betsy, her mind racing as she thought more and more about this. "If I do invite him, it'd be amazing to have you there."

"Yes. My mother is excited. She still raves about your mother's snickerdoodles."

"So then you can help me play interference if things get bad?"

"Absolutely."

"Then I'm doing it, but I think I'll make sure it's a surprise for Mama. This way, she can't prepare to torture him. It'll just have to be spur of the moment."

"Adding someone to her perfectly placed table at the last minute might actually infuriate her and make her hate him more."

"It'll be fine. I'll sneak a place setting when she isn't looking. She won't notice." Scarlett took her phone out, then called Greyson up.

"Hello, Scarlett, what can I do for you?"

"Greyson, hi, how are you?"

"Splendid, just leaving work."

"Really? At this time?" Scarlett glanced at her watch. It was almost eight at night.

"I've been doing some additional work for my foreman. Making some elaborate carvings, that sort of thing."

"Oh, well, I'm sure it'll all turn out fabulous. Anyway, I guess it's my turn to invite you out."

"What did you have in mind?"

Scarlett took a deep breath, trying to steady her voice so he couldn't tell how nervous she was. "So, every year, my mother throws this big Christmas party. She calls it a cookie decorating party, but she just places cookies out and you can put toppings on them to take home. Mostly, she hosts it because another family in our circle throws these extravagant Christmas party. She loves Christmas and wants a piece of

SARAH FISCHER & KELSEY MCKNIGHT

the entertaining pie, too, but can't copy and call it a holiday party. Anyway, I'd like for you to come."

"Meeting the parents? So I guess you fancy me a little bit?"

Scarlett felt her cheeks flush as she tucked her pajama-clad legs beneath her. One of the things she "fancied" about him was he kept her on her toes. "You could say that. Show up and maybe I'll tell you in person."

"I wouldn't miss it, but when is it?"

"Oh, right. It's Sunday."

"I'm off this weekend already."

"So that means you can't use work as an excuse not to go."

"Then I suppose I'll be there. Uh, am I supposed to bring anything? I've been working on my cooking. You'll be impressed. I'm sure I could manage to whip something up."

Scarlett would be impressed if he managed to make anything without burning it, but she knew his best attempt would definitely be a turn-off to Mama. "Why don't we try your cooking another time? My mama has been preparing for this meal for at least a month."

"She cooks the whole dinner? No catering or anything?"

"That's not exactly how we do things here. Did your mother cater for your big meals?"

Greyson laughed. "Let's just say there's a reason I don't know how to cook."

"Well, then I'm glad you're coming."

"So am I."

CHAPTER SIX

2, Scarlett

THAT FRIDAY AFTER yoga, Savannah came home. Her attention was drawn to the bare corner in her apartment where a Christmas tree should sit. She had been so wrapped up in charity work, running away from Mandy, and getting to know Greyson, that December got away from her. It was almost shameful. If she didn't do something quickly, she'd be ordered to change Blitzen's name to something like Rover or Fred.

She could get a fake tree, one with pre-lit lights that fit neatly into a box, but then she would be abandoning the magic of having a real pine with the scent filling her living room. And Blitz would miss out as well, as he loved the act of picking one out. He had a fabulous knack for finding the perfect one with the best shape and the fullest branches. He'd sniff each trunk, winding between the displays, until coming to sit at the base of the one she'd buy.

Then she thought to Greyson. She didn't know if he had any family in the area, but she assumed he didn't. He probably didn't have a Christmas tree either.

He picked up on the first ring. "Don't tell me you've called to cancel my invite to the illustrious cookie party?"

"Of course not. I was calling to see if you had a Christmas tree."

"Is this one of those bad jokes about a running refrigerator?"

Laughing, she hooked a leash to Blitz's collar for a walk. "No, it's a serious question."

"No, I don't. I didn't see the need for one this year."

"Oh, okay. Well, I was just asking because I'm going to go to this Christmas village tomorrow to get a tree, and I wanted to know if you needed one as well."

"I don't, but I'll gladly lend my pickup for your use."

"Really? That would be amazing."

"You cook, I lug big trees about. It's a give and take."

Scarlett locked the door behind them, Blitz pulling at his leash. "Thank you, really. I was going to go borrow my daddy's truck, but I'd much rather go with you."

"When shall I collect you?"

"Does noon work?"

"Of course. See you then."

Scarlett hung up with a smile. She loved the feeling of togetherness she had with Greyson, the comfortable reality of having someone to do those kinds of things with. She never thought of herself as a lonely person, but after every date and their afternoons, she would immediately miss him. It was a nice thing to feel.

SCARLETT WAS OUTSIDE before Greyson had a chance to park the truck to go up to her flat. She looked the part of a beautiful lumberjack ready to cut down a tree in jeans and a red-and-black button-down shirt. He liked the casual side of her when her hair was up in a ponytail and she ran about in trainers with Blitz. She could seamlessly fit in the ballroom and at the dog park.

Speaking of Blitz, the dog sat beside his mistress, a red-and-green bandana tied around his neck. He barked once in greeting when Greyson stepped from the truck to open the door for them.

"Good morning, you two," he said, helping Blitz climb into the seat.

"I hope you don't mind I brought him."

"Of course not. It's only fair, as he's been more than kind to share you."

"Great. We're not going far, just a half hour. Want me to drive?"

"No need. I'm fantastic at being told what to do and how to do it."

When she was seated, he went to the driver's side. Blitz licked Greyson's face when he sat, the dog poking the window with his nose. He seemed more excited for the outing than Scarlett, but Greyson could hardly blame the dog. He was just more open with his feelings. In truth, Greyson felt ecstatic he could be spending two days in a row with Scarlett.

They weren't on the highway more than ten minutes when Scarlett told him to get off on the next exit. When they turned down a wooded road, he knew they were coming near their destination. A billboard sign read *Elton Christmas Towne* in bright red letters. The radio began to dim as well.

He fiddled it to the next station, which was apparently the Elton Christmas Towne station. It blasted covers of popular holiday song, and Scarlett began to sing along.

"You have a lovely voice," he said when she finished "I'll be Home for Christmas."

Her cheeks took on a flattering shade of pink. "Knock it off."

"I mean it."

"You're just being nice."

"It's better than I could do."

"Oh yeah?"

"Yes." He turned up the radio, which began playing "Baby, it's Cold Outside."

Greyson sang the man's part with gusto, stumbling over some of the lyrics he'd forgotten. She joined in through peals of laughter. Soon, Blitz added his voice to the mix. The truck's cab was filled with howls and giggles as Greyson pulled into an empty spot beside the arched gate framed in fake holly.

All three hopped out of the pickup. Greyson opened the bed, pulling out an ax.

"What's that for?" Scarlett asked.

"Aren't we… We're here to cut down a tree, correct?"

"Yes, but they're precut. We just pick one out."

He put the ax back, feeling rather silly. At home, the groundskeeper would venture out to the royal forest with a line of trucks and axes on the first of December. They would return hours later with the first of the castle trees, one for the family's private quarters and another for the grand foyer.

"Greyson, I appreciate you came prepared. I like that about you. You're ready for anything."

Greyson flushed, sure there was no way to hide the blush. It seemed like every time he made a mistake, she found a way to find him endearing. She was never angry or annoyed when he got things wrong. And it was one of the things he liked about her.

"Just wanted to show off my manly skills, chopping the tree down for the fair maiden."

Scarlett laughed, placing a hand on Greyson's forearm. "You're right. I should've planned for that. I guess you'll just have to suffer with us regular folks and our precut trees."

"I rather like the idea of being a regular folk with you." And he meant it. Being regular with Scarlett had been the best time he'd ever had in his life. He just wasn't sure how long he could keep it going. And that thought constantly left him on edge. But today, he didn't want to be on edge. He just wanted to be Greyson.

"Here, before I forget, put this on." Scarlett held out a gold wristband. She already had one on.

"What's it for?"

"Entry to the village, unlimited snacks, and a tree."

"I see," he said, putting his on. "How much do I owe you?"

"Nothing. My friend Betsy gets a ton of these because her daddy works on the Georgia tourism board. You know, I should've registered yours under your last name, but I'm embarrassed to say I don't know it."

He opened his mouth, his full name nearly spilling from

his lips. "It's Montgomery."

"And mine's Calhoun. I'm glad we got that out of the way. I was beginning to wonder if we were going to stick to first names only."

"Of course not," Greyson said, shifting from one foot to the other. He had purposefully kept his last name out of the mix. One look on Google, and he'd be done for. But he didn't want to lie about his name. So far, he hadn't lied to her, just left out some bits of the stories, adjusted things slightly. That was allowed, right? Where was the etiquette book for masquerading as a regular person whilst having royal blood? Surely enough royals had tried it that there'd be a precedent. But without that guidance, he was flying solo, unsure how much to tell Scarlett, wanting her to know everything about him, yet still scared of what would happen if she were to know the truth.

As they neared the fences and had their wristbands scanned, he could hear the tinkling of bells and the shrieks of children. It was so warm it was almost strange to step into a winter wonderland. In Aldora, he would be wearing a coat instead of a jumper and the falling snow would be real, not whatever fabricated soap the white flakes were.

Still, he was charmed by the picturesque village. Small storefronts that seemed more in line with something out of a colonial village lined the cobblestone road where families milled about with their holiday shopping. Garlands wound around lampposts and looped overhead, interspersed with oversized glittering snowflake decorations.

He turned to tell Scarlett to look at a reindeer on a nearby roof he almost thought was real, but his voice caught. The magic of their surroundings glittered in her eyes, spreading an expression of absolute wonderment over her delicate features as she seemingly drank it all in. While he always thought her beautiful, he found her stunning in that moment.

"Come on," she said suddenly, making him jump. "There's a place over there that makes fantastic apple cider."

They went to the stand, each showing their wristbands for a cup. Even Blitz got a treat, a bit of whipped cream he lapped off his nose. The cider was piping hot, but just as delicious as Savannah promised. He normally wasn't a cider drinker, but it was more dessert than beverage.

"Ready to get a tree?" she asked, and they meandered down the cobblestones.

"Certainly. What kind do you fancy? Tall and thin? Short and squat?"

"Blitz picks them for me. He's great at it."

"Haven't you only had him two years? How many trees has he picked?"

"Seven in total. He loves car rides, so he always came with me when I went with Betsy or my parents or another friend."

"You said you found him on Christmas, yes?"

"Yep. Betsy and I do this thing where we collect toys for families and deliver them late Christmas Eve, so the kids are surprised. So two years ago, I had just dropped off the last bag when I saw a box on the side of the road. Actually, it was more *in* the road, so I pulled over to move it so no one would hit it in the dark. But the box wasn't empty. Little Blitz was in there without a mama or daddy in sight. I was going to bring him to the rescue, but…well, how could I? He was so tiny and perfect."

"He is a wonderful dog."

"The best. And now you get to see him in action."

They reached the part of the Christmas village that boasted row upon row of brilliant green trees from the tallest ones that would fit nicely in an Aldoran ballroom and the smallest ones meant for a desk decoration. But there weren't only the handful he had expected, but dozens of them, some already cut and others still growing, stretching father than he could tell.

Scarlett unhooked the leash, and Blitzen's nose immediately went to the ground. He sniffed, then crouched like a bloodhound fresh on the scent. Greyson had to laugh as the dog darted from tree to tree, pausing at the base of each one before casting if off and going to the next.

"What talent," he said as Blitzen smelled one, then snorted to show his displeasure. "Is it wise to let him loose like that?"

"Shh. Let the genius work."

But instead of sticking close by, as Scarlett said he would, Blitzen had other plans. He suddenly stood, his ears at attention and his tail straight. Letting out a small woof, he set off at a run, kicking up dirt as he went.

"Blitzen, you get back here," Scarlett called, her hands on her hips. The dog skidded to a stop, looked at her, then ran off again. "Oh, no."

"I'll fetch him."

Greyson tossed his empty cider cup in the trash, then set out at a jog after the dog. He was in good shape, but apparently not as good as the dog because he soon lost the runaway animal in the throng of people and trees. Greyson quickened his pace, not wanting to return to Scarlett without Blitzen.

He paced the rows, going back into the village in search of the dog. With every passing dog-less space, the pit forming in his stomach grew. What if Blitzen had slipped through the gate or run off into the wood beyond? He had a collar, but that meant little if whoever found him decided to keep him or if he managed to wriggle it off. If Greyson came back without him, Scarlett would be heartbroken.

But just as he turned the last corner in the field of trees, he saw Blitzen sitting at the foot of a rather nice fur. Six feet tall and pleasantly plump, Greyson had to admit it was a fine pick and perhaps the dog did have a gift.

Scarlett poked her head from around the tree and grinned, a sale tag in her hand. "There you are. We've been waiting for ages."

SCARLETT LAUGHED AS Greyson fought to untangle a line of lights that weren't even tangled to begin with. When they had gotten back to her apartment with the tree, Greyson had carried it in and helped her set it up in the stand. Then, as the branches settled, she had fixed a shepherd's pie.

Since meeting Greyson, she had begun to research English dishes. She wanted him to feel at home, and she found she enjoyed the meat-and-potato recipes. It was a twist on the home-style meals she'd grown up on in the South. Greyson had proclaimed it a taste of home. After they ate, she tasked him with lighting the tree while she fixed hot chocolate.

He unwound each strand, tucking it between the branches. When the last of the lights were in place, he asked, "Now do we drink hot chocolate and call it a day?"

"No, the ornaments. If you're good, I'll even let you put the star on top."

"Then I shall be on my best behavior."

They started with the normal glass balls first. She always chose the colorful ones, the mismatched things she found at yard sales and craft tables at the fair. Her mama always had a decorator come set up perfect trees with themes like *angels in flight* that had bright blue ornaments and a plethora of white feathers, or *colonial Christmas* where everything was made of wood and miniature colonists in Santa hats with American flags graced the trees.

"You know, I've never done this before," Greyson said, studying an ornament of a crescent moon.

"What?"

"Decorated a tree."

"I thought you told me you celebrated Christmas back home?"

"I did—*do*. But my mother was very…particular."

She smiled, putting a hand on his arm. "Me too. It sounds more and more like our mamas would be the best of friends."

"To be honest, I'm not entirely sure my mother has friends. At least not ones she'd trust to decorate her trees for the holiday." He shook his head. "No, I think I like your style much more."

"Do you?"

"Of course. I don't know what's going to come out of this box yet. So far, I've hung a moon, a raccoon, three tropical birds, a Leaning Tower of Pisa, and more than one Disney character. I've no idea what I'll find next."

"Only one way to find out. Let's hurry and get them all on so we can light it up. Nothing's better than that. It's the beginning of Christmas."

As they continued to dress the tree, her conversation with Betsy nipped at her subconscious. Scarlett didn't know anything about his family, other than he had one. "You know, you haven't told me anything about your parents or your brother."

"What would you like to know?"

"Anything, I guess."

"Well, Harrison, my brother, he's a top-notch lad. He's a good cook, much like yourself. But he has a mouth on him that gets him into more trouble than not."

"Sounds like my friend Betsy, actually. If he crosses the pond, they should meet."

"As lovely as I'm sure your friend Betsy is, Harrison has a best mate. As soon as he realizes he loves her more than a friend, I'm fairly sure the two will be wed."

"Aw, so cute."

"Not if you've had to watch it for years. I want to grab him and shake the lad."

"Do you two look alike?"

"Yes and no. People say I favor our mother while he resembles our father." He stared at the glass ball in his hands. It wasn't a particularly fancy one, just a golden shiny thing, but Scarlett felt as if he could see something in its depths. "My parents and I have a difficult relationship."

"Is that why you came here?"

"Yes and no. Things are complicated between us at the moment, and my mother doesn't handle change well. With my father, you wouldn't know anything bothered him, but I know he isn't pleased I'm here."

"So why come?"

"It was important for me. I want my own life. To experience more than just what their circle has to offer. Don't get me wrong, they are lovely people. Well, Mum's a bit dramatic and my dad's quiet, but I'd never know what I want from life if I only do what they expect of me."

"Sounds a lot like my parents, including the dramatic mother."

"Can she faint on command? It's one of my mother's favorite tricks."

"She can. In fact, there's a chair, a chaise, or a couch in every room so she can dramatically fall without getting anything on her immaculate clothes."

"Now I think my mother has found her match. She hasn't quite gone to furnishing the house for her fits, though. She just falls straight to the floor." He hung the ornament, then picked up his hot chocolate, holding it up for a toast. "To parents."

"To parents," she said with a smile as they tapped mugs.

They worked to dress the tree, pausing every so often for Scarlett to tell Greyson about a particular ornament. The sun drifted lower and lower until the city was cast into night. When everything was hung, she passed Greyson the star, a glittery silver one her grandmother had left her. When he affixed it to the top, Scarlett flipped the switch. The tree glowed, the lights sending multicolored glimmers from the ornament across the room.

She settled onto the couch with Greyson, fresh mugs of hot chocolate in their hands and Blitzen asleep by their feet. And as she sat in the quietly comfortable afterglow of a perfect day, she wondered if that was what love felt like.

CHAPTER SEVEN

G REYSON SPENT THE week leading up to the cookie party in his makeshift workshop. Scarlett had told him not to bring anything, but he wanted to do something to sway her family. Back in Aldora, one never went to a celebration without some kind of gift for the hosts. It was usually something related to one's family, so when the hosts looked at the gift, they thought of who it had come from.

While he wasn't in Europe or attending a royal celebration, he still figured the idea held merit. So he stuck with something he was good at. However, instead of a basket, he figured he could make the Calhoun coat of arms.

Scarlett had once talked about how proud her family was of their history. He decided to make them a coat of arms they could display for everyone to see. Or at least, he hoped they'd display it. They might end up relegating it into a closet forever. But either way, it was the best he could do.

It was just time that kept him from knocking it out in a night or two. He'd taken on some jobs for a couple of lads from the construction site to supplement his income. One wanted this grand entertainment system and the other a rocking chair for his wife as a surprise for their new baby.

It only took a few hours of research and some long nights

for Greyson to create one of his most intricate works to date. On a large oval piece of dark wood, he had engraved the shield first, crossing it with an oversized X. Then a knight's helmet was added above it, and a small stag's head on top. Along the sides were clouds of filigree, a more detailed take on the shields he had seen online. Finally, before the layer of finish was added, he carefully carved the name *Calhoun* on the bottom.

Greyson was just getting ready to leave for the party when his mobile rang.

"Greyson," his mother began sternly. "I will come to the United States and drag you home by your ear if you don't check in more often. I've tried to keep my nose out of it, but I can't anymore. Do you realize how dangerous it is for you to be there without a bodyguard or anyone watching over you? I fall asleep every night in a panic. At least let me send a driver over there. He can take you around and watch you from afar."

Greyson ran a hand through his hair, then held the phone between his cheek and shoulder to finish buttoning his shirt. "No. I'll make more of an effort to ring you. But I have plans, so I'm going to need to hurry off."

"Ah, yes, ever the socialite. Tell me—is it Thanksgiving, the prized American holiday where they celebrate when their people left Europe and went to the United States for a new life? Your auntie Elizabeth thinks it terribly inappropriate. I bet you can understand that mentality."

"It's not. That's in November, but—"

"Well, Greyson, what are these plans that are more important than speaking with your mother?"

"I'm accompanying a friend to her family's holiday party."

"Is this the female friend you briefly talked about the last time I was forced to ring you out of parental concern?"

"Yes, it is the female friend."

She huffed into the receiver. "So you're going to meet her family, but you refuse to even tell me her name?"

"Her name is Scarlett."

"Is there a surname as well, or must I wait several more frantic calls before you grace me with that knowledge?"

He rolled his eyes at the receiver. "Calhoun. Scarlett Calhoun."

"Well, I insist you bring her to Christmas."

"Pardon?" He was certain he heard his mother wrong. She always insisted Christmas was for family only, no guests outside of nobles, politicians, and dignitaries, and definitely no dates one wasn't engaged or married to.

"I said you should bring her to Christmas."

He *had* heard her correctly. His throat feeling dry, he went to the sink for a glass of water. "I can't."

"And why not?"

"As I told you before, I'm keeping things quiet here. I haven't even told her who I am or who our family is."

"Oh, just tell her. I'm sure she's sorted it out by now."

"No, she hasn't, and I've worked hard to keep it as such," he said firmly, hoping his mother would drop it.

"Like any girl wouldn't wish to be with a royal. Just tell her who you are. Although, do make it clear we have prenuptial agreements in place in the event you wed."

He choked on his drink, taking a moment to compose himself. True, he'd grown fond of Scarlett, was maybe even considering love, but he wasn't ready for the family lawyers to begin the prenup agreements. Had his mother gone mad? And then he realized what her comments meant—he'd have to tell Scarlett who he was.

No, he wasn't ready for that yet. If he didn't do it, then he could just sit in their perfect bubble with Blitzen and continue going on as if he hadn't been hiding something from Scarlett. "Her family has money, and she is definitely not interested in me for ours. Scarlett doesn't even know we have wealth. She only knows me as a poor construction worker, and she fancies me anyway. I don't want to ruin that by introducing her to—"

"First, you don't want to be our prince…and now you're too ashamed of our family to bring your girlfriend home for holiday? Will you keep this up forever and never visit again? Am I to take your picture off our walls and pretend I do not have a son? Are we to make an announcement Greyson Charles Rudolf Leopold Montgomery never existed and is a figment of everyone's imagination? Would that make it easier for you to reject us?"

"Mother, keep it together. Please stop."

"Greyson, I just don't understand why you despise me so much," she said lowly, her voice tinged with sadness.

And just like that, the queen was gone and his mother was back. The sadness, the pain in her voice, it didn't sound dramatic. It sounded real. He hated making her feel like this.

But he needed to stick to his plans. Scarlett was worth it. If he brought her over, it just gave his mother the chance to try to manipulate Scarlett, push her straight from his life to open a spot for the royal of his mother's choosing. No, it couldn't happen, no matter how distraught she seemed.

"That's not the case. Things are still new with Scarlett, and...I'll think it over. How about that?"

"I suppose you should consider if she is appropriate. I would hate to have her cause a scandal for us during the party."

"Mother, she is one of the most elegant and sophisticated women I have ever met, and that includes the ones back home."

"An *American*? Really?"

"Trust me, you'll approve."

He promised to speak to her again in a few days, initiating the contact instead of ignoring her. Mother was right— he didn't want to be the king—but he did still want to be in the family. They had their quirks, but he still loved them and didn't want to keep any future relation from them forever.

He thought about it as he wrapped the coat of arms. At home, all holiday and birthday purchases would be seen to by the staff, perfectly sorted to be put under the tree or presented at dinner. Wrapping things was just another average task he had no idea how to accomplish.

After going through half a roll of wrapping paper and most of the tape, Greyson decided it would be better if he just abandoned it completely. Next time, he would buy a gift bag and make it simple. Or maybe he'd make something in the shape of a square so it would be easier to wrap.

His mobile rang as he was tossing the last of the hopeless wrapping paper in the bin.

"Hi, Greyson. I'm outside. Are you ready?"

"Scarlett, of course. I'll be down in a moment."

Scarlett sat in her convertible with her big sunglasses on and a bright smile.

When he opened the passenger door, he slid inside and kissed her once on the cheek. It was a customary greeting where he was from with people one was familiar with. Yet, when he leaned in, he smelled the floral scent of her perfume, the slight hint of strawberry from her hair, and something delicious he couldn't quite name. "Something smells amazing. It smells almost as lovely as you do."

"Hey, easy on those cheesy lines. Save them for Mama," Scarlett said, but her cheeks brightened slightly as she reached behind her. "I think it's the pie—my famous apple pie. What do you think?" When she lifted the cover off the dish, the mouthwatering aroma overtook him.

"How upset would your mother be if we ate this on the way and showed up without your famous apple pie?"

"She would consider canceling dinner, as this is one of the main reasons people come. Well, and to be graced by my presence, I suppose."

"Then I guess I'll just have to suffer through the actual dinner and wait until dessert."

"What did you bring?" Scarlett asked, pointing to the coat of arms.

He picked it up, then shyly handed it to her. The slab of

oval wood almost hit the rearview mirror as he did. "I didn't want to come empty-handed. You said your family is proud of your name, so I did a little research."

"This is perfect. Oh my goodness," Scarlett whispered as her delicate fingertips gently stroked the knight's helmet, following the indentations, circling the carvings, and feeling the border. "My parents will love this." She transferred it to him carefully, as if she were afraid something would happen to it. "Flowers would've worked. You didn't need to go through this much trouble."

"Did you mother hire a florist?"

"Well, yes."

"Then my flowers would've been inferior, lessening the effect. I couldn't afford to get a bouquet made to the caliber she probably ordered. I figured it would be more personal this way, so she would know I put thought behind it."

"Like the picnic basket?"

"Just like the basket. You're worth the extra effort, and I want your family to approve."

Scarlett just stared at him for a few seconds. She didn't say anything, nor did he. He didn't know what to say. His heart pounded in his ears, and he wished to desperately to kiss her. But he couldn't. Their first kiss should be a special one with the perfect backdrop or under some carefully placed mistletoe. She deserved fireworks and roses, the things the old him would have been able to extend. The new him needed to get to work.

"My parents, Woodward and Delia, probably invited twenty to thirty people to this party. A lot of them will be there, so I hope that doesn't overwhelm you," Scarlett said after a few minutes of driving.

"Back home, my mother threw similar parties, so don't fret. I can handle myself amongst a crowd. And if your mother's cooking is anything like yours, then I will have to steel myself so I don't challenge someone to a duel for the last piece of turkey."

"Oh, trust me, that won't be a problem. There is always so much leftover food. No need for a duel today."

"Fair enough. I didn't bring gloves, so I'd have no way to challenge someone. And really, what is a duel if you don't set it up properly?"

"I agree, a proper Englishman like you couldn't start a duel without following all the protocol."

"A proper *Aldorian*," he corrected without thinking.

"What do you mean by Aldorian?"

Greyson froze, realizing he'd lost himself. He hadn't been paying attention to what he was saying. He'd just wanted to keep Scarlett smiling. As the awkward seconds ticked by, he began to think about the possibility of just telling her.

But it was too soon. He knew she was interested in him, but there was no way of telling if she, too, felt…he didn't want to say love, not yet, not until he was sure, down to his marrow, that he loved her. Until he felt she did, he didn't want to break the news of his true identity. On the other hand, the longer he took to break the news to her, the higher the chance she'd be distraught about him keeping secrets.

"I just mean…dueling used to be a large part of Aldorian

culture. That's how the royal family got into power, actually. Seven hundred years ago, a blacksmith didn't approve of the king or his cruel methods, so he challenged the king to a duel for the kingdom. The blacksmith won and took the crown. The people and the crown have lived in peace since then."

"Wait…but what's Aldorian? I must admit I'm not great at geography."

He cleared his throat, trying to figure out how to explain things without lying. "The country of Aldora is a small nation island near the western coast of England."

"But didn't you say you were from England?"

He was glad her gaze was firmly on the road since he was sure the panic rising in his chest was visible across his features. He had gotten too comfortable, too sloppy. If he weren't careful, he'd let his princely persona slip and then he'd be forced into the truth before he could find a way to do it properly. "I did. I—I just know quite a bit about history. It's a bit of a long story, really."

"Well, I guess we have to catch up on geography better because this is my parents' home," she said as she turned into a long drive made up of stone.

The black iron gate was open, allowing them to enter the charming estate. Greyson, used to the grand and elaborate style of Aldorian architecture, had to admit even he was impressed as they drove up the tree-lined driveway. The house was not just large—it was extravagant. There was a fountain in front of the rounded drive, with a mermaid in the center and two massive fish on either side of her. The water flowed into the rotund fountain with elegant speed.

Behind it, the house stood proud, boasting three-story towers on either side with pointed roofs topping them. The stone-work along the façade was flawless, suggesting they were high quality and probably European. *Italian*, Greyson thought as he squinted, examining it a little closer while Scarlett parked the car.

"This is beautiful," he said. "Architecture and the various types around the world have always fascinated me. And your home is similar to many of the country estates where I grew up."

"When you meet my mother, say that. She spent an exorbitant amount of money remodeling this house when she and my father got married. She even flew in an architect from Italy to draw up the plans. The stones were all brought over on a ship."

"Her taste is to be commended," he said, taking in the carvings and giant bronze handles on the double doors. Elaborate wreaths hung on each, decorated with gold bows and red Christmas balls.

"Are you sure you're ready for this?" Scarlett asked, this time breaking him out of his trance. "I know we just met and all."

"Well, actually, before we walk in…how are you introducing me to people?"

"What do you mean? Do you want to go by something other than Greyson? Mr. Grey maybe?" Scarlett laughed, but Greyson didn't get the joke.

"No, no, Greyson is fine. I just mean I don't want to cause any problems for you. Am I your friend or maybe something more?" He paused, trying to decide if he was being too presumptuous in asking. They had only known each other maybe a month.

Scarlett turned to Greyson, her eyes wide as she seemed to catch his meaning. "I didn't think that far through this. Um, I guess I could just say—"

"Because I'd like to be introduced as your boyfriend, but I don't want to make any assumptions. I've greatly enjoyed our time, and I would truly be honored if you wanted to take this step with me." He took her hand and brushed his lips against her knuckles, trying to control the shake in his fingers as he waited with bated breath for her answer.

"Yes, I think *boyfriend* would be a sufficient title for you," she murmured, sounding pleased.

The vise squeezing his chest released, and he breathed a sigh of relief.

"You have a deal. As long as when we meet your family, I'm introduced as your girlfriend."

"I wouldn't have it any other way."

Greyson extended his other hand, brushing a stray hair out of Scarlett's face. Then he leaned in, his tall frame bending to meet her petite one. He closed his eyes as he neared her lips. Those red full lips he had wanted to kiss since he almost ran her off the road. She was his *girlfriend*. The statement produced so much elation in him it was hard to contain. He had wished their first kiss to be surrounded by Christmas lights, beneath a starry sky, or beside the ocean with the waves lapping against the sand. But he couldn't deny his need to express his adoration of her any longer. And after the new title—the best he'd probably ever have bestowed upon him—it seemed like the perfect time.

"Scarlett," a voice said, causing Greyson to jerk back. "Who is your *friend*? You didn't tell me you were bringing anyone."

When Greyson turned, he couldn't help but smile. He was staring at an older version of Scarlett. They looked exactly the same with the salon blown-out blond hair and wide blue eyes. "Mrs. Calhoun, nice to meet you," he said, extending his hand.

She reached out with a smile, though it seemed quite forced, similar to the society smile his own mother frequently put on when she was entertaining. But Greyson was determined to impress her. He took her hand, then kissed the top of it.

"My name is Greyson, and I am ever so grateful you've so graciously accepted me into your home. Without you, I'm afraid a tin of store-bought chicken salad was my dinner date."

He thought he saw her cheeks pinken. "Oh, no. Even if you aren't a Southerner, that simply won't do. Why don't you come in? We have plenty of food. Of course, it's no problem to have an additional guest." She sidestepped away from the door, motioning for them to enter.

Greyson was about to accept her invitation when he remembered the coat of arms. "If you'll only give me a moment, I brought you and your husband a gift, but I'm afraid I've left it in Scarlett's car. Scarlett, do you mind accompanying me to your vehicle? Then I'd be happy to escort you inside."

"Yes, I'd love to Greyson. Mama, we'll be right back."

"How am I doing?" he asked quietly as they stepped onto the drive. He'd been too distracted by the house initially to remember to grab the gift earlier.

"Too early to tell. But it was definitely good to throw in store-bought chicken salad. Wait…didn't I make you a fresh tub the other day? Are you out?"

"Oh yes, I've been out for days. But I cannot go back to the store-bought kind now I've tasted yours. I just figured she'd be as horrified about it as you were."

"Clever man. I'll fix you up a nice big batch for work this week."

"That's kind of you, but really, you don't need to."

"What are girlfriends for, if not to ensure our boyfriends eat real food?"

"Ah, you've got me there. Thank you. I am the envy of the other men in my crew." Greyson opened the passenger door, grabbing the coat of arms.

"Then I'll have to add some homemade cookies to make them jealous."

Greyson took her hand with his free one as they strolled to the front doors. "Are you ready to make everyone in the party jealous of you now? I'm about to be quite charming and terribly British in the cheeky Hugh Grant sort of way, yet as refined as the beloved Prince William. Prepare yourself."

"I'm looking forward to it," Scarlett said with a small laugh.

"Here you are, Mrs. Calhoun," he said when they reached the front door. He presented the gift, hopeful that first impressions were wrong and she'd warm to him. "It's the Calhoun coat of arms."

"I know." Scarlett's mom accepted it and seemed to be investigating it with a careful eye. "We used to have one, but it fell off the wall during an awful storm. I've always wanted to replace it, but I just haven't found one I liked. Wherever did you get this? It's stunning."

"Actually, Mama," Scarlett cut in. "Greyson made it. He carved, assembled, and then painted it."

"Did you really?" Mrs. Calhoun closed the door behind them, then placed the gift on the side table. "Well, you've done a beautiful job. Thank you."

"No, thank you for the compliment, Mrs. Calhoun."

"Please, call me Delia," she said before excusing herself to the kitchen.

"Mama," Scarlett called. "Would you take my pie? I'm going to greet Daddy."

The woman turned and took the pie, not looking at Greyson or the coat of arms she'd left on the table. He and Scarlett stood in the entryway beside the massive Christmas tree, the white lights twinkling in the branches. He supposed this year's Calhoun tree theme was snowfall, an almost laughable concept, as he didn't think it every snowed in Savannah.

"She didn't like it?" Greyson asked Scarlett in a hushed tone. Her mother was an especially difficult woman to read. For all he knew, the moment they left, she'd toss it in the fireplace. Part of him was a little gutted. He'd worked hard on the crest, hoping it'd be a key to getting the Calhouns to like him. Scarlett may have described her parents as a bit dramatic, but he knew she still valued their opinions. If they didn't like him, would Scarlett give him the time of day? Worry flowed through him at the prospect.

"Oh, she did. You saw the expression on her face change when I said you made it. You must have. She's a bit of a snob sometimes, and she definitely needs to work on her poker face. You'd think a society woman like Mama would have mastered it by now, but no. Don't let it bother you. I'm going to bring it to show my father. I know he'll appreciate it. And if he doesn't, then I'm going to steal it and hang it in my apartment because it is beautiful."

"Works for me."

SCARLETT TOOK THE coat of arms, with Greyson following behind her, and went to her father's study. The guests hadn't started to arrive, so Mama wouldn't have forced him to put his work away. She knocked on the massive door, then pushed it open and entered when he responded. The familiar scents of leather, oiled wood, and the faint smell of cigars he promised he never smoked surrounded her.

"Hello, Daddy." Hurrying to his side, she then placed a kiss on his cheek.

He put down the stack of papers he had been reading and smiled, leaning back in his desk chair. "And hello to you. Who is this gentleman? Is it the one Mrs. Hartman told your mother about?"

"Yes, Daddy. How many men do you think I'm entertaining?"

"Well, your mother had quite a few callers when I was pursuing her. Since you're just as beautiful, I expect they are interested as well. It's one of the reasons I don't want you living in that apartment on your own."

Scarlett fought the urge to roll her eyes. Her father brought up her apartment every time they saw each other. She secretly wished for parents who celebrated their empty nest as opposed to hers who hated every minute of it.

"Daddy, this is my boyfriend, Greyson. The only man I am...entertaining," she said, using his word. "Greyson, this is my father, Woodward Calhoun."

Greyson and her father shook hands, their grips appearing very firm to Scarlett. She placed the coat of arms on her father's desk, careful to not make a mess of his carefully piled files. "What do you think of this?"

"It's the Calhoun coat of arms, of course. It's very well crafted and amazingly accurate. Top-notch craftsmanship."

"I'm glad you think so," Greyson said.

"You made this?" Mr. Calhoun looked up from the coat of arms for the first time since it was placed on his desk.

"Yes, sir, I did. I wanted to make something to show your family my appreciation for allowing me to join the festivities."

"Greyson, this is a work of art." Her daddy extended his hand to Greyson, and they shook again. This time without the death grip. "Scarlett, please tell your mother I would like it up in the dining room before the guests come over. I bet half the people in attendance have never even seen their own coat of arms, let alone own a custom one of this caliber. Greyson, you may leave here with some special orders for these."

"That would be fantastic. I have a workshop in my flat, so I could whip them up for any of your friends who try to be as prestigious as you."

Daddy laughed. "You'd better watch what you say, son. They might hear you and realize the truth."

Just then, the phone rang. "Darlin', go have your mother hang this. I need to finish a little business before she locks me out of my office for the rest of the evening."

Scarlett smiled, knowing it was no idle threat on her mama's part. When she motioned for Greyson to follow and closed the door behind them, she said, "He likes you. Definitely."

"One out of two isn't bad, correct?"

"Mama *will* like you. Give her some time. She's cold with most people when she first meets them. Then she realizes they are worthy of her presence and warms up considerably."

"And if I'm found not worthy?"

He sounded worried, so Scarlett tried to reassure him, touched he genuinely seemed to care. "But you are. Therefore, I'm not worried."

Scarlett settled Greyson in the library. There were several filled bookcases. Since Greyson told Scarlett he liked to read, she figured he could find something while she went to the kitchen to help Mama finish up the cooking and be interrogated.

As soon as she walked into the kitchen, she was met with the delicious scents of her mama's cooking. While actually a Christmas cookie party, there was always a full buffet of stuffing, baked chicken, potatoes two ways, four vegetables, cornbread, and more than enough gravy.

"You know how hard I work every year to make this party perfect," Mama said quietly, not turning away from the potatoes she was aggressively mashing. "I spend hours on the seating charts, the place settings, everything. And then you knowingly bring a date without giving me any kind of warning. What would happen if I didn't have enough gold-rimmed china plates? Or if I made miniature pies like last year and was one short when dessert came?"

Scarlett cringed, realizing she'd maybe made an error in deciding to add Greyson without her mother's knowledge. "I wanted to surprise you."

"Why?"

"I just wanted you to meet him without any preconceived notions you would undoubtedly think up on your own. This way, it's all fresh."

"Scarlett Anna-Beth, how dare you suggest I wouldn't give that man a fair chance in my home? I did not raise you to think that way about me."

"I'm sorry, Mama," Scarlett said, trying to end the tense moment. "What did you think of him?"

"Well, I don't know him yet." Her mama moved to the stove, stirring the gravy, smelling the cranberries, then checking on the chickens in the double oven.

Scarlett slid onto one of the barstools at the granite island. "What do you want to know?"

"Let's start with the basics. What does he do besides make coats of arms for people and show up to parties without a formal invitation?"

"He's a construction worker. He likes to work with wood, and he wants to do carvings and build furniture when he's more settled. He told me one day he wants to maybe even build the house he'll live in with his family."

That fact was one of the reasons she was glad she'd shown him the old house she would love to have made into a bed and breakfast. She could imagine him working on the roof, refinishing the hardwood floors to their former beauty, carving intricate designs into the railings down the grand staircase they would have, and building furniture to put in a nursery. Like Betsy said, Scarlett was imagining their future. It was too soon, and she wasn't marrying him tomorrow, but the images felt nice.

"He'll have to build one, since he won't be able to afford to buy one with that kind of job."

Scarlett gasped, horrified her mother would say something so callous. "Mama, you can't speak like that."

"What? Do you want me to pretend he wasn't wearing secondhand pants?" her mother replied, nose snootily tilted up.

"What does it matter? He's a gentleman. He treats me well, and I like spending time with him. Really, I'm surprised you're being like this."

Mama sighed heavily, a wooden spoon still clutched in her hand. "All I'm saying, darlin', is boys like that are fun to date, but you don't marry them. You're getting older. I think it's time the fun ended, and you began to think about your future."

"I do think about my future. And I have plenty of money, so I don't see how I need someone else's," Scarlett protested.

"Right." Her mother put down the spoon, then crossed her arms. "And there's one more flaw in the grand plan to have invited that boy into my home for the cookie party."

"What?"

The doorbell sounded throughout the house, the music announcing another guest. Her mother glanced at her gold Cartier wristwatch and said, "Someone's punctual."

"It must be Betsy and her parents," Scarlett said, glad someone in the house beside Greyson would be on her side. "I'll go let them in."

"No, darlin', I don't think it's Elizabeth and her family. I invited another guest who has arrived on time, but who will now make things a little uncomfortable."

"Who?" Scarlett had a sinking feeling in her stomach.

"Well, I'm going to say I obviously didn't expect you to bring a man, so this may be a bit awkward. Nonetheless, I do hope you will be polite and open to this."

Confused, Scarlett trailed her mother out of the kitchen and down the hall to the front door. "Mama, what you talking about?"

Ignoring her, Mama swung the door open. Standing

there was a tall man with dark features, wearing an immaculately tailored suit. "William, how lovely it is to have you join us. I hope you've brought your appetite."

Scarlett's throat tightened, her face flaming with anger. Her mother just couldn't let her make her own choices, or even respect them once they were already made. It wasn't William's fault, of course, but Scarlett didn't know how else to end her mama's dreams of her marrying him without being blunt.

"Along with some imported Swiss chocolates." He grinned as he handed her mother a gold box wrapped with a red ribbon. "And Scarlett, it's wonderful to see you again."

"William...what are you doing here?"

Her mother closed the door, beckoning them to follow her while shooting Scarlett a narrow-eyed glare. "I ran into William and his mother at the club yesterday. Now, Scarlett, be a big help and come assist me in the kitchen? William, you'll find Woodward in the study."

As soon as William had gone off in search of her father, Scarlett rounded on her mother. "Mama, what is going on?"

Her face was placid, devoid of embarrassment or any other emotion. "I obviously didn't know you'd be bringing that construction worker here, so I took the liberty of invit—"

"*William?*" Scarlett whispered. "Mama, what in the world were you thinking?"

"I was thinking William is a nice young man from a good family who has a *real* job."

"He's my ex-boyfriend's cousin, and I already told you it wouldn't work."

"I know, but I always thought Scarlett Birmingham had a lovely ring to it. If yow married him, we wouldn't even need to change everything we already had monogrammed when you were dating Reginald."

Scarlett stood frozen in place, her heart beating so rapidly she thought it must be audible to everyone in the house. Emotion swirled in her chest, a tornado of sadness, humiliation, and red-hot anger. Scarlett balled her fists and bit her lip, trying not to cry. She was mortified for so many reasons she didn't even know where to begin. But the emotion that was winning in her heart was a deep devastation. No matter what she did, no matter how many times she said something, no matter how Scarlett tried to live, it was never good enough unless it went in line with her mother's plans. Why was Scarlett such a source of disappointment to the woman? She went to church, did charitable work, was polite to everyone she met, and tried so hard. But it didn't matter. Being the best person she could be didn't matter. Scarlett felt something breaking inside her.

"Mama, why don't you listen to anything I say?"

"Because I know what's best for you. You can't just write someone off without getting to know them. You're a silly child who thinks the world is a perfect place. The world is cruel. If you don't act right, it will swallow you up and leave you with nothing. You don't want to end up alone, do you? Because it sure seems like you're headed down the spinster path."

Scarlett took a step back, feeling like she had just been slapped across the face. While she knew her mother to be a little overbearing and judgmental at times, Scarlett had never expected she would be so cruel and hypocritical. She wouldn't give Greyson a chance, but demanded Scarlett give her ex's cousin one? The nerve! It was then she decided store-brand chicken in the park with cooking wine was a more agreeable dinner than the elaborate one her mother had planned.

Scarlett turned sharply on her heel and stalked into the library, where Greyson was thumbing through an encyclopedia. She knew she needed to get out before she fell apart. "Come on, we're leaving."

He shut the book. "Leaving?"

"Yes, I just want to go home. Just…come on, please." Tears began to well in her eyes, her hands shaking with a combination of anger and sadness.

Greyson carefully slid the encyclopedia back onto its shelf before moving to her side. "What's happened?"

"Can we talk about it later? I want to get out of here."

"Of course." When he took her hand, she began leading him toward the front door when her mother appeared.

"Scarlett, did I hear correctly you are leaving my Christmas cookie party before the guests even arrive?"

"Yes, Mama," Scarlett replied, her voice quavering as she spoke. "I brought Greyson here tonight so you could meet the man I've been spending so much time with, who has been nothing but polite, supportive, and romantic since the first day we met. I thought if you just met him, you'd like him just as much as I do and wouldn't look down your nose at him like you insist on doing to everyone else you deem beneath you. But I was wrong. For now on, you will no longer have a say in who I choose to keep in my life."

Her mother's cheeks flushed the same red as her lipstick. "Scarlett, I—"

Scarlett held up a hand, interrupting her mother in a way she never had before. "No. We're leaving."

Scarlett pulled Greyson from the library, brushing past her mother as she tried to make it outside before she started to cry. She was so focused on escaping she didn't even think to say goodbye to her father, who was just coming out of his study with William by his side. Scarlett thought she heard Greyson call out something to her parents as she yanked him out the front door, but it was like she had temporarily gone deaf.

When they got to her car, her fingers shook as she tried to get her keys from her purse. When she got them free, she dropped them onto the paved driveway. But as she bent to get them, Greyson stopped her.

"Here, let me drive."

With a shaky nod, she allowed him to escort her over to the passenger side. As he opened the door for her, a sleek black Mercedes pulled into the long drive and stopped just beside hers. Betsy and her parents emerged from within. In her haste to get away, Scarlett hadn't thought to call her best friend and warn her about the nuclear zone they were fixing to walk into.

Betsy was grinning ear to ear as she bounced over to Scarlett's car, eyes on Greyson. But her friend's smile faced when she caught sight of Scarlett. Turning to her parents,

Betsy called out, "Go on ahead." Then she drew closer and asked, "What's going on?"

Scarlett sniffed. "Mama was just being… She's just so…"

"Mrs. Calhoun has upset Scarlett, so she's chosen to leave the cookie party early," Greyson said.

"Wow, whatever happened must have been pretty bad." Betsy glanced toward the Calhoun manor, then opened the back door of Scarlett's car and slid in. After she clipped on her seat belt, she leaned out the open window. "So…where are we going?"

GREYSON GLANCED AT Betsy in the rearview mirror as he drove. "This isn't the best way to get acquainted, but I'm pleased to meet you just the same."

"Likewise," Betsy said with a smile. "You probably already know, but I'm Elizabeth Sicklerson. Betsy for short."

"Sicklerson? Why does that name sound so familiar?"

"Oh, that would be because of my dad. So you've probably seen the name Chris Sicklerson on a billboard for real estate or on the cover of *Forbes.*"

"Her daddy was just named the top real estate broker in all of Georgia," Savannah said softly. "We're all very proud of the hard work he's done."

Greyson liked she was joining the conversation a bit, but in the light of the streetlamps they passed, there were obvious tears in her eyes. Reaching over the center console, he took her hand in his before addressing Betsy. "Now that you mention in, I do believe I've seen the issue of *Forbes* you speak of. It was the September volume, right?"

"Wow, how did you know that?"

"At home, I made it my business to know…well, how others did business."

"Aspiring businessman or interested in stocks?"

His mind flitted to his rather full stock portfolio, and he smiled. "A bit of both."

In traditional Southern fashion, the moment they arrived at Scarlett's flat, both women had hurried into the kitchen to begin making dinner. While not the elaborate one he'd imagined, Greyson thought the simple meal of fried chicken, corn on the cob, and mashed potatoes was one of the best he'd ever had. While he had offered many times to help cook, he'd been firmly told to stay out of the way, not that he could blame them. Instead, he'd made himself useful by taking out the trash and walking Blitz.

When they finished eating and he had tended to the dishes, Betsy rang a cab to take her home. Scarlett had stepped out onto the balcony for some air, leaving Greyson alone in the kitchen. He wasn't all too sure how to help her, so decided to do so in the way his governess always had. By making tea.

To his horror, there was no kettle to boil the water, not that he'd ever actually made tea before. So he filled a mug with water and placed it in the microwave, then rummaged in the cupboard. Instead of loose tea to steep, he found a box of small teabags. When the water was warm enough, he plopped one inside before adding sugar and a splash of milk.

"Tea?" he offered as he stepped on to the balcony and

held up the cup.

"How British," she said with a small smile. She took the mug, cupping it in both hands. "I want to apologize for tonight."

"Although I don't know what's going on, I can assure you there's nothing to apologize for."

"But there is." She paused, taking a sip of the tea before placing it down on the small café-style table. "Did you see that man with my father when we were leaving?"

"Yes, I did."

"To make a long and very messy story short, he's my ex-boyfriend's cousin. When my ex and I broke up last year, it upset my mom. You're the first guy I've dated since then, and I thought the cookie party would be a good time to introduce you. In my mind, I had this idea we would all come together—like everyone I cared about would just get along like on television. It was stupid."

"No, it wasn't."

"I didn't even tell you the worst part," she admitted with a grim expression. "My mama invited that guy because she wanted to play matchmaker. Even though she knew I was seeing someone, seeing *you*, she went behind my back because she can't handle not being in control."

"I see." Greyson leaned against the railing, resting his elbows on the smooth metal. He gazed over the darkened skyline of Savannah. For the first time since his plane had landed, he felt like he didn't belong. At work, he was just one of the lads, respected and friends with everyone at the site. He'd even been yelled at by the foreman for being five minutes late once. Greyson had never been chastised by anyone outside his parents before. And since then, he'd shown up fifteen minutes early. Nearly everyone he'd met in Savannah had welcomed him fully, and while he assumed Scarlett's parents would be a little more difficult to please than his foreman, Greyson hadn't thought he'd be so clearly disliked. "She doesn't think much of me, does she?"

Scarlett placed a hand on his arm. "I don't care what she thinks. You're hardworking and funny and sweet…I've had so much fun with you over the past few weeks. If she can't see what an amazing guy you are, then it's her loss. You and I are a package deal now. If you're not welcomed in my mama's house, then neither am I."

The pale glow of the moon and the many lights of the city around them lit her face. In all his life, he hadn't ever imagined anyone standing up for him the way Scarlett had. Of course, he had a care team at the castle who would cater to his needs and quell any bad press he might attract, but no one did it simply because they cared deeply for him. They did it because it was their job. Scarlett had just stood up to her mother and walked out of a family holiday because she… Well, he couldn't say for sure it was love, but he could say it felt like the closest thing to it. And if he had any chance of having her in his life for good, he needed to take a gamble. He just hoped it paid off.

"Scarlett," he began, bringing his hand up to cup her cheek. "Would you do me the honor of coming home for the Christmas holiday with me?"

CHAPTER EIGHT

S CARLETT STARED AT her luggage, wondering how much more she could fit into her two full-sized suitcases. While she would only be staying at Greyson's family home for a week, she had no idea how to pack. She knew England would be cold, but that was about it. He wasn't much help either, as all he'd suggested were clothes to keep her warm and comfortable.

"Maybe ditch the dress with the puffy skirt?" Betsy suggested, picking through the pile in the bigger of the suitcases. "It's taking up way too much room."

"But I was going to wear that if their Christmas party was on the formal side."

"Then what's this other dress for?"

"What if they go to church? I need to have my shoulders covered. Or if I need to dress nice for brunch. Or if his family turns out to be very conservative."

Betsy pursed her lips. "Okay, here's what we'll do. You'll wear this jacket on the plane and this chunky sweater, so we can at least get this shut. Here, sit on it and I'll try to zip it."

Scarlett closed the lid, then sat on the suitcase as Betsy struggled to close it. "You don't think I went overboard?"

"Oh, no, not at all." Betsy replied sarcastically as the zipper sealed. "But what if you buy anything there? You won't be able to bring it back."

Scarlett groaned. "Ugh, fine. I'll lose the dress with the puffy skirt *and* two pairs of shoes."

"Good. It's three AM. I'm too tired to help you sort through pants for the third time, and we need to leave for the airport now. Do you have everything else ready?"

"Yep. You'll stay here to dog sit and water plants, I have my passport, wallet, cash to exchange, and I set up international calling on my phone."

"Perfect. What about your tickets?"

"Greyson took care of them."

"What airport are you guys flying into? Heathrow Airport has the best little shops."

"Hmm, I don't know. We'll ask Greyson when we pick him up." Scarlett took off her T-shirt, then pulled on the sweater that hadn't fit into her suitcase. Then she slipped on a pair of black riding boots over her leggings before tying her hair into a high ponytail. Shoving a green-and-black plaid scarf into her Louis Vuitton bucket bag, she scanned her bedroom for anything else she might have missed.

When she declared she was packed and ready, the pair dragged the heavy suitcases noisily to the elevator and struggled to put them in the trunk of Betsy's BMW. But once they were on the way to pick up Greyson and Scarlett no longer needed to stress over if she'd brought the right outfit for meeting his mother, she began to silently freak out. She was about to fly across the Atlantic Ocean with a man she had only known a month in order to spend Christmas with his family in his home country.

In a lunch meeting at the club, she had told her daddy why she wouldn't be home for the holidays. To her surprise, he understood her loyalty to Greyson and was just as surprised as she was to know William had been invited to the cookie party. Scarlett's mother...well, they hadn't talked since that night. Scarlett hoped by the time she got home after Christmas, her mama would be a little more open to realizing how terribly wrong she was. And if not, maybe they could have tea at one of the hotels downtown and talk. Mama couldn't make too much of a scene if they did it in public.

Greyson was standing on the sidewalk below a streetlight when they pulled up in front of his building. But to her surprise, she saw he didn't have any suitcases. He was dressed in a pair of jeans with a plain gray sweater. A leather jacket was tossed casually over one shoulder, and he looked more like he was about to run to the store than fly internationally. But the outfit suited him. She liked the rebel side of him revealed in the leather jacket. Well, the way it gave him a rebel persona at least, since Greyson would probably never get involved in any kind of crazy adventure.

"Good morning, ladies," Greyson greeted as he climbed into the backseat. "Lovely day for a flight."

Scarlett turned to face him. "Aren't you forgetting something?"

He pulled two boarding passes and a deep burgundy passport from his jacket pocket. "No, I have everything I need right here. I even did the pre-flight check-in."

"Love how organized you are," Betsy began. "But where are your bags?"

"I'm going home. I don't need anything. Besides, if I decline to bring luggage, that gives me two free hands to carry Scarlett's. Really, only two? I'm impressed."

"I could have done one with a little more guidance," Scarlett murmured under her breath.

The drive to the airport was a short one. Before Scarlett knew it, Betsy had pulled up to the *departures* lane and put the BMW into park.

"Call me as soon as your plane lands, okay?" Betsy asked, hugging Scarlett.

"I will, don't worry. And take extra good care of Blitz for me."

Greyson exited and went to the trunk. He popped it open, then took both suitcases out with ease before slamming it. Then he opened Scarlett's door for her. "Betsy, thank you for driving us to the airport."

"Anytime. Have a good time, you two!"

"Come, we need to get through security rather quickly," he said as he began maneuvering Scarlett's suitcases through the automatic doors of the terminal.

She followed, digging her passport from her oversized purse and joining the check-in line. The process went smoothly, with them dropping off her luggage and going through security in near silence. The act of walking through the scanners and metal detectors always made her feel tense. Not that there was ever anything in her suitcase to cause concern. Well, one time she'd inadvertently brought a full tube of toothpaste, but no one had stopped her. Actually, now that Scarlett thought about it, maybe that was why she was nervous. If they'd missed her toothpaste, what else were they missing?

But once they were cleared and free to go find their gate, Scarlett took note of the number on her ticket. With the preholiday crowds and the rush of the security lines, she hadn't even thought to study their gate number. But as she read the fine print, she saw the words *Savannah International to Aldora International* and *First Class*. "Greyson, I think our tickets are wrong. It doesn't say we're going to England…and it says we're first class."

He shoved his hands in his pockets. "Well, Scarlett, that's because we're not going to England. We're going to Aldora, where I'm from."

"Wait, I'm confused. I thought you were from England."

"It's easier to tell people that than explain where Aldora is. Most people have never heard of it."

"I fall into that category."

"Well, as I said before, Aldora is an island near Ireland. It's not part of Great Britain, but it's still in Europe."

"All right, so that wasn't too hard to explain. Why not just say that?"

"Because I have an awfully lot more to explain, I'm afraid. We're almost at the first-class lounge. We can talk more privately there." Confused, Scarlett raised an eyebrow in question, but Greyson only took her arm and guided her to a door with gold writing across it, alerting everyone it was only for those passengers carrying first-class tickets.

They entered, showed their tickets to the concierge, and then found seats alone by the window. As she settled into the red leather armchair, Scarlett's puzzlement with the situation and Greyson's cryptic remarks only got deeper as she waited for him to explain. What did he mean he has an awful lot more to explain? The confusion she'd felt earlier was shifting to more of a panic. What could he need to explain that was making him so nervous? There was sweat on his brow, and the forced smile he kept flashing her was definitely not the Greyson she was used to.

And then she thought about the implications of their tickets. First-class seats to Europe could not have been cheap. Had he felt like he had to get the most expensive seats because of her? Had there been something she'd said that suggested she'd expected him to? She would have gladly paid for a coach ticket to meet his family. Scarlett didn't want him to think he had to pull out all the stops financially for her.

"Wait, Greyson, these tickets…I'm sure they were quite expensive."

"Yes, they definitely were. In fact, we'll have the whole plane to ourselves." And there was the forced smile again. Lacking the warmth and brightness his infectious grin usually had, there was no joy behind the expression.

Hot guilt flooded her chest as she tried to calculate how much me must have paid. She needed to find the words to explain that even though she came from money, she wasn't a snob. She'd flown first class before, but usually used her credit-card points for economy seats. And then his words clicked in her mind. They'd have the whole plane to themselves.

"What do you mean?" she asked. "How do we have the whole plane to ourselves?"

"I mean we will be flying Aldora Air as the only two passengers."

"What?" She tried to do the math in her head, attempting to figure out how much he must have spent. "First of all, Greyson, you didn't have to do this. I would've been just fine on coach. This is all too much. I mean, I know this is very rude of me, but how were you able to afford that? I've seen your truck."

Surprisingly, Greyson laughed and shook his head. "First of all, the truck is a classic. Second, my mother actually purchased the tickets."

"Oh, well, she didn't need to go through all this trouble. I'd be happy to pay her back for my ticket." But this didn't make sense either. His apartment was tiny, his truck was breaking day by day, and he was on a tight budget. If his mother could afford an entire plane, what was going on between them that had him cut off? Was that what he wanted to discuss? If they were family problems, she was no stranger to those.

"You can always offer, but I promise she will never accept it. But this isn't what I wanted to discuss with you."

His face grew serious as he leaned toward her. Her heart pounded. Was the shoe ready to drop and ruin their fairytale romance? She tried to brace herself, taking a few deep breaths and folding her hands in her lap in an attempt to keep them from shaking. He was taking her to meet his family. His mother paid an exorbitant amount for those tickets. Nothing he said could be that terrible…or so she hoped.

"I haven't been honest with you about my life before Georgia. I want to be clear my past is the only thing I've ever lied about, and I only did it because I wanted you to get to know the real me."

Her stomach dropped. Maybe it could be that bad. She felt like she was going to vomit. Words like those were never followed by anything good. Did he have a secret wife? Was he wanted by the law? Did he have six months to live or a career as a black-market diamond smuggler? Her breath sped up. "Please don't tell me you're some kind of criminal. Betsy will never let me live it down if she was right and you're on the run."

Greyson chuckled. "Uh, no, but we'll get back to why Betsy thought I was a criminal later. I mentioned my family was in politics and I didn't want to go into the family business, correct? Well, my family's business is royalty." He winced, his expression somehow sheepish and ashamed at the same time. "Well, um…my father is the King of Aldora, which makes me the—"

"The prince?" Scarlett's eyebrows shot up, and she felt silly for even saying it. Greyson wasn't a prince. There was no way. He was a construction worker in the USA on a work visa. "You're joking."

"I do believe I have a brilliant sense of humor, but I assure you this is no joke."

"You're a prince?" She could barely get the absurd question out, much less wrap her brain around it. How could he possibly be a prince? How was a prince running around Georgia like a regular guy? No, it was impossible. Scarlett opened her mouth a couple times to tell him to stop messing around, and then closed it, words escaping her. It had to be a prank. There was no other explanation.

"I am, for the time being, the crown prince. However, I will be abdicating my throne and moving back to Savannah, hopefully securing permanent residency in time." Greyson said it matter-of-factly, like it was the most normal thing in the world.

Scarlett felt as if she'd been dropped into a reality show without her knowledge. Any minute, some celebrity would pop out and show her where the hidden cameras were. "You're leaving your family?"

"I'll still be family, just without the prestigious title and all the public works that accompany it. It's why I have no money, drive that truck, and work the construction job. I'm starting a life without my family's help or influence. I want my own life."

Scarlett nodded, able to at least understand exactly where he was coming from, even if it was on such a ridiculously grand scale. But there was the matter of him keeping the secret from her. They had spent so many days and nights together, and she thought they were really getting to know one another on the deepest scale imaginable. She had never lied to him about anything and had assumed he gave her the same consideration.

"I get that," she said quietly. "But why lie? Why not just tell me the truth?"

"To be honest, I didn't want to chance the crown coming between us before you got to know the real me."

"But why?" She couldn't understand. She wasn't shallow or fame hungry. And it wasn't as if she would need the money a royal boyfriend could offer. Scarlett was many things, but not a gold digger. "Did I do something to make you think you had to lie to me?" Hot tears began to well. The more she tried to fight them, the faster they came. She thought everything between them was so pure and uncomplicated. It was all becoming too much. Their happy little bubble was completely burst.

He reached over and took her trembling hand. "No, Scarlett. Don't you ever think that. Women have always been drawn to me because of the crown. For my entire life, I have never been sure if people liked me for me, or if they just liked the crown and the idea of being a princess. When I came to the States to try to have a regular life, I met you and chose to leave out a few pertinent details. I wanted you to like me. The *real* me."

"But now I feel like I don't know the real you," Scarlett murmured. It was true. She looked at him and saw his eyes, the eyes she'd spent hours staring into. They'd always made her feel comforted and safe. And now, looking back at him, she wasn't even sure she recognized the man before her.

"But you do. You know me better than anyone else on this planet. You know my heart and my soul, and you've liked all of it. Before now, didn't you think that?"

"I did."

"So what's changed?"

"You lied." She nearly pulled her fingers from his grasp, but knew she would miss his comforting touch. Frustration flowed through her body as she tried to sort through the anger, hurt, and shame. Greyson lying to her seemed to be the grossest injustice after she had bared her hopes and dreams to him.

"I did, Scarlett. And I understand if you hate me, but please just listen. I...I was scared. I didn't want a loveless marriage with a woman my mother picked out. Surely you can relate."

Scarlett's hardened shell softened a tiny bit at the earnestness on his face. She looked down at their hands, the rough construction hands hiding the truth she now knew. But were they really hiding the truth? He really was a construction worker, a man who loved working with those hands. A man who worked hard to live off his salary when he could've easily bought the company if he had stayed royal. He seriously couldn't cook, but he walked Blitz in the rain, and held her close as they talked about their dreams. He was her Greyson. Not Prince of Aldora. And Greyson would never do anything to hurt her. She knew that, deep inside. So, to hide his past, he must've been desperate.

Scarlett tried to imagine she was in his shoes. What would she have done? He was trying to keep his mother at bay, just like she was. He didn't want a "proper" marriage, but the right one. It was a desire she knew all too well. As she considered Greyson's position, she couldn't help but realize they weren't all that different. Who would've thought, the Southern belle and the prince had just as much in common as the dog mom and the construction worker.

"When we get on the plane, I'll be more than happy to answer all of your questions," he offered, ducking his head a bit so she could see him, despite her lowered gaze.

"No offense, but I don't think I can board that plane without all the details beforehand. You owe me that."

His jaw tightened. "If you wish to go home, I understand."

"I didn't say that. I just want to know more to try to sort all this through before I get on a plane that's taking me halfway across the world."

"All right, ask away," Greyson said, face drawn.

Scarlett took a moment, trying to organize her scattered thoughts. She had millions of questions but she'd start small so she could wade carefully into his reality instead of jumping right in. "So your family has a castle?"

"Three, actually," he replied, lips quirking slightly for only a second. She wasn't sure, but she thought he looked rather relieved she was beginning with the easy ones.

"And you have a crown and, like…horse-drawn carriages and people who bow to you?" she asked, flashes of animated princess movies coming to mind.

He nodded.

"And your name's still the same…right?"

"Yes…well, sort of. My name is Greyson, yes. But my full name is Charles Rudolf Leopold Montgomery. But Scarlett, I'm still Greyson."

Scarlett took a few minutes to digest what he had told her. She studied him, noting the worry in his brow, the sheen in his eyes suggesting he was fighting back tears, too. He really was still Greyson, the one she knew deep down in her heart of hearts.

"Okay, you really sprang this on me and I'm going to probably ask a lot more questions as I think of them. First, though, I want to say this doesn't change anything between us."

His eyes widened, his shoulders noticeably relaxing. Then he asked quietly, "It doesn't?"

"Okay, it changes things a little. Like, I'm probably going to need to go shopping for a nicer dress to wear for your family's Christmas party. But other than that, you still seem like the same man I knew before you dropped this truth bomb on me." She gave him a tentative smile, hoping what she said was true.

"There is a seamstress who will be glad to assist you." He shifted his hand to intertwine their fingers. "Does it still bother you that I lied?"

Scarlett exhaled. "A little bit, but I can understand why you did it. I'm sure you have women fawning all over you, itchin' to get to your title. I mean, who doesn't want to be a princess or...a queen? I assume you wanted me to get to know the un-royal you, the person you hope to become. But you don't have to worry. I like him. I like you. Just promise me there will be no more lies. As long as you're honest about everything from here on out, I'll see you as the Greyson I met in Savannah. The man I can't wait to spend Christmas with."

Greyson's smile was huge as he lifted her hand, placing a kiss on her knuckles. "I cannot express how grand it feels to hear you say that. And I promise you I won't lie about anything else, nor have I. If your cooking tastes burnt, I will tell you straight off."

"My cooking is never burnt, so that example is moot," Scarlett said with mock haughtiness.

He laughed. "Good, because my cooking is still consistently burnt, and someone in this equation needs to keep us fed."

"Ah, that makes sense now. You never cooked before coming to America, right? You had chefs and a staff, probably." Greyson's admittedly odd quirks—not knowing how to cook even the basics, choosing wine they couldn't drink, designer accessories on a construction worker's salary, and the myriad of other small things—were suddenly becoming easy to understand.

"Correct. I hadn't even poured myself a bowl of cereal before. My brother Harrison can cook well enough, but the staff always chased us from the kitchen."

"Then it's a good thing I'm so understanding, or you just may starve."

"I couldn't agree more. In all seriousness, I don't know what things are going to be like when I get home. My parents are furious about my decision, so it may be quite tense."

"You don't need to worry about me. I can handle tense." While it was true she could handle issues at say…the country club, she was entirely unsure of how to handle issues in another country. Still, he seemed so nervous, his knee bobbing up and down and his grip on her hand firm, so she felt the need to reassure him that she could handle anything.

"I know you can. Just promise me we'll be a team. I feel like I'm constantly relying on you for so many things, yet here I am, asking for your assistance again. Help me get through this week, and, just as you told me not to stress over your mother's behavior, please don't stress on mine. She is a tad dramatic."

"It's not something you need to ask me. It's something I'm happy to do," Scarlett stated. He smiled, running his thumbs in circles on the back of her hand. It was soothing, and she felt herself relax.

"Then I am lucky to have found you."

"I feel that way about you, too, Greyson."

"But might we circle back to why Betsy thought I was a criminal?"

Scarlett only giggled.

CHAPTER NINE

S CARLETT HAD TRAVELED first class to Europe before, but it hadn't been like this. Having an entire plane to themselves meant they didn't have to wait in a line of pushy people to board or have to sit there while some lady tried to shove a giant bag into the overhead compartment despite being told on multiple occasions it wouldn't fit. It meant she was sitting in a cushiony first-class seat, holding Greyson's hand, with the promise of the best English breakfast she had ever had and then an amazing lunch of a perfectly cooked steak and real potatoes later.

The flight was eight hours long, and Scarlett spent the first three hours glued to the window as the sun began to rise. Sure, all she saw were clouds and later the ocean, but, eventually, she would be gazing over Aldora. Frankly, she'd never even heard of the country. She repeated that thought in her head—she'd never even *heard* of the country, yet she was sitting beside its crown prince.

She hardly even had time to Google it before the plane took off, finding a photo of Greyson in full military uniform. While he explained it was nothing more than tradition and Aldora had no need for a military presence, it was a shock. Scarlett wished she had more time to do some research. She needed to see what his parents looked like, learn if there were any Christmas traditions, or any customs she needed to be aware of... Being unprepared didn't sit well with her.

Scarlett turned to Greyson, feeling a bit of panic begin to rise. "I know nothing about Aldora. You should've told me in advance, so I could've done research to make sure I didn't break any kinds of rules or procedures. What if I do something that offends your mother?"

"You will almost certainly do something that will offend my mother, but that's mostly her personality as opposed to your behavior."

"Ah, so your mama and my mama were cut from the same cloth?"

"Sounds like it."

"But seriously, jokes aside. What do I need to know about Aldora?"

"My younger brother Harrison will now be taking over the throne from my father, Leopold. He will be expected to wed by the end of next year to keep tradition. There will be tons of women trying to throw themselves at him over the coming months. It's going to be entertaining to watch as he has no interest in dating, let alone marriage."

"And what do I call your family? Like, do I refer to your brother as His Majesty, or do I call him Harry?"

"Well, I haven't abdicated the throne yet, so, technically, I am still the crown prince. Besides, we already have a cousin we call Harry, and if he comes to the ball, things would get rather confusing. You may, though, call me Your Highness." He winked.

Scarlett laughed, slapping a hand over her mouth. "Sorry, I'm not doing that."

"I was only teasing. Call everyone by name, but no nicknames. We don't do nicknames in the royal family. The first time you meet them, they'll probably be introduced with their titles, but since you are with me, I'm going to insist on familiarity while in private."

"That's lovely you insist on it, but what if they insist on something different? You already like me since I've fooled you into thinking I'm amusing company. But since I haven't had the chance to charm them, I'm willing to do whatever they want."

"My mother, Philipa, will probably prefer the addressed as Your Majesty. If you truly insist on being polite and all that, you may use the title until she tells you different. My father…well, he's trickier. While he may insist on Leopold, my mother will probably prefer you refer to him as Your Majesty as well. So, for now, just refer to them both as Your Majesty until my mother asks you to call her something different."

"And your brother?"

"Harrison is fine still."

"All right." She half wanted to pull out her phone and take notes, but she thought that might be a little on the dramatic side. But then, another thought made her gasp. "Greyson, the gifts."

"What?"

"I made your parents and your brother these tins of Christmas cookies. Now…oh my God, I can't give chocolate chip cookies to the king and queen." She slumped, feeling ridiculous. They were going to hate her. She just knew it.

"I'm the crown prince, and I find your cookies spectacular."

"But I didn't *know* you were royalty. I can't just show up to a castle and present cookies to a bunch of royals. I could have gotten…like…um…" Her mind blanked. While her mama had taught her to never go to someone's home empty-handed, she'd never said what to bring when invited to someone's castle.

"There's nothing you could bring they don't already have, aside from homemade cookies. Trust me."

"Can we just stop at the store on our way from the airport, maybe?"

"And go to one of the stores my mother owns?" Smiling, he shook his head. "Let it go. Your presence is the only gift required."

Scarlett tried to ignore the impulse to rush order an elaborate flower arrangement. "So, what events should I expect?"

"I haven't seen the calendar as of yet, but we do have a few traditional events. We'll have a royal parade just before Christmas. On Christmas Eve, we have a grand ball. Truly, it's lovely. And since you'll be here for New Year's…well, there'll be another ball then, too, as well, a larger one."

"Aw, I love watching parades. Will I get a special seat?"

"Yes, next to me in the carriage."

"Seriously, I get to be in the parade?" She couldn't help but grin. The last time she had been in a parade was when she'd been crowned *Miss Teen Peach*.

"If you want to, that is. I'd be honored to have you riding beside me."

"Whatever you got me for Christmas, return it. That is the best gift ever."

Greyson smiled. "My gift for you is back in my flat in Savannah. I wanted to give it to you when we were back in our real world, if you don't mind?"

"I like that. But seriously, the parade, even doing it once, is going to be a highlight."

"There will be a couple of boring dinners you'll have to sit through before then. Hopefully nothing too painful."

"I've sat through plenty of boring dinners. I can smile and bear it."

"And you have the prettiest smile." Greyson reached a hand out to gently stroke her cheek. "I'm just so happy you're here."

She leaned into his feather-light touch. He could calm her nerves in an instant without more than a brush of his hand or a soft word. Never before had someone had that kind of effect on her. He'd just revealed a massive secret that should have sent her reeling, but since it came from him, it was somehow easier to manage.

But then again, she was going to a castle to meet his family. Scarlett had already been nervous about that before she'd found out she'd be referring to them as Your Majesties. How was she supposed to impress a queen? She had to find a way. It mattered to Greyson, so it mattered to her. This trip to his home was going to be hard on him, she knew. She had to find a way to make it bearable, to impress his family, to show them she was good enough for their son, while still making their first Christmas together beautiful. She had to. That was what people did when they possibly loved someone. But she didn't have the slightest idea how to do that.

"I am, too. I know we talked about this, but please be upfront with me about everything while we're there. I want to know if your parents hate me, or if the other royals think I'm simply a rude American. I need honesty since, you know…I haven't had a chance to get used to the whole prince thing."

"I will never lie to you again. I swear to it."

"I hope not. I do understand the prince lie, but I think trusting you will be impossible if there are any more. I was raised to be courteous, but honest."

"I can respect that. Now, back to the prince thing. I forgot to go over some additional aspects of it, and I feel I must ask something of you."

"Okay, what is it?"

"Please, are you able to keep my lineage to yourself for now? In order to keep my life the way it is in the United States, this must stay a secret. At least for a while longer." He seemed pained to ask, but firm about the request.

Scarlett frowned. "I just told you I don't lie, especially not to those I love."

"And I'm not asking you to. At the Christmas Eve ball, when my father makes the announcement Harrison will take the crown, I won't be a prince and it won't be a lie. I'll be a man from a wealthy family in Europe who gave it up to follow his own path. There will be no pressure to keep my title to make others happy."

"So what do I tell my family?"

"You had a lovely time with my family over the holidays. We live in a nice area, and we went out of our way to make you feel welcome. I would just prefer you to not bring up the royal part until I am nothing more than a son of the king."

Scarlett thought of her mother learning about his title. If she'd thought Reggie the Veggie was a catch, she'd scream in delight if she knew where her only daughter was spending Christmas. "You know, Mama would like you a lot better if you *were* a prince, even if it's just for a week. Maybe telling her wouldn't be the worst thing in the world?"

"That's the point." He took her hands in his, holding them tightly. "If you mother hates me, I don't want to fix it by telling her I'm a prince. That's the very reason I didn't tell *you*. I want her to like me for the man I choose to be. What will she say when I take away her daughter's chance to be a princess? I have a feeling she wouldn't handle that well."

"You would be correct," she admitted.

"Please, it's not forever. I'll share it with them when I'm ready. I promise you it won't remain a secret."

"Okay, I'll do it."

Greyson grinned, giving her fingers a final squeeze before releasing her.

Scarlett turned to the window, a little uncomfortable with the request. On one hand, she wasn't speaking to her mama, so it wouldn't be hard not to tell her. On the other, she also knew this prince secret could change everything. How much easier would life be if her mama knew he came from such a prestigious background? She would bend over backward to please him. True, she would be upset Scarlett missed her chance to be a princess, but she already was, at least in the debutante world. But for now, she would follow his request. When he opened up to her parents, it would make things easier. She could hold out until then. Right?

CHAPTER TEN

A S THE PLANE began its descent in to Aldora, Greyson watched Scarlett eagerly press her forehead against the plane's small window to try to take in the scenery from above. The day was sunny, but a thick layer of clouds hid the country from view until almost the moment when the landing gear hit the runway of the small airport. So he knew all she probably saw were several other planes and the nondescript gray building that made up the terminal.

He had no idea how he'd gotten so lucky as to have met such a darling woman in the few weeks he'd been in America. While some might have pushed him away and never spoken to him again after he came clean, she'd tried to understand. She was always trying to understand, and it was something he loved about her. When things could have gone so terribly wrong, Scarlett was a firm figure of poise and curiosity. She held his hand on the flight, dozed off gracefully on his shoulder, and randomly peppered him with questions. She was constantly surprising him with her depth and layers. It was almost like he was getting to know a piece of her every day. The thought he could've lost all that by exposing his secret sent a chill to his bones no fire could ever warm. Yes, he was lucky, and he'd never forget it.

When the plane had taxied to a halt, the cockpit's door opened and the pilot emerged from the cabin. He strode up to their seats, then bowed briefly at the waist. "Your Highness, madam, it has been my pleasure to pilot you home today."

Greyson stood, then placed a hand on the pilot's shoulder. "Thank you. Your skills are impeccable, and I don't recall ever having had a smoother flight."

The pilot smiled as the attendants opened the door. "It was my honor, Your Highness. Welcome home."

Greyson pulled on his jacket, then took Scarlett's hand to help her down the set of stairs that had been rolled to the door. Cold mountain wind whipped past them, and he inhaled deeply. The familiar scent of home was one he could never forget, and he relished the cool hint of snow and pine in the air drifting down from the far-off range.

A black Range Rover was parked a few dozen yards from the plane, flanked by police vehicles. Outside, a lone man in a nondescript black suit stood at attention, dark sunglasses covering his eyes. When he saw them, he pressed his earpiece and said something into his sleeve before bowing.

"Wow, is that our ride?" Scarlett asked as they stop beside the truck.

"Yep, this is my old bodyguard, Robert."

"Good afternoon, Your Highness, Miss Calhoun," Robert greeted, opening the back door of the Range Rover. "I trust your flight was a smooth one?"

"Perfectly," he replied as Scarlett slid into the seat.

Then she placed a hand on Greyson's arm. "Wait, what

about my suitcases?"

"Taken care of."

He sat beside her, and Rob took the front seat. A man in an orange vest popped the boot, then gently placed both pieces of purple luggage in before closing it. Scarlett immediately relaxed beside him, although he saw her nervously toying with the little gold locket she wore around her neck. Fearing she might snap the delicate chain, he took her hand and weaved their fingers together as the police cars turned on their lights, one taking its place before the Rover and the other following behind as they left the airport.

Scarlett's blue eyes were massive as she stared out the tinted windows. He loved watching the wonder overtake her face as she took in the small city they drove through.

Greyson tried to appreciate his home as she did, but his mind was on her instead. He was fortunate to have found someone who cared for him without knowing his birthright, who still did even after she found she'd been deceived. He had almost felt sick to his stomach while explaining his royal background to her in the Georgia airport, but she surprised him again with her ability to forgive and accept him—all of him. He only hoped he could continue to earn her adoration.

SCARLETT TRIED TO maintain her composure as the castle came into view. She had been to Disney World and had visited Cinderella's castle, went to Buckingham Palace where the queen of England lived, and even attended Hogwarts for a day. She was no stranger to castles, but the sight of Greyson's childhood home took her breath away.

Upon a gentle slope covered in lush greenery sat a sand-covered castle that could have come straight out of a storybook. Surrounded by a tall stone walls and backlit by the late afternoon sun, the many turrets and battlements loomed overhead, casting shadows on the winding road that led up to the massive gate. In the background, a white-topped mountain range completed the postcard-perfect picture.

She saw traces of medieval architecture in the arrow-slit windows and tall pointed towers. Burgundy and gold flags flapped in the wind, and she noticed smaller versions of the same colors were flown on the front corners of the truck. While Greyson had told her he was a prince, it was like she was just presented with the physical proof of his royalty.

A small crowd of tourists, all bundled up against the cold and clutching cameras, parted as the police car let out a small wail, but they still snapped away. Two guards in burgundy-and-gold livery bowed in unison as the cop car in front veered to the left and the Range Rover slowly drove through the black gates, under a stone archway with the name *Montgomery* emboldened in gold atop a mural featuring a fierce lion.

"Welcome home, sir," a man in a traditional butler uniform greeted as he opened the Rover's door for Greyson.

Greyson had to practically drag Scarlett from the backseat. She was so overtaken by the sheer enormity of the castle. They were in the outer ward, framed by the tall protective walls. The cobblestones beneath her feet made up the winding drive where a convoy of matching black Range Rovers had all been parked to one side.

She clutched Greyson's hand as she craned her neck to see the entirety of the massive keep, feeling like she might fall over. It rose taller than the flanking and corner towers where she spied security forces keeping watch. The tallest turret sat maybe eight-stories high. From the corner of her eye, she saw a team of maids and footmen lining the set of stairs that led to the oversized double doors.

"Goodness," she whispered as Greyson began leading her inside.

The staff bowed and curtseyed as they passed. One broke formation to fetch Scarlett's bags from the car. She felt bad having a stranger carry in her things, but she didn't have time to dwell as they entered the grand foyer. It was a huge room with high arched ceilings and a shiny marble floor. The windows were framed by deep red velvet curtains that let natural light stream in. On the walls were paintings of men and women so elegant she could imagine them hanging in any museum. Their gilded frames glinted in the sun, and she realized they were not just images of random people, but most likely were of Greyson's ancestors.

"A bit pompous, is it not?" he asked her in a lighthearted whisper. "Usually I take the family's entrance round back, but I assume my mother insisted Robert bring us through the main gates."

"Oh, I see."

"Ready to run?"

She shook her head, her eyes flitting from the crystal

light fixtures to the carved stone arches above the entrance to the massive staircase. "No, I'm just a bit…overwhelmed."

"Then I'll show you to your room so you can collect yourself and rest before dinner. Come." He led her through the grand foyer, and they began climbing the stairs. "I've instructed the staff to place you in the Princess Diana suite."

"Wait…Princess Diana like *the* Princess Diana?"

"Yes, the rooms were named many years ago. She and my aunt were childhood friends. Diana visited quite often, staying in those very chambers."

Scarlett thought she would faint right there on the stairs. She was not only dating a prince and spending Christmas in a real castle, but she would also be sleeping where Princess Diana had. She longed to call her mama and tell her, as she had always held Princess Di up as the ultimate lady, claiming if she'd been an American, she would have definitely been a Southerner. It was something they shared, an admiration for the woman. But Scarlett hadn't spoken to her since announcing she wasn't spending the holidays at home. Besides, Greyson had asked her to keep everything a secret. So, true to her promise, Scarlett left her phone in her purse.

The stairs led to a landing, and Greyson pointed to the left. "This is the West Wing where we keep the informal library, the Princess Cecily Room, and the game room." They continued down the hall, one side inundated by a dozen oversized windows, the other hosting several doors. All empty wall space was filled with framed portraits and several landscapes. He stopped before the double doors at the end of the hall. "Your rooms."

"My *rooms?*"

Scarlett gently turned the elaborate handle, then pushed. There was a sitting room with dove-gray walls and plush white furniture. A gorgeous crystal chandelier filled the room with more light than the single tall window overlooking the darkening mountains ever could. A set of white bookcases flanked a low-burning fireplace, above which hung a practically life-sized picture of two young women in similar sundresses with giant hats upon their heads. One Scarlett immediately recognized as the late Princess Di, but the other she couldn't place.

"Is that your mother?" she asked, pointing to the dark-haired woman.

"Yes, that was taken before I was born. Actually, it was taken before either one was married. Here, I'll show you into the bedroom. I believe the footman managed to spirit your luggage in through the servant's stairway."

Tearing her eyes away from the picture of the laughing girls, she went to the next room. If she could describe it in one word, it would be opulent. A massive four-poster bed with pale blue bedding edged with gold was against one wall, a matching chaise at its foot. The walls were the same shade, the one opposite the bed boasting a series of windows overlooking the setting sun, which was beginning to dip behind the mountains. There was more framed art, which, to her somewhat practiced eye, appeared to be painted by Claude Monet. Beside yet another fireplace, this one decked with a gigantic winter wreath on the mantle, was another door she presumed held the bathroom.

"Ah, I was right, here are your suitcases," Greyson said, breaking her out of her daze. "The footman's put them in the dressing room already."

She peered past him at an open door she hadn't realized was there. It was a sizable but empty walk-in closet. "So he did…"

"Are the rooms all right?"

"You can't seriously be asking me that."

He held up both hands with a smile. "I'm glad you like them. Do you need anything? Are you hungry?"

"No, I'm fine. I ate a lot on the plane. I'm just a bit tired. Jet lag."

"We dine at seven. I'll come to collect you just before then, so you don't get lost." His tone was cheerful, but she knew he was serious about her getting lost.

"Wait…what do I wear for dinner? I only brought, like, one semi-formal dress."

"We're only having a very informal dinner with just the family tonight. No need to overdress. Besides, you could show up in a paper bag and still look fantastic."

When Greyson had left her to own devices, Scarlett noted she had almost an hour and a half before dinner. She didn't know how she was going to fill the time, as she wasn't exactly in need of a nap. But when she decided to explore the bathroom, she saw a classic claw-foot tub. Above it sat a shelf lined with a dozen bottles and jars of soaps and tonics. Pulling her phone from her purse, she texted her daddy and Betsy to say she'd gotten there safely and would call when she could, then began to fill the tub.

GREYSON HOPED HE hadn't overwhelmed Scarlett by placing her in the Princess Diana suite, but he'd just wanted her to have the best. He figured at least one of them should spend the afternoon in comfort, and since he had to go face his family for the first time in weeks, he knew it had to be her.

The assorted staff all bowed and curtsied as he passed them on his way to his father's study. When he'd left Scarlett, a footman had told him where he could find his parents. He wasn't surprised they hadn't greeted him at the door when he'd first arrived. No doubt they wanted to meet on their own ground, the imposing study where he had received all of his childhood admonitions.

He rapped on the door once before his father's deep voice called out, "Enter!"

The room was just as it had been the day Greyson left, as was his family. His father sat behind his imposing mahogany desk while his mother stood just before it, her wide eyes teary. Harrison was wearing one of Greyson's favorite suits, and he nodded in greeting. All three of their of faces held various emotions, and Greyson wasn't sure where to begin.

"Greyson, you're home." His mother stepped forward to throw her arms around his neck.

He returned her hug tightly, careful not to muss her hair. "Hello, Mother." When she released him, he went to the desk and held out his hand. "Father."

The king's eyes softened as he stood, clasping Greyson's hand. "Son. Your country missed you."

"Just my country, Father? I'm sure Harrison did well in

my absence."

Greyson held his hand out to his brother. He shook it eagerly, the smile on his face like a dagger in his heart. Greyson hadn't kept in touch with him. He hadn't talked to Harrison about all the pressures he would be under once Greyson abdicated. Truthfully, he'd wanted to. There were multiple instances when he'd picked up his mobile to ring his brother but had then decided against it. How could he reassure Harrison he would make a good king when Greyson was running from those very responsibilities? He knew they would need to sit and have a proper visit before he left again.

"Of course not just your country, Greyson," his mother said. "We have all missed your presence. But I can't help but notice there appears to be a certain presence missing. Where is your...*friend*?"

"Scarlett is in her room having a rest. I thought it best because of the long flight and the time change. You will all meet her at dinner."

"I think that's just lovely. Now we can have a visit with just the family. I think we have many things to discuss," she said, walking over to the velvet chaise and sitting. She looked expectantly at the three men in the room, who quickly followed suit and found their own seats.

"Philipa, need I remind you about the meeting I have with Portugal?" His father nodded toward the grandfather clock. "It is due to start any minute."

"This won't take long, darling. So, Greyson, have you changed your mind about abdicating the throne? You have three days until an announcement must be made."

"No, I have not," he replied firmly, so as to leave no doubt his decision was final.

Her face fell. "Yes, well, I don't want a shock like this affecting the people during the holiday season. So many of them are looking forward to your leadership, and to know you are abandoning them will truly break their hearts. Especially when you consider you are moving to America. It may make the people think you believe Aldora is beneath you."

She continued to groan and guilt him, and while he wanted to ignore her, those words were hitting heavy on his heart. Was it selfish he'd never considered how the people would handle his departure? He looked out the double window in the study at the rooftops, the church cross, and the countryside he'd always loved riding through. Yes, he would miss it, and he needed to acknowledge the people would miss him, too.

How many times had he ridden through town and had shopkeepers say they looked forward to his rule, or had a farmer praise his diplomacy? They believed in him. They trusted him to do well by Aldora, the country he was born and raised to govern. Too bad he couldn't be the man they needed him to be.

"Greyson, are you even listening to me?" his mother snapped.

"Yes, Mother, I am. I just don't know what you want me to say. Life on the throne just isn't for me. These past few weeks have shown me that while life as a non-royal can be difficult, it's more rewarding than I ever could have dreamed."

"As you've said before. You know, part of being a royal is making sacrifices for your people," his father said. "That's part of having Montgomery blood in your veins."

"But should you sacrifice yourself in the process of ruling?"

"Enough," his mother interrupted just as his father opened his mouth. "I don't wish to discuss it any further at present. You've just returned, and I want to enjoy your company as we all digest this information. But I want to make it clear this is not to be discussed with the media, as we will still make the formal announcement at the ball."

Greyson agreed, feeling some hope in his heart. It seemed his family, though upset, was beginning to respect his decision. Maybe there was a chance he could abdicate without causing too much pain.

Howard entered the study, bowing slightly in the doorway. "I'm sorry to interrupt, Your Majesties, but the meeting with Portugal is slated to begin in three minutes."

"Yes, thank you, Howard." His father cleared his throat and stood, straightening his suit jacket. "Greyson, as you are no longer going to be a ruler in our country, I must ask you to leave."

Greyson stared at the king, feeling his words as if his father had physically slapped him in the face. The Portuguese Ambassador was a great friend and mentor of Greyson's. He'd wanted to speak to him, wish him a happy Christmas. Their relationship wasn't a secret, yet Greyson was being thrown out of the room like a...well, like a construction worker from Georgia.

He held his head high as he walked out of the study, trying to keep his pride. Moments like those were going to be his reality, and he needed to accept it. He was no longer privy to the inner workings of the royal study as he had once been trained to be. Greyson just hadn't thought the knowledge would hurt as much as it did.

SCARLETT EMERGED FROM the bath feeling like her body was mush. She knew she smelled of rose petals, but it was the lavender that had the most impact. It had left her relaxed and feeling better about meeting Greyson's family. But if she'd learned anything from her mama, Scarlett knew dressing the part was one of the best ways to convince herself she could do it.

Scarlett took out her dark jeans, then placed them on the bed. Greyson had told her to dress informally, and she cursed herself for not bringing more outfits befitting a castle. However, she had a beautiful satin cream top with tiny gold polka dots to pair with them. After Scarlett found the blouse, she took out her traveling steamer to make sure she was wrinkle free. With her outfit crisp and hanging up, she was ready to start with her makeup and hair.

Forty-five minutes later, Scarlett stared at her reflection in the mirror. Her makeup was tasteful and natural with her hair falling in graceful, even waves. She'd added a pair of purple heels to dress up her outfit, and she was satisfied she would maybe look as if she belonged. It was the nicest she could appear without wearing her only semi-formal dress. She'd considered putting it on, but she didn't want to seem like she was trying too hard. Also, she figured she would probably need it for another occasion and didn't want to be an outfit repeater.

There was a knock on her door. Scarlett rushed to open it, hoping to see Greyson. Instead, a woman in a gray uniform with a stony expression stood there. "Hello, madam, I am here with instructions to take you to His Majesty, Prince Greyson's chambers."

"Oh, yes, no problem." Scarlett grabbed her cell, then placed it in her back pocket out of habit. "All right, I'm ready."

Scarlett followed behind the maid—errand woman— valet? She wasn't sure what to call her, other than *speedster.* The woman moved so quickly, snaking through the halls like a mechanical train that Scarlett was almost running to keep up. Then, suddenly, she stopped in front of a door and Scarlett nearly ran into her back.

The woman knocked on the door. Within a few seconds, Greyson appeared in a designer sweater and perfectly pressed slacks. His shoes were so shiny Scarlett could probably see her reflection, and his usually wavy and loose hair was slicked back with an awful lot of gel. Scarlett had to do a double take. She hardly recognized this royal Greyson. She kind of missed seeing him in his T-shirt and jeans. Casual and carefree suited him. But the royal persona suited him, too. It was fascinating to her that Greyson had two separate worlds. What would it be like to walk around, straddling assorted identities?

"Scarlett, you're a vision," he said, taking her hand and brushing another kiss on her knuckles like he had on the plane. She liked the sentiment, not able to help feeling warm and excited. With the brush of his fingers, she could feel the butterflies forming inside her. His gray eyes were so focused on hers, she almost wished he would blink to break the spell.

"Thank you," she said.

"Allow me to escort you to dinner." He offered her his arm and she took it, feeling a little silly in such a formal pose.

As they walked down halls she hadn't seen yet, she tried to not come off as overwhelmed by the sheer lavishness of her boyfriend's childhood home. But that was fairly difficult when the art and carved wooden pieces of historic-looking furniture framing the Oriental carpets made her mama's taste in décor look positively shabby in comparison. Generations of royalty, Greyson's own family, had walked these very corridors.

A twisting nervousness began to build in her stomach as she remembered she wasn't just meeting Greyson's mom, dad, and brother, but the king, queen, and soon-to-be crown prince of Aldora. "Hey, so should I…curtsy the first time I meet them? Is there a rule at dinner that you stop eating when the queen does, like they have in England? Am I too underdressed?"

They stopped before a dark oak door, and he patted her hand. "Scarlett, you'll be perfect. Just be yourself and they'll adore you."

"Easier said than done," she mumbled as he pushed the

door open, revealing the informal dining room.

The board and batten walls were shades of cream, trimmed with gold leaf that seemed to touch everything in the room from the edge of the fireplace to the crystal chandelier above the white-covered table. It appeared to seat twelve, by the number of red velvet chairs, but it was only set for five. The three royals she was meant to meet stood below a painting of a man on horseback.

Mustering all the courage she had and calling upon everything she'd learned at Debutante school, Scarlett crossed the room with her head held high. Stopping before Greyson's family, she fell into the rusty, but still acceptable, curtsy she'd had instilled in her by her instructors. She counted to five in her mind before rising. "Good evening, Your Majesties. Lovely to meet you all." When the queen smiled, Scarlett's rapid heartbeat began to slow.

"Hello, Scarlett," the queen greeted in a polished British accent. "We're so pleased you've come to spend the holidays with us."

Scarlett actually felt welcomed, her nerves dissipating a little. Something about the queen just set Scarlett at ease. Maybe it was because Greyson and his mother had the same light-gray eyes. "It's such an honor to have been invited."

A young man who looked remarkably similar to Greyson, but with a slightly rounder face and brown eyes, grinned and held out his hand for Scarlett to shake. "Harrison, Greyson's brother. So glad to meet you."

"Oh, you as well. Greyson's told me you are a huge soccer fan. Or, wait, do you call it *football* here?"

"Yes, we do say football."

"I love watching at home, although I'm far from an expert."

"It's too bad it's the off-season. Otherwise, I'd see about getting us some tickets. Perhaps we could all go see their winter training facilities."

"I'd like that."

Then the king came forward. He didn't extend his hand as Harrison had, nor did he give off the same warmth as the queen, but he wasn't exactly glaring, which was okay by her. "Hello, welcome to Aldora. Our country in winter is when it is at its most beautiful."

"Yes, I couldn't tear myself away from the window when we were driving here. It's so different from Savannah. I always thought Savannah was historic, but coming here...wow, my whole home country is basically just a preteen."

The king chuckled. "I like the way you view the world. Very refreshing."

"Shall we sit?" the queen suggested, sweeping her arm toward the table.

Scarlett fell beside Greyson as the family took their seats. The king was at the head, the queen and Harrison to his right, with Greyson and her to his left. She made an extra effort to ensure she was sitting straight as she surveyed the table. Vibrant pine branches dusted in white spread the length of the tablecloth, interspersed with pinecones and red candles. The dishes and cutlery were white with gold-and-red trim, and the crystal goblets were finer than at any of the best restaurants in Savannah.

"That went well," she whispered to Greyson as she unfolded her napkin and laid it across her lap.

"Very. You were perfect."

"Stop calling me perfect. It'll go to my head, then I won't be able to fit it into any of my shirts."

"Then I'll buy you new ones."

To start, there was a salad of mixed greens, goat cheese, and cranberries topped with champagne vinaigrette as well as a fishy-smelling soup she only pretended to eat. The conversation was light with Greyson, Harrison, and their father talking about horses and the queen focusing her polite attention on Scarlett. By the time the main course of chicken, asparagus tips, and roasted new potatoes was served, Scarlett thought the queen knew almost everything there was to know about her. Scarlett had talked about her father's insurance business, the charities she frequented, her mother's love of Italian architecture, and even her dog Blitz.

"Greyson has always adored animals. Every year, he'd beg for a dog for Christmas or his birthday."

"He never said if he had one."

The queen paused as the footman delivered their desserts of pound cake and fresh fruit. "A pet would hardly be practical while attending boarding school. He and Harrison were only ever home for more than a week or two at a time."

"But I did have a horse," Greyson cut in. "So my childhood wasn't a complete farce."

His mother rolled her eyes. "Oh, such a terrible upbringing you had. Holidays in Florence, trips to Japan, not one but *three* of the finest Arabian stallions in the country—"

"Yes, I am aware, Mother."

"So why lament the ownership of a dog when you had the world at your fingertips?" The queen's voice was sharp, making Scarlett cringe. "I bet you filled this poor girl's head with horrible stories about your family. I'm surprised she even stepped foot in this castle after what you must have told her."

"Actually, I didn't tell Scarlett anything. Until we arrived at the airport this morning in Georgia, she had no clue I came from royalty. She thought I was a poor construction worker, nothing more. She agreed to come and meet my family because she wanted to be with me, not because I am—was—a prince."

"Well, then I guess you got your sneaky romance. Did you have to go all the way to the United States just to fool some trusting girl into thinking you're someone you aren't?"

Greyson slammed his silverware down, and Scarlett placed a hand on his arm. She had never seen him the least bit angry.

"It's who I am. It's who I want to be," he vehemently replied.

"It is *not* who you are," the king snapped. "You are the crown prince of Aldora. And we are *not* going to have this discussion at the dinner table. We'll have a proper meeting in my study for our Christmas Eve announcement when dessert is cleared."

The table fell into a terse silence and Scarlett wondered if everyone could hear her heartbeat. She had expected some tears and tense words, but not that small explosion she had just witnessed. Greyson's jaw worked as he stared at his water glass, and she wanted to do something—anything—to lighten the mood. But for some reason, her mind was blank and she couldn't think of anything to say.

"Scarlett," Harrison began in a breezy tone. "What do you do for work?"

Scarlett cleared her throat, trying to shake off the small confrontation she had just witnessed. Then she explained about the charity world and how active she was in it. "I just love being able to help people who need it."

"That's wonderful," the queen said, back to her pleasant self. "It sounds similar to what I do with my queenly duties. You and I will have to trade methods."

"Your Majesty, I would love that. I'm sure there is so much I could learn from you."

"And I am intrigued to see yours. The newer generations have different methods of doing things, and I'm sure I could adapt. And please, call me Philipa."

"Thank you, Philipa." Scarlett looked down at her plate, trying to hide her joy. She'd gotten the first name. If that wasn't a victory, she didn't know what was.

AFTER DINNER, GREYSON, Harrison, and the king went to his study to have their meeting. That left Scarlett sitting across from Philipa at the dinner table. While Scarlett was sure the queen at least liked her, she knew she was still under review.

"Scarlett, I suppose you are not prepared, sartorially speaking, for this week, is that correct? How could you be with Greyson keeping his secret?"

"Yes, I'm afraid I didn't pack anything for formal dinners or balls. If I'm being honest, I even feel underdressed for dinner."

The queen was wearing an expensive-looking pink skirt suit. There wasn't a wrinkle in it, and the brooch on the left side was an elaborate snowflake covered in diamonds. Scarlett ran her hands against her jeans, hoping they would magically turn into satin slacks. But, of course, they weren't magical pants.

"I'll call for the seamstress. She can come tomorrow to make you the perfect gown." Pausing, Philipa tapped her chin. "Although that will take some time, so perhaps we will go shopping and see if we might find you a few staples. Let me get my bag."

Scarlett's watch said it was well after eight. "The stores are going to be open this late?"

Philipa laughed, a tinkling sound that echoed in the dining room. "Darling, I'm the queen and I pay well over the asking price to help our economy. If I ask, they'll stay open, especially if I mention Greyson's girlfriend is accompanying me. The people just love him, you'll see. He has such a way with them, and everyone will clamor for the chance to see you."

"Your Maj—Philipa, that's so considerate of you. Let me just grab my purse and a jacket from my room."

"Are you able to get back on your own?"

"Yes, I think I can manage."

"Wonderful. Come to the main hall in fifteen minutes."

Scarlett nodded and tried to hold her composure long enough to leave the room, but she was unbelievably excited. She was going shopping with a *queen*. It was her mother's dream coming true. Scarlett was dating a prince, sleeping in the same rooms as Princess Diana, and was about to have a shopping trip to rival any she had ever been on.

Then it hit her—she couldn't tell her mother any of it. They were still fighting after the cookie party fiasco. And even if they weren't, she still had to keep Greyson's secret for the foreseeable future. The balloon of joy inside her started to deflate.

"No, Scarlett," she told herself quietly, stopping in the hallway. "You will tell Mama about it when things have improved, and she can celebrate with you. But if you don't have an amazing time, Mama will never forgive you for wrecking this."

Feeling better, she walked to her room, hoping she had a few minutes to check her hair and possibly refresh her makeup. Scarlett assumed when one went out with the queen, it was required to be as polished as she was.

THE RIDE TO the store was pretty quiet. Philipa was on the phone with someone, chatting in rapid French Scarlett couldn't keep up with.

Scarlett looked out the window of the town car, thinking about the idea of being a queen. The job never ended. Sure, they always looked gorgeous on television and in the tabloids, but no one ever considered the work that went into it. They were all smiles and waves, but then again, so was Scarlett. Their lives were similar, and Scarlett knew from experience that managing that kind of social life was hard work. Add that to assisting the king on diplomatic duties, while still trying to make sure her people were taken care of, and the mere idea was overwhelming.

They pulled up to a little boutique in the heart of the darkened village. By the light of the streetlamps, Scarlett could see the lattice trim on top of the stone store. The awning appeared to be purple with a white *fleur de lis* painted across it. She couldn't see the sign below, but in the lit windows by hidden lights, she saw several mannequins garbed in floor-length satin evening gowns.

She wanted to reach through the window and feel the soft fabric, see how it cascaded down her body and flowed dramatically behind her. On the right side of the front door were three smart suits. The pencil skirts appeared as if they would hit just above the knee, and they were in varying colors. The blazer on one was lined with velvet, another had what appeared to be diamonds in the buttons, and the last was a gorgeous plaid of red, black, and gold.

"I already want everything in this store, and I haven't stepped inside," Scarlett said.

"Then you have excellent taste. This is my favorite boutique, and I've declared it the official dresser of the queen, which is why it has the royal *fleur de lis* upon it, my personally adopted emblem. Everything is one of a kind, and they only make one of each piece in each size. It's wonderful. The owner's name is Gerta, and she's a friend."

"I will make sure to treat her with my highest respect."

"Oh, I know you will. I am usually quite harsh with the girls Greyson and Harrison bring home. As their mother, I like to think that is my right. But I have a good feeling about you, Scarlett." With that, Philipa pressed a button next to the door. "Jasper, we're ready to go in," she told the driver through what Scarlett assumed was a microphone somewhere in the back of the car.

"Thank you for being so welcoming, Philipa. I have to be honest—I was nervous about meeting you, even before I knew he was a royal. I care about Greyson, and I wanted you to like me."

"Well, darling, who wouldn't like you? Let's get some shopping done and bond like all women do. You'll need five dinner outfits, two formal ball gowns, a dress for the parade, the Christmas Eve ball, and another for…well, if you stay on through the New Year, you'll need something, but we'll sort it."

Scarlett bit her lip, thinking about how much money she had in her purse. "Do they take credit cards here? I haven't changed over enough cash at the airport for all of those outfits."

Philipa reached out, ignoring the open door to her left, and placed a hand on Scarlett's knee. "This is my treat. I want you to be as loved by the people as my Greyson is. Looking the part will help them welcome you immediately. Now, let's get you out of that jumper and into something made of silk and velvet."

When they entered the boutique, they were immediately greeted by two women with eager smiles. The elder of the two dipped a small curtsey. "Your Majesty, thank you for coming. It's been too long since we've seen each other."

Philipa reached out, then shook the woman's hand. "No, thank you for doing this for me, Gerta. I'd like to introduce you to Scarlett," she said, placing her fingers on Scarlett's shoulders and pushing her forward. "She is Greyson's girlfriend, here for the holidays. We need to get her ready for the week. Did my assistant send you the itinerary?"

"Yes, ma'am. May I get you anything? Coffee? Tea, perhaps?"

Scarlett was dying for a strong coffee. The jetlag was getting to her, but she wanted to follow Philipa's lead. She asked for tea, so Scarlett did, too, hoping the adrenaline of a shopping experience of the ages would boost her energy levels.

While Philipa chatted with Gerta and her assistant Carla, Scarlett began wandering around the store, teacup and saucer in hand. Browsing through the racks, she was amazed at the individual quality of each piece. She'd never seen anything like them before, and she was no novice shopper.

There were velvet cocktail dresses draped in pearls, silk shirts with price tags she dared not look at, and skirts with such impeccable embroidery she knew they had to have been hand stitched. Each thing had been lovingly made, and she saw the queen hadn't been lying that there was never more than one thing in each size. The boutique had earned its place as the royal dresser.

Then, as if it were a dream, she saw the perfect dress alone upon a wall. The only one of its kind, it was a gorgeous shade of midnight blue. The bodice was sheer, made of silk flower appliques in the same color of the flowing skirts. The flowers drifted down the sheer sleeves.

"Philipa," Scarlett called, trying to keep her voice calm, despite the excitement in her veins. "Philipa, have you seen this dress?" Scarlett placed her teacup on a nearby counter, moving nearer for a closer look. The satin fabric was some of the softest she'd ever felt. As soon as she touched one of the delicate blooms, she felt a spark. It was fate. In the middle of each flower was a shiny blue gemstone that glinted in the boutique's overhead lights. Was it a sapphire? A *real* sapphire? Her fingertips brushed it. She didn't see any glue around it, and it was exactly in the middle. It was perfect. The dress was *perfect*.

"Oh, Scarlett. Gerta, Gerta, we're going to try this one on," Philipa called, taking the dress off the rack before pushing Scarlett into the fitting room.

CHAPTER ELEVEN

G REYSON AWOKE EARLY the next morning, his mind filled with snippets of his late-night meeting with Harrison and their father. Words were exchanged, bribes offered, threats made, but Greyson had stuck to his guns and made it clear he could not—would not—take the crown. It wouldn't do to dwell, so he sat up.

He thought he could go for a ride on his bike to reacquaint himself with Aldora. Breathing in freshly frozen country air sounded perfect. And he thought it was early enough he could be home before Scarlett woke up. Greyson found a pair of jeans, a thick sweater, and his heavy leather jacket. But just as he opened the door, he stopped short. Scarlett was standing there, her hand up like she was going to knock.

"Good morning. Did you sleep well?" he asked.

"I did, thanks. I mean, your mother and I were out shopping until pretty late, but it was worth it."

"Oh, really?" He tried to hide his surprise at his mother taking her on a solo excursion so soon into her visit. "Did you two have a nice evening?"

"We did. She is an unbelievably wonderful woman. I cannot even express how much I needed a fun night out like that. I was worried she wouldn't like me, but she made it clear she does."

Greyson felt warmth flow through his system. His mother may be a little theatrical—sometimes unreasonable—but he still adored her. Seeing Scarlett get along with his mother just confirmed how perfect he truly felt his girlfriend was.

"Anyway, I wasn't sure what was going on this morning, so I just wanted to knock and see if you were up."

"Actually, I'm going for a motorcycle ride through the countryside. It clears my head, and it's a terrific way to see the kingdom. Are you interested in coming with? If not, I'd be honored to take you to the kitchen, where they'll sort breakfast for you."

"The ride sounds great, and I'd love to see the kingdom. Maybe we can stop somewhere to grab a Danish or something. You know how I feel about pastries."

"I do, and I know just the right place. Why don't you go get changed? I'll be by your room to pick you up in what—maybe twenty minutes? Remember gloves, please."

Greyson watched her go, trying not to focus too hard on the fact she was the first girl he'd take on the back of his motorcycle. It was his alone time he never shared with anyone, but something made him want to make an exception for her.

When he went to her rooms, he saw she had dressed for the occasion in jeans with riding boots, her thick black winter coat, and a blue-and-gray plaid scarf wound around her neck. "So what's on the agenda today?" she asked as they walked through the main hall to the informal foyer that led to the garage.

"Well, we're fairly free until after lunch. We have a dinner party with some of the members of Parliament tonight, but nothing too formal. It'll be dull for a little while, as we have to follow a certain protocol. But after dinner, I have a little surprise planned for us."

"I love surprises," Scarlett said, a grin spreading over her face. "Tell me what it is."

"It's more of a surprise for everyone, but I did it with you in mind."

"How about a hint?"

"Let's just say if you thought Aldora looked like a winter wonderland before, then tonight will truly define the term."

"I quite like the sound of that," Scarlett said, leaning into him. "This is the best trip I've ever been on."

"And I like the sound of that."

SCARLETT WAS ON the back of Greyson's motorcycle, her arms wrapped around his waist. The freezing winter wind rolled over her gloved hands and the top of his spare helmet as she watched the countryside flow past. There were rolling hills topped with snow and livestock in penned-in valleys. At one point, they rode over a small stone bridge that went over a babbling brook trimmed in ice.

She loved watching the kingdom pass by on the bike, barely feeling the chill. Her indescribable link with Greyson was warming her from her toes to her fingertips. She felt like they had connected since he had entrusted her with his secret, and the level of trust filled her soul.

After a time, Greyson turned down a nondescript street and the countryside began to disappear. Instead, it was replaced by a picturesque village that seemed untouched by time. It wasn't the same one she had gone to the previous night with Philipa, and it didn't have the same modern feel. But she found it even more charming.

The houses, stores, and buildings were all the same gray stone. Their doors were painted bright red, brilliant blues, and deep greens, adding splashes of color to the streets. It was like she had stepped onto the pages of the illustrated *Beauty and the Beast* picture book she had loved as a child. People waved to one another as they stepped in and out of shops, most of which were decorated with ropes of garland and deep red bows. She could see almost all the roofs were lined with Christmas lights, and she longed to see the village when they were lit.

Greyson stopped the bike in front of a smaller buildings. It said *Patisserie* on the side. "Hungry?"

"Yes," Scarlett said, sliding off the motorcycle. Her legs felt a little like jelly from the ride.

"They always say the way to a man's heart is through his stomach, but, truth be told, it was the way to yours. Good thing I can buy you some tasty treats, because my cooking skills are still seriously lacking."

"Your Majesty," a gentleman said as he opened the door to the bakery. "It is so nice to see you again. And I want you to know the roof is still holding up brilliantly. I cannot thank you enough for helping."

Greyson reached his hand out, greeting the man as soon as he was off the bike and had his helmet off. "I'm glad the roof is still safe. Did a palace guard come check on it as I ordered?"

"Twice since you left."

"Good. I can't have snow coming down on your family. By the way, how are your children? Did Kathryn get over her cough you were so concerned about?"

"Oh, yes, she is feeling much better now."

Scarlett watched as the conversation between the men continued. Philipa hadn't been kidding when she'd said Greyson was good with the people. He had an ease about him that made it clear he cared about his subjects.

She couldn't help but wonder why he didn't want to be king if he loved helping his subjects so much. It wasn't her place to say something, but she cared about Greyson and didn't want him to make a mistake. She wanted to talk to him to better understand why he wished to abdicate. Sure, he wanted to build things and work with his hands, but she didn't understand why he couldn't do both.

Then she thought to the realities of him taking the throne. He'd have to move back to Aldora, and he would have to trade in his tool belt for a ceremonial saber like the one he wore in his royal picture online. He wouldn't just be Greyson anymore, not her Greyson. He would belong to his country. And she'd be in Savannah, broken-hearted and alone. Would he ask her to move here? *Would* she move here? Could she be a queen? Scarlett shook her head, reminding herself she was creating problems where there didn't need to be any. Right?

"Scarlett," he called, catching her attention. "Wait until you try his wife's pastries. They are some of the greatest treats you'll ever taste. Her work is so impressive she's the one making the cakes for the gala dinner tomorrow night."

They hung their helmets on the handles of the bike before following the man into the little pastry shop. The warmth enveloped her as she stepped in, the scent of their wares making her mouth water. There was a long glass display case filled with rolls, glazed buns, and twisted baked confections she couldn't name. She wanted to try one of everything, but she knew she couldn't handle eating so much.

"Order for us?" she asked Greyson, who was pulling off his gloves.

"Can't decide?"

"How could I? Everything looks amazing." He stepped up to the register, where a portly older woman stood in a flour-dusted apron. He rattled off several things to her. When it came time to pay, the couple tried to refuse Greyson's money. But, in his own quiet way, he got them to accept about double what the costs of the pastries were.

Scarlett shrugged off her outerwear, then sat at a table near the window and gazed out. It was beginning to snow, draping the historic town in a perfectly picturesque cloud of Christmas. "I'm not gonna lie, Greyson, I enjoyed the ride here, but I think I'll freeze if we ride the bike back."

"Yes, I shouldn't have suggested it, but I was too excited at the thought of getting on the road again. I didn't think it through. It won't be safe on the bike in the snow, but I'll get it sorted."

The baker's wife came up to the table, holding a tray. She seemed a bit nervous as she placed a plate of baked goods between them, then placed hot coffees in front of them. As soon as she was finished, she scurried behind the counter.

Scarlett picked up a giant creampuff pastry. She carefully took a bite, groaning in ecstasy. It was the most decadent thing she had ever eaten in her life. The filling was the perfect consistency, the crust was flaky, and the flavors overtook her. The honey, caramel, and a hint of lavender was otherworldly.

"We need at least two more of these," Scarlett between bites. "I am nowhere near done."

WHEN THEY HAD finished their breakfast and drank their coffees, Greyson rolled his motorcycle into the baker's garage with a promise to pick it up as soon as he was able. He had called for a car to come collect them after they had a chance to explore the village a bit. It gave them plenty of time to look around while still getting back to the castle well before dinner was slated to begin.

The flurrying snow fell around them, and the delicate flakes clung to Scarlett's hair and lashes as they walked out of the bakery. It was falling just enough to cover the streets and the tops of houses, but it wasn't so much the people fled to their respective homes.

Their gloved hands clamped, they stepped into several

shops. Greyson greeted each owner as he had so many times before. In almost every store, the storekeepers offered their wares free of cost. There were postcards, hand-knitted scarves, perfumes, and many other objects they tried to give to the potential future princess.

After her late-night shopping trip with his mother, word had spread like wildfire. The newspaper asked who the American beauty was. People whispered behind their hands about the young girl who had captured the prince's heart. He wasn't used to having someone so publicly attached to him. As long as he ignored the media's implication she was to be his bride, he could enjoy the effortless way she interacted with the Aldorians.

But the more he mulled it over, the more he could see how her grace and firm handshakes would fit seamlessly into the role of a royal. He had to remind himself several times that even if he was fortunate enough she decided to be a permanent fixture in his life, he couldn't promise her a crown, just his heart. He hoped that would be enough.

Scarlett was firm in refusing their gifts, insisting she pay. But Greyson had a pocket heavy with Euros, and he made sure she didn't spend a single coin. While in Aldora, he had the prince's salary to spoil her with. So by the time the car pulled up to the bakery where they had begun their day, he carried several heavy shopping bags.

"I'm so full from breakfast, I can't even think about lunch," Scarlett said after they climbed into the waiting town car that now wove through the snow-covered streets toward the castle.

"Might be for the best to skip it. We'll have so much food at dinner and an amazing dessert to follow."

"I'm glad your mom took me shopping so I have something appropriate to wear tonight. I want to fit in. I mean, it's clear I'm an American and not from Aldora, so I don't want anyone to think I don't belong."

He squeezed her fingers gently. "You've won over the king and queen. The hard part is done."

When they got back to the castle, Scarlett left to retire to her chambers, followed by a footman carrying her bags. Greyson went the opposite way to search for Harrison. While Greyson had seen him the previous night at dinner and at the rather tense meeting that followed, he wanted to speak to his brother privately.

He knocked on Harrison's bedroom door, which opened at once. "Afternoon, Greyson. Have you been on a ride?"

"Just got back, actually. The snow mucked things up a bit. Can I come in?"

Harrison nodded and stepped back, closing the door once Greyson was inside. "What's on your mind?"

Greyson sat on the green silk couch in the small formal sitting room. "I have a lot to say…and a lot to apologize for."

"Apologize?" Harrison echoed, falling sideways into the armchair, upsetting a stack of cooking magazines piled on the coffee table.

"When I made the decision to abdicate, I didn't even ask you how you felt about it. I was so concerned with making my own life I didn't give a thought to how it would affect yours. I left all the responsibility of my station to you without any consideration. For that, I am sorry."

"Don't be," Harrison said, grinning and a waving a hand. "I've always been 'the spare to the heir,' and it's nice to be in the limelight a bit, innit?"

"But it's not temporary. When I formally abdicate on Christmas Eve, you'll be in line for king. You're only twenty-two, barely out of university."

"And I'm a prince, same as you. Was I surprised you wanted to leave? Yes. But I suppose it's nice to be needed in this way."

"It's the ultimate way. You're going to have to do everything. It's not just smiling and signing orders someone else wrote." Greyson didn't wish to scare him off, but he wanted to convey all the work and sacrifices that went into being the crown prince.

"Greyson, where do you think I've been these last ten years? I've been next to you, listening to everything Father said. I'm not just scenery," he said, his jovial expression rapidly replaced with firm indignation. It was clear on his features with the lowered brow and tight-lipped mouth that reminded Greyson so much of their father. Harrison was the jokester, the one with a lighthearted comment to smooth over an argument. He didn't frequently get offended, yet he very clearly was.

"I'm not saying you are scenery, but there's a lot to go into this. I'm not just giving up for jollies."

"To be honest, I never thought you were. I get it."

"So you're...you're pleased, then?" Greyson asked carefully, studying his face.

"I get to be king of Aldora. It's a bit more responsibility, but I welcome it. Just as you feel you're better suited for a simple life, I've found rising every day with meetings to attend and memos to read to be oddly fulfilling."

"Strange to hear, coming from a man who used to refuse to do his schoolwork."

Harrison laughed. "It's quite a bit more fun to run a country than it is to solve algorithms in a classroom. I mean, when are you actually going to use those algorithms?"

"I use them about every day in my construction work," Greyson said.

"Then I guess it's good you did the coursework and I didn't." Harrison reached over and shoved Greyson playfully, and Greyson punched him back. Then Harrison grinned, motioning to his face with a hand. "Besides, I'm obviously the better-looking one, much more suited to being on a coin than you."

"I'm so glad to hear you say all this. I've honestly been having second thoughts about if I made the right choice in abdicating, but having you say it's what you want solidifies I made the right decision."

"Just don't ignore my calls again. If you do, I'll be forced to follow you to Georgia. I'm far too busy for all that."

"Who knows—maybe if you do, you'll find your own Southern belle. They're pretty terrific over there."

"Are you trying to give Mother a heart attack?"

"What? She seems to like Scarlett. Am I missing something?"

"Not sure. Maybe she doesn't want to push you away,

but she had some choice words to say about the 'wannabe Princess Di commoner,' assuming she can get in with the royals."

"Your assumption or her words?" Greyson asked, not knowing if he wanted the answer.

Harrison was silent, and Greyson knew what that meant. If he were being honest with himself, he'd sensed something was off from the moment Scarlett had been introduced to his family. Mother was being too nice, too welcoming, and too understanding. Her faux dramatic behavior was more natural than this façade she was putting on. But for a few days, he'd just wanted to believe it was true.

He had been a fool to think his mother would be any less judgmental about Scarlett than she was about anything else. If her own children weren't good enough in her eyes, how could he have thought she would accept his girlfriend? The reality of the situation hit him square in the gut. Scarlett had never stood a chance. Was he foolish to think she had—an American with no title of her own? His mother hadn't had a title when she'd married his father. Greyson had assumed she wouldn't care Scarlett didn't either. But then again, hypocrisy ran strong through these halls, so he shouldn't have been surprised.

"I should've known." He sighed, rubbing his temples.

"Hey, relax. Don't think on it. You'll be back in America soon enough, and they invented the *end call* button for a reason."

"That is true. Though I promise I'll ring you more regularly this time."

"Now that we got that out of the way…" A sly grin passed over Harrison's face he held out his hand, his signet ring flashing. "Bow to your future king."

Greyson let out a booming laugh. It was good to be home.

CHAPTER TWELVE

S CARLETT TOOK A deep breath and studied herself in the three-sided, full-length mirrors in the walk-in closet. She was wearing one of the semi-formal dresses she had bought with Philipa. It was a pale pink with a square neckline, long sleeves, and a hem that hit just above her knees. She pulled on a pair of nude-colored heels over her stockings, then fastened the pearl necklace she had gotten for her sixteenth birthday around her neck. It matched her earrings, which shone among the softly waved curls of her hair.

She had just started practicing her curtsies in mirror when there was a knock on her door. It was nearing dinnertime, and she thought it might be a maid like the night before. Instead, Greyson stood there in a perfectly tailored black suit. His hair was again slicked back, and he smiled broadly as he took her in.

"Scarlett, you look beautiful."

Her cheeks flamed, lips tilting up. "Thank you. You clean up rather nice yourself."

"It's the good breeding. Don't worry, it washes right off."

"Oh, good. For a second, I was concerned I'd lost my jeans-and-T-shirt man."

"Give me a few days. I'll be back. Though if I'm being honest, the jeans are from Calvin Klein."

"With some sawdust on the knee, no one will notice."

"May I have the honor of escorting you to dinner, madam?" He bowed dramatically as he spoke.

"That would be delightful, Your Highness," she said with a giggle as she placed a hand on his arm. When they began down the corridor, she continued, "Is that what I call you tonight? You said it was more formal than before."

"Me? No, don't bother. It'll be known by our attachment we are familiar. Although, I think it would be best if you addressed my parents as such when before the Parliament."

The reminder of the formalities expected of her made Scarlett's stomach drop. When she was busy practicing her table talk in the mirror and doing her hair, it was easy to ignore the realities of the night's events. She wasn't just having dinner with Greyson's family, but all sorts of Aldorian bigwigs. "Good thing I practiced my curtsies."

He laughed. "Have you?"

"Don't tease. I want to make a good impression on everyone, like I said."

"You're right, I adore you're making such an effort. You make it fitting into this world look so easy."

"Well, it's important to me to fit in wherever you are."

"This is just a practice one anyway, less formal than tomorrow with all the pomp and circumstance." He was quiet for a moment, then asked, "How were things with my mother last night?"

"I told you, she was lovely. We have such an enjoyable time shopping."

"She wasn't rude or snobby?"

He was choosing his words too carefully, speaking slowly. She peered at him from under lowered lashes. "Why do you ask?"

"I just want to make sure you have a wonderful Christmas."

Instead of going to where they had dinner before, Greyson took her to another dining room that had been set for twenty. It was much larger than the other with even more gold on the walls between portraits of kings in finery and nobles on horseback. A giant chandelier lit the table, where candles and fresh white roses made for a romantic scene. A trio of violinists added to the experience as they played a gentle melody that wrapped around her and made her feel as though she had stepped backward in time.

"Greyson, Scarlett." Philipa glided toward them. She was dressed in a shimmery purple dress with a matching jacket. "You're just in time for the receiving line."

"Receiving line?" Scarlett asked Greyson in a whisper as they walked with the queen to where Harrison stood. "Like at a wedding?"

"In a way, yes. Everyone will come in on their way to their seats to pay their respects. My father is usually late to these things. I think he likes to make an entrance."

"Oh, should I go sit?"

"No, stay with me. It's a good time to make introductions."

"Do I curtsy to them?"

He shook his head. "A handshake will be more than sufficient."

As if on cue, a footman opened the door beside them. Men in suits and women in dresses filed in. They approached the royals, bowing and curtsying to them, while giving Scarlett interested looks. But she was used to meeting relative strangers, so she greeted each with an introduction of her name and a firm handshake. By the time everyone was ushered to their assigned seats, her fingers had been squeezed half to death.

When Greyson, the queen, Harrison, Scarlett, and the other guests all stood behind their chairs, the door swung open and the king stalked in. He had a commanding presence that his sons seemed to have had inherited, and when he stopped before his chair at the head of the table, all assembled called out, "God save the king!"

Scarlett was taken aback, almost feeling guilty she hadn't said it, too. But it seemed no one noticed, and they all sat. The first course was served—an artfully filled plate of tomatoes and mozzarella, some sort of pâté spread on a seasoned crostini, and a salad of thinly sliced apples and arugula with a sweet dressing.

Greyson sat to her right, and the wife of one Parliament member was on her left. Scarlett thought her last name was something like Johannes, but she couldn't be sure. The woman seemed pleasant enough, though. When Scarlett turned to ask the lady to pass the salt, she said, "Are you visiting Aldora for long, Miss Calhoun?"

"Until New Year's Day."

"And did I hear correctly you're a guest of His Majesty, Prince Greyson?" There was a glint in her eye as she asked, obviously eager for a bit of gossip.

"I am. He wanted me to meet his family, and it's a lot easier for me to come here then it is for the entire royal family to come to Georgia."

"And how did you meet the prince?"

Greyson chose that moment to politely cut in. "Honestly, Mrs. Johannes, we met when I nearly ran her off the road."

"Did you?"

"I did. She was lovely enough to forgive my driving and, well, now we're here."

"And what were you doing in America? I've noticed you've been gone for several weeks, but no one told us why."

Scarlett looked from the woman to Greyson, wondering how he was going to explain away his absence. But, ever the royal, he seemed at ease. "Travel and getting to know all our friends in other nations is important for our growth as a country. America is an eclectic and interesting land I admittedly knew little about. But seeing as we'll soon be entering into a trade deal in the coming months, it seemed prudent to become better acquainted."

Mrs. Johannes nodded, seemingly mollified with his answer, and turned to the second course. Scarlett didn't know how she'd missed the changing of the dishes. Before her was a neat row of beef tenderloins, a collection of cooked carrots, and artfully molded flowers made of mashed potatoes. She took a deep breath as her neighbor dug into her plate.

"Thanks for saving me," she said so only Greyson could hear.

"I know when to step in. Although I have faith you would have been able to handle it on your own."

"Maybe, but it's so hard to lie."

"It's only until after the holiday, then all will be sorted. You won't have to worry about it again."

She nodded, then focused again on her meal as the conversation flowed around her. Sometimes, when she was sure she could contribute, she said her bit and involved herself in topics such as literature or current events. But when people conversed about Aldora and its goings-on, she stayed tactfully quiet, listening carefully in order to glean what knowledge she could about Greyson's homeland. By the time they had finished the next two courses of salmon and lamb respectively, she was comfortably full of knowledge and more food than she thought she could handle.

WHEN EVERYONE APPEARED to be finished with their desserts of whipped apple sorbet, Greyson stood. He tapped his glass with the edge of his spoon to gain everyone's attention. "Good evening. I trust you've all eaten your fill, as my mother's menus are always exquisite."

Everyone nodded in approval as Philipa smiled demurely, obviously pleased with the compliment.

Greyson continued. "Now, I have a special surprise to officially mark the beginning of our Christmas holidays. If everyone could follow me to the main hall, your coats are waiting."

As the Parliament members and their spouses stood, chattering excitedly as they readied to leave, Scarlett squeezed his arm. "Wait. My coats are all up in my room. Do I have time to go get one?"

"While my picnics in America leave much to be desired, I am much more capable of planning a surprise in Aldora. I have your coat and gloves ready with all the rest."

"Can you tell me what it is?"

"I think I'd rather you see for yourself."

Once everyone was assembled in the great hall, butlers, footmen, and maids began bringing out outerwear like an assembly line. In only a few moments, all twenty of the assembled were bundled up. Greyson helped Scarlett into her thick jacket. He'd had this outing in mind since the night he had asked her to join him in Aldora for Christmas. Having his family and Parliament there as well was merely the cherry on top.

A pair of footmen in matching red livery opened the double doors wide. A burgundy carpet had been rolled from the stairs, through the courtyard, and out to the main gate. All around them were whispers of winter, and a blanket of fresh snow covered all available surfaces. In a line, they strode out to the outer rim of the castle.

Scarlett gasped beside him as they stepped outside the gate. A line of horses stood waiting, each matching pair heading up a sleek black sleigh. They were waiting for their passengers, their breaths coming in puffs in the cold. Above the seating area sat drivers in the traditional capes and top hats, looking straight out of a Dickens novel.

"Everyone," Greyson bellowed, "four to a sleigh, if you please."

"We're going for a sleigh ride?" Scarlett asked excitedly as everyone found a place.

"Of course. If you thought the motorcycle was a fantastic ride, you'll adore this. The snow-covered mountains lit by a full moon…it's a side of Aldora I've wanted to show you."

He had set it up so they were the last two in line, giving them a smaller sleigh to themselves. The rest had dashed off for a tour of the grounds, and they were alone. Greyson had grown up driving and riding horses, and he didn't need someone to ferry him about. He had ordered a two-seater sleigh with a single white stallion to pull it. Just as he'd imagined, the beast with its red bell-covered reins and the golden sleigh was a magical sight.

So she didn't chance dampening her shoes by stepping on the few stairs that led to the open-topped buggy, he placed both hands on her waist and swung her up. She immediately sat, her mouth drawn into one of the most brilliant smiles he had ever seen. His heart swelled as he studied her, committing her expression to memory. If he could pick one sight to see for the rest of his life, it would be her in that moment, snow in her golden hair, framed by the mountains and the starry night sky. If she asked for the moon, he'd have no choice but to issue a royal decree to bring it back to earth.

"Greyson, this is so amazing," she said as he settled beside her, draping a faux fur mantle over their legs.

"You haven't even seen anything yet."

"Then I guess it's time you show me what I'm missing."

He clicked his tongue and the horse began to canter, making Scarlett squeal in surprise. They raced around the edge of the castle walls. He could barely make out the other sleighs, each holding a lantern for additional light. But he didn't care. He wanted some alone time with Scarlett, not to stay in a single file line.

They rounded the rest of the castle and then sped down the gentlest slope of the hill to light forest beyond. The fit trees were all coated in snow, making them sparkle in the moonlight. And he saw her blue eyes darting from the woods to the castle above.

"This is just like the Christmas carol," she said before beginning to sing, "*Dashing through the snow, on a one-horse open sleigh, over the hills we go, laughing all the way—*"

"*Ha, ha, ha,*" he bellowed dramatically, the sound echoing off the landscape.

She giggled. "Don't quit your construction job for a singing career any time soon."

"I do admit your voice is much more melodic than mine. Care to drive?" he asked, holding out the reins.

"The only horse I've ever been in charge of was a pony at my eighth birthday party."

"Come on, these are the finest trained in the country and I'm right here."

Biting her lip, she slowly took the reins in her gloved hands. He could feel her instantly tense, although the horse was just walking at that point. To comfort her, he threw one arm over her shoulder and pulled her close. She seemed to relax, even beginning to smile again as they made their way through the gardens.

He couldn't believe he had set up something special for her that went even better than he'd dreamed. Sleigh rides through the snow, being pulled by a purebred stallion from an ancient bloodline, wearing a fantastic gown…that was what Scarlett deserved. She made him want to give her the world, and then some. With his arm around her, their mingling laughter filling the air, the promise of a few more days together was enough to make him want to pull the horse to a stop, kiss her soundly, and confess his love.

There it was. Love. He knew it to be true in his heart for the first time since he'd felt the initial spark when he'd set eyes upon her on the side of the road. Never before had he had someone in his life who seemed to be his perfect companion in every way. He just wished he had the guts to put his feelings into words.

He had taken the reins back and turned them toward the main gates when it began to snow again. Fat flakes settled on them, and they filled the air with more of the winter magic he longed to show Scarlett. She seemed just as entranced at the sight of the castle as she gazed up at it, her head lying upon his shoulder.

Greyson hoped it could always be like that between them, no matter what country he was in or who he was. Because it seemed as if she was content with him, no matter who he chose to be.

AFTER THE SLEIGH ride, everyone reconvened in the main hall to warm up. There was some mingling and small talk over hot chocolate, coffee, and tea, but it didn't last long. Midnight was fast approaching. As everyone started to make their exits, Greyson escorted Scarlett upstairs. While she was perfectly capable of finding her way to her room, she wanted to spend every spare moment alone with him that she could.

"Wow, Greyson," she began as they strolled arm and arm through the hall. "That was an amazing surprise. I've always wanted to go on a sleigh ride like that."

"After the picnic, I wanted to do something romantic."

"Greyson," Scarlett said as they stopped before her door, placing a hand upon his cheek. "The picnic was not a failure. I know you tried, and the effort was what made it so amazing. The sleigh ride was beautiful, but the picnic is still my favorite date."

"Really?" Greyson asked as a smile spread across his face.

"Yes. The palace is beautiful, but we'll be leaving in a couple of days. Then, we'll be back in our town where we'll go back to our real lives and I will make a third attempt to teach you how to bake chicken without burning the house down."

"You're a very brave woman."

"Am I?" She grinned. "Maybe I'm secretly hoping to meet a fireman and leave you."

Greyson shrugged and pretended to think for a moment. "Then we should be more ambitious and try to bake bread as well—put your double ovens to good use."

"No, no. I'd like to be alive when the fireman gets there to save me."

"I don't know. It could be exciting if he rescues you from the brink of death."

"Goodnight, Greyson." She giggled, pushing him away playfully. "I'll see you tomorrow."

"Actually, my mother has made arrangements to take you on a spa trip so you two will be relaxed and beautiful for the dinner tomorrow."

"Oh, a spa trip. I definitely like the sound of that."

Greyson frowned, his eyes drifting away from her. She thought he might want to say more, but somehow couldn't. His expression worried her.

"What's wrong?"

"Scarlett, my mother has been nice to you, right? She hasn't been degrading or insulting to you in any way?"

"What? Why do you keep asking me that? She's been nothing but nice to me. You must be confusing her with *my* mother and the way she treated you."

"Good, I'm just checking."

"Did someone say something?" She was terrified. Was someone badmouthing her to him or the rest of the royals? Had she done something wrong? What didn't she know?

"No, no. I just want to make sure. I want you to have the best week in Aldora, and I want to ensure that you're treated with nothing but the utmost respect."

"Well, everything seems to be going smoothly, and the spa trip tomorrow will be just as smooth. What will you be doing while we're out being pampered all day?"

"I have some work to do with my father and Harrison. Some things he needs to be caught up on to make Harrison's transition to crown prince a tab bit more seamless."

"Official royal duties, all right." She had been thinking about him as a prince and a king since she'd first seen him in the village, and she couldn't keep quiet. "I know it's not my place, but I just wanted to make sure you felt you were making the right choice by abdicating. The people seem to love you and I can see in your face you love them as well."

"I do love them. But it's a different kind of love than that of a ruler. It's hard to explain, but yes, I'm making the right choice. I have no doubts about that. I've spoken to Harrison, and he's keener to take over than I ever was."

"Good, I just wanted to make sure. You know, it's a big decision."

"I know it is, Scarlett, which is why I'd been thinking it over for more than a year before I made my choice known."

The romantic moment was gone, but her questions hadn't ruined the evening. She had her answer, and she felt good about his response. But it also felt strange to be standing in that beautiful castle, knowing he was going to give it all up. Would she be willing to give up everything for a different life? She thought about her dream of owning a bed and breakfast. The idea of making a warm home for tourists, cooking for people every day, learning about their families, hearing their stories, and preparing the best tours...she would give anything to make that a reality.

"Greyson," she said suddenly, stepping forward and placing two hands on his chest. "I know my dream house is gone, or going to be soon, but I want to open that bed and breakfast."

"Okay. That's great."

"When we get back, will you tour some places with me, maybe give me an estimate of what you think it would cost to get them up to code? I have some money, an inheritance my grandmother left me, and I think it's time I spent it on something I want."

"Of course. But just for your ears, I know a handyman willing to work for food."

Scarlett smiled up at him, realizing this man had the potential to make all of her dreams come true. Without daring to think more, she wound both arms around his neck and pressed her lips against his. Brilliant sparks erupted in her chest, but the feeling of elation continued when they parted. As she went into her bedroom and closed the door, she thought he might just be the one.

CHAPTER THIRTEEN

S CARLETT AWOKE TO a series of sharp raps on her chamber door. She blindly groped for her phone on the nightstand as she tried to sit up. The jetlag had come in at full force and she realized she had managed to sleep through her alarm, the one she set so she woke up in time to meet the queen.

After she threw the heavy coverlet off her legs and dashed through the bedroom and the connecting sitting room, she threw the door open. She half expected to see an angry Philipa, tapping her designer shoe in disapproval, but it was merely a maid. She stood there, holding a flat, nondescript box.

"Good morning, Miss Calhoun," the maid began. "Her Majesty has sent these for you to wear for your appointment, and she instructed me to wait until you are ready for me to escort you to her chambers."

Rubbing her eyes, Scarlett stepped back. "Please, come in. I overslept. I didn't actually know when I was supposed to meet her, only that I was going to have a spa day with her... Am I late?"

"Not at all, madam."

"I'll be right back." Scarlett took the box, then scurried

to her bathroom.

She set the box on the marble countertop and lifted the lid, finding a pale gray velvet tracksuit and a pair of matching slippers. To her surprise, everything was in her size. But the most striking part was on the left breast, beneath the gold-and-burgundy lion crest—her initials, embroidered in gold.

No matter what Greyson had implied, she found the gift to be very adorable and thoughtful. If the queen didn't like her, then she wouldn't have gone through the trouble of finding out her sizes and even her middle name. The thought of them bonding over nail polish warmed Scarlett's heart, and she hoped she might even be able to find out a few embarrassing childhood stories about Greyson. Had he gone streaking down the hall in the middle of a Parliament meeting? Or maybe thrown up on a dignitary from Japan?

After she brushed her teeth and hair, she threw her curls into a ponytail and met the maid back in the sitting room. Silently, she led Scarlett out to the hall, then down several more, away from the one that would have led them to the main entrance and the dining rooms. She knew the castle was massive, but it seemed like the corridors were never-ending and there were dozens of closed doors. If she were on her own, she knew she would get lost.

Finally, the maid stopped at the end of one long hallway and knocked on the white double doors. "Your Majesty, I have Miss Calhoun."

"Enter," Philipa trilled.

The maid allowed Scarlett entrance. Her jaw dropped as her slippered feet sank into the plush cream carpet. Everything was pink or silver in the lavish sitting room that was twice the size of hers. There was a tall, roaring fireplace, over which sat a massive landscape of a field of pale pink flowers. Beneath it, upon the mantle, were dozens of photographs in identical frames. She itched to examine them closer look, longing to see what Greyson might have looked like as a child.

At first, she didn't see the queen, but then realized the woman was camouflaged perfectly, her tracksuit matching with the pink armchair she sat in. It was clear the shade was her favorite color. Even dressed for a spa day, her face free of makeup, and her dark hair wrapped into a polished bun, she still oozed the authority of her station. Scarlett fought the urge to curtsy.

"Good morning, Scarlett," Philipa said, rising to her feet. "I hope you slept well?"

"Very, thank you. I'm not late, am I?"

"Oh, hardly. Today is for pampering and immersing ourselves in the finest spa treatments Aldora has to offer. Come, the team is waiting in the washroom."

Scarlett couldn't contain her excitement as she followed Philipa through one of three doors into an immense bathroom. Actually, it could hardly be called something as simple as that. Filled with fresh roses, floor-to-ceiling marble, and the three people who bowed and curtseyed surrounded by rolling tables of tools, it was like Scarlett had stepped into a swanky salon. She couldn't even see a tub or a toilet.

The queen immediately sat in one of the matching spa chairs the team had been standing before. "Hello, everyone.

This is Greyson's girlfriend, Scarlett. She's visiting from America, and we'll just be doing a tad bit of prep for tomorrow's events. Scarlett, this is Tim. He's a master of skin care. Hannah is nails, and Peggy excels in the world of hair, although she's marvelous at massaging kinks from your shoulders and has a bit of a special treat for us today. Would you care to explain, Peggy?"

Peggy was a tall, thin woman with wide green eyes. She bobbed her head, then addressed Scarlett. "I am the royal perfumer, and I mix all the scents Her Majesty wears. If you'd like, I could help you create your own signature perfume."

"I'd like that, thank you." Scarlett looked from one to the next. "It's lovely to meet you."

"Care for breakfast?" Philipa asked, waving her hand to a counter holding pots for coffee and tea, cups, glasses, plates of freshly cut fruit, and small baked goods.

"Thank you. And thank you so much for this outfit. I love that we match."

"Well, I've never had a girl around the house to do these things with. Harrison and Greyson would never allow me to dress them up and paint their nails." She laughed a bit, and Tim handed her a cup of tea without her needing to ask. "What better way for us to bond?"

Scarlett felt her heart would burst as she busied herself with fixing a cup of coffee. Philipa was just so kind. Greyson had obviously been worried for nothing. If his mother came on a strongly, it was only because she was excited to have another woman in the castle. It seemed the queen wanted

Scarlett to feel welcomed. She could see why the royal family was so beloved.

They ate and chatted as Tim whipped up special face-masks and creams while Hannah did their nails. There were even pedicure basins. Scarlett had her nails done tastefully in a neutral color, only having Hannah paint the tiniest of snowflakes on her ring fingers.

While Tim worked on buffing the queen's face, Peggy brought forth her kit to Scarlett. Peggy opened the large box filled with tiny pots and droppers. There was essence of sandalwood, dried lilac leaves, many ingredients Scarlett couldn't name, and decorative bottles to put the mixture in.

Scarlett hardly knew where to begin, so she just stuck with the scents she could identify. She settled with a potion of tea tree oil and lavender essence with faint undertones of vanilla and cinnamon. It sounded amazing—and smelled even better—but as soon as Peggy handed her the gold-and-ivory perfume bottle and Scarlett took a big sniff, she realized what it reminded her of. It was like she had a plate of the decadent crème puffs from the previous morning. She stifled a laugh as she wondered what Greyson would think.

"Scarlett, would you like to take a little walk with me while Peggy begins to prepare the restorative hair masks?" Philipa asked, placing her teacup on the counter.

Scarlett thought back to the line of family photos. "I'd like that. I noticed some pictures on the mantelpiece when I came in. Are any of Greyson?"

"Would you care to see them?"

"Very much so."

They went back to the sitting room to allow Scarlett to look at photos. Most seemed like they would have belonged to any America family in the suburbs. A glamorous young mother with two small boys on the beach smiled up at the camera in one, those same boys in matching sailor suits in another. The next featured a toddler Scarlett knew at once to be Greyson. He was maybe three, wearing a small suit with a massive crown upon his head while a younger version of the king looked on, laughing.

"That one's my favorite," Philipa whispered, stroking the frame. "This was taken while I was still pregnant with Harrison. The nanny would always bring him in before events, and he just adored wearing his father's crown."

Scarlett smiled. "It looks so big on him."

"We always joked he would grow into it, and…and…now that he has…" Philipa made a little choked sound in her throat, her eyes shining with unshed tears. "He was born into the crown, carried it before he even knew what it meant to be king. Now his time has come…if only he knew how much the people loved him."

Scarlett's throat tightened. While she was always a sympathetic crier, something about the queen's soft tone touched her deeply. She feared not only for her son, but also for her people as well. "He does. And he loves them just as much."

"I fear that may not be true. If he did, then he would stay and be the ruler we all longed for him to become. He has the skills, the education, the bloodline, and the unconditional love of the people. When—*if*—he leaves, I worry it will all fall apart without his kind and steady leadership."

Scarlett bit her lip, hating to see how torn the queen was. "Aldora is strong, and Greyson just wants to do what's best for everyone."

"Without him, the orphanage in his name may close. And if Harrison decides to take after his elder brother and abandon his station…" She shook her head, retreating from the fireplace. Then she turned to Scarlett with a smile that seemed forced. "No matter. Let us speak of other things. After all, today is just about fun. It's nearly Christmas, hardly a time to sulk. Come, come."

While Scarlett tried to brush their tense conversation from her mind, Philipa took her through the center door, which led into her bedroom. It was the picture of luxury with pink and silver all around. The immense four-poster was one of the largest beds Scarlett had ever seen, and a line of windows overlooked the mountain range. To her surprise, a huge flat-screen TV was mounted on one wall, but she supposed even queens needed to unwind.

"My closet," Philipa announced as they stepped through an open doorway.

The size of Scarlett's condo, the closet had rows and rows of perfectly color coordinated clothes hung neatly, lit by overhead lights in the form of small chandeliers. Shelves of hatboxes were nearly labeled with occasions and types. The racks of shoes were enough to make Barbie jealous. Nearly five hundred pairs sat polished and waiting to be worn, framing a plush dressing sofa. Beside that was a professional makeup table and seat that could have come out of any New York City salon.

But she didn't have time to explore because Philipa said, "This way."

Scarlett followed her around the corner to a wall holding nothing but a framed print of a woman in a ball gown. Scarlett wasn't sure what she was supposed to say, so she said, "Great painting."

Philipa laughed. "You Americans, always joking." She tapped the bottom of the frame, and it slid up to reveal a keypad. While Scarlett politely averted her eyes, the queen typed in the code and the entire wall swung to one side.

At first, all Scarlett could see was darkness until Philipa pressed a button and the small room lit up. It was like a jewelry store with display cases of tiaras, ruby necklaces and emerald broaches sitting beneath glass, and rows and rows of ring cases. All around her were glittering tokens of Aldora's wealth, all in the form of the queen's private collection.

"Welcome to my favorite room in the house."

Scarlett tried to speak, but she was too overwhelmed by the sparkling jewels.

"I thought you could find a few things to borrow for the dinner. Some earrings, perhaps? I have a brilliant diamond cuff an oil sheikh gave me for my thirtieth birthday. But maybe we should stay within the sapphire realm to match the gown? Take a look around, please."

"Philipa, this is all so beautiful," Scarlett whispered as she peered into one case that held an exquisite tiara. Made of silver, every inch was dripping in diamonds, the shimmering stones covering the twisting metal of the many arches, which were tipped with pearls. From each peak hung yet another pearl, vibrant white against the red velvet.

"Oh, darling, you must try it on."

"No, I-I couldn't."

"Yes, you should. Here, take a seat." She set Scarlett on a small tufted stool before a mirror. "You know, in almost every kingdom, it's a rule that no one, save married royal women, may wear a tiara, and only after dark. That's why I will be the only person wearing one tomorrow night."

"Oh, I didn't know that. Then are you sure it's okay if I try one on?"

"What's the fun of nosing about the queen's closet if you don't put on at least one crown?"

"Well…if you insist."

Scarlett watched as Philipa carefully opened the case and picked up the tiara. "This is the oldest in the royal collection. Boasting thirty-eight pearls and seventy-three total carats of diamonds, this was the first tiara brought into the Montgomery family in sixteen-nineteen."

Scarlett held her breath as Philipa pulled out Scarlett's ponytail and arranged her hair around her shoulders. Then the queen placed the tiara upon Scarlett's head, the weight catching her off guard. But when it settled and she looked at herself in the mirror, she almost didn't recognize her own reflection. The diamonds glittered in the lights surrounding the glass, the pearls swaying gently with every slight move of her head.

"My, my, my…" Philipa tittered, bending to look at Scarlett over her shoulder. Their faces were so close they nearly touched. "It's a perfect fit. Look at you, my darling, you're simply glowing."

"The closest I've ever come to a tiara was when I was runner-up for Miss Georgia. It's so gorgeous I'm afraid to even move."

"It suits you more than I could say. You carry it like, well, like a queen."

"That's so kind of you to say."

"You know, you remind me of myself."

Out of all the things the queen had said that day, that one statement surprised Scarlett the most. "I do?"

"Why, yes. You see, I wasn't born a princess, or even a duchess. I was just a common girl, although I do hate the phrase as I think everyone is extraordinary."

"But the portrait of you and Princess Diana—"

"Well, I wasn't just a shop girl, by any means. I did have a fine education and a family to be proud of, as do you. And then a chance meeting with a prince changed my life." Philipa placed both freshly manicured hands upon Scarlett's shoulders, her mouth lifting into a small smile. "The way you carry yourself, the good you do with your many charities, how people are drawn to you…it takes a special kind of woman to join the Montgomery royal line and carry such a burden this delicate piece of art stands for. But you have that in you, Scarlett. You have the bearing of a queen, and it's a shame you won't be one."

"Well, I don't know about that, but I respect Greyson's decision, even though it *would* be fun to walk around in a tiara." Scarlett laughed, brushing her fingers over the precious jewels in awe.

"It is." Philipa tucked a stray lock of hair behind Scarlett's ear, the queen's eyes taking on an aura of a long-suffering woman, full of sadness and brave resignation. "But…no, it's probably not my place to say anything."

"No, please. I always want you to speak your mind around me."

"Well, I just hoped you could talk to Greyson about this decision. He is such an important part of this country. Our international relations depend on him, and I honestly believe we need him here as crown prince. Harrison isn't ready. He's so young. And with my husband's health declining, I'm just not sure how much longer we'll have with him."

"The king is sick?"

Philipa nodded, a tear forming in her eye. "We haven't told the boys yet. We had hoped to get Greyson settled on the throne first."

"Do you think Harrison could do it? Be the king?" Greyson said his brother was ready to be king, but her brief time in Aldora had begun to truly make her consider how much the people, and the royal family, relied on her boyfriend. It made her assertion he was making the right choice waver, and she didn't like how that felt. She wanted to believe Harrison could do it. As long as she believed in him, she could support Greyson's decision to leave the throne. But without Harrison, Greyson would be deserting his people. And a man who could do that wasn't someone she could love.

"Greyson and Harrison are so different. Greyson has been trained and prepared for this role his entire life. He has the relationships with foreign dignitaries, and he has established trade agreements our little country desperately needs. Harrison hasn't had the chance to do that yet. Maybe if Greyson could rule for a few years, give Harrison time to grow and study, then Greyson could go off and live his life."

"Would he be allowed to do that?"

"My husband is stepping down early. Greyson could do the same."

Scarlett thought about this contemplatively. What if Greyson was king for a couple of years? Then he could go off and build his own construction empire or open a specialty shop selling his wood creations. He had voiced his longing to live his own life, but if it would only be for a few years, how could he not look after his people?

"That doesn't seem unreasonable to me," Scarlett said carefully.

"Exactly," Philipa said eagerly. "So you will talk to him, my darling girl?"

"What?"

"Yes, I've tried to speak to him, and he won't listen to me. I've seen the two of you together. You have his ear."

"I have, and it didn't work."

"Try again. For me. Will you, darling?"

Where Scarlett once saw light and elegance in Philipa's eyes, now she saw the lines on her face, the creases of stress in her forehead. The queen was gone, and a mother concerned for her children stared back. But it was more than that. It wasn't just her children she was worried about—it was also her people. "Of course I will," she said. "I can't promise he'll listen, but I do promise to try."

"I am just so grateful you're here. I have faith you'll be able to swing his vote. Now, let's look at the other jewels. I can't have you showing up without sparkling bright."

Scarlett smiled, but she couldn't ignore the guilt flowing through her. Talking with Greyson would have to be delicate. She knew he was pretty adamant about his decision. But at the same time, she also knew he had a good heart. If he felt his people were at risk, Scarlett knew he wouldn't abandon them. Maybe he just needed to be reminded how much they needed him. Some celebrities lost touch with reality because they'd distanced themselves. He could be in the same situation with America. It'd been less than two months, but maybe it was enough time for him to have forgotten how valuable he was.

GREYSON AND HARRISON strolled along the row of stalls in the royal stable, taking a look inside each one. Greyson had missed the horses greatly—had been worried his favorites would have forgotten him. If there weren't two feet of snow upon the ground, he would take each one out for a ride about the paddock. But he would need to make do with just giving each a pat and a carrot.

"What do you think they're doing up there?" Greyson asked while he stroked the mane of a dappled gray pony. "Do you think Mother's torturing Scarlett?"

"I doubt it's as bad as all that. Scarlett is an American, after all. Standing up to overbearing royals is sort of their forte. The worst that'll happen is Mother's favorite tea will be tossed into the pond."

He laughed. "You're right. I'm just worried, is all."

"Don't. They're probably up there gossiping and poring over all your baby pictures."

"Do you think?"

"I hope so. I only selected the best bath time photos and embarrassing school portraits to be left on Mother's dresser."

Greyson struck out, playfully trying to snag his little brother with a sharp left hook. "You think you're funny now, but just wait until you bring a girl home."

"And what'll you do about it? You'll be back in America."

"You can't hide your future wife from me forever."

"Future wife? First, I'd have to find a bird to meet my high standards."

"Oh, you mean like…Gina?" Greyson asked innocently, pretending to inspect a recently oiled saddle hanging on the wall.

Harrison's face hardened. "Gina? She's just a friend, a mate like anyone else, innit?"

"If you say so."

"Stop worrying about my life. Instead, worry about Mother and Scarlett."

"And I thought you said I had nothing to worry about?" Greyson countered. He loved teasing Harrison. The timeless game of sibling rivalry always cheered Greyson. He would miss it when he left for Georgia, and he hoped the stress of being the crown prince didn't take away his brother's fire.

"Harrison, do you think Father will ever forgive me for leaving the throne?"

"Perhaps one day, if I don't make a mess of things. But even if I do, you'll be long gone. We've just the dinner tomorrow, the parade the day after, then the Christmas Eve ball when Father will announce me as the future king, then you're a free man."

"I suppose you'll get all my ornamental medals and whatnot. I'll even have to have my jackets made up for you. I know you fancy my red riding one."

Harrison shrugged. "I suppose. I can't seem to find the belt that matches. I might have one I left in your closet."

"In my closet? Why would it be there?"

"Well, I have been in there quite frequently."

"You've been messing with my things?"

"Brothers share, do they not?"

SCARLETT FELT RELAXED as she lay in bed that night. After playing dress-up with the royal jewels and having her hair trimmed and covered in some kind of seaweed wrap that made it glow, she had enjoyed an early dinner with the queen. They had sat in her sitting room, looking over a pile of photographs that just happened to be on her dresser, and eating bowls of pasta. Philipa had told her loading up on carbs the night before a dinner was important, as they were often too busy dressing and socializing to worry about eating.

She was thinking about turning in early when her phone rang for the first time in two days. When she looked at the screen, a picture of Betsy flashed. "Betsy," Scarlett said as she answered. "I miss you!"

"If you missed me, you'd pick up the phone and call your best friend."

"I know, I'm sorry, I've just been so busy. Everything at the castle is—"

"*Castle*?"

"Oh, right, you don't know anything." She sat up against the pillows. "Wow…I don't know where to begin."

"Um, the castle part, I think."

"Well, it's Greyson's…okay, not Greyson's. So, don't freak or say anything to *anyone*, promise?"

"Girl, have I ever ratted on you?"

"So have you ever heard of Aldora?"

There was a pause. "Isn't that a small country near Ireland?"

"How did you know that?"

"I watch a lot of *Jeopardy*. What about it?"

"That's where I am. We were never going to England. Greyson…Greyson's the crown prince of Aldora."

"Get outta here," Betsy said through a laugh. "Greyson's a *prince*? Back to the question about if he has a brother. I'm not greedy—I could take a cousin or something."

"He is. Well, was. It's complicated and a long story, but he's abdicating the throne and didn't want to tell me he was royal."

"Are you pulling my leg?"

"No, but I need to talk to you. Listen, Greyson wants to abdicate his throne but his mom, the queen, wants him to be king, like, soon, and it's all a mess."

"Well, it is the holidays. It would be boring if there were no family drama."

"It's more than that. I promised the queen I'd talk to Greyson about reconsidering his decision to abdicate his throne." She paused, waiting for Betsy to respond. "Are you there?"

"Sorry, I didn't hear anything you said after *queen*."

"Betsy!"

"All right, all right. You and Greyson just started getting serious. Isn't it too soon for you to be taking sides in a family matter?"

"I know I shouldn't, but it's not just something, like, will we celebrate Christmas in the Alps or in Hawaii? This is about ruling a country full of people who rely on him."

"Yes, so shouldn't you leave it to the rulers to sort out?"

"I want to, but the queen said she needed my help. She's concerned her younger son isn't up to ruling the country. He just graduated college."

"I definitely wasn't ready for a pet when I graduated college, let alone being responsible for a whole country."

"That's what I thought, too."

"Then I guess you have your answer. You're coming from a good place, and that's what should matter."

"I hope you're right."

"Me too. On a more serious note, can you Facetime? I wanna see the castle."

"Sure." Scarlett slid out of bed and turned on the light before pressing the Facetime button on her phone. When

Betsy answered, Scarlett saw it was still daylight in Savannah. "Okay, it's late, but I'm going to give you a tour of my *chambers*."

Betsy raised a brow. "Your *chambers*?"

"The Princess Diana Room. As in *The People's Princess*... Yeah, she was a childhood friend of his mom's." Scarlett turned the camera outward, giving Betsy a good look at the bed and art on the walls. "Here, the sitting room is amazing." She opened the door, pointed the camera at the picture above the fireplace, then flipped it around to show the crest on door.

"Wow, I don't know what to say, Scarlett. How...why didn't he tell you?"

Scarlett sat on one of the armchairs, then shrugged. "He just wants to live a normal life like a normal guy. That's why he came to Georgia, since, chances are, no one would recognize him. Him introducing himself as just a regular construction worker was part of him building a life for himself. He didn't want to tell me who he was because he just wanted me to like him for himself—not his title."

"I can respect that. Although, it would have been a lot easier to win your mama over if he showed up to the cookie party wearing a crown."

Scarlett giggled. "You're right, but it won't matter soon. After Christmas, he might just be...him."

"Christmas in a castle. That's amazing."

"I know. I'll send pictures and everything soon, I promise. It's just been one thing after another. How's everything at home?"

"Pre-Christmas is always a rush at my house. You know how it is. With my grandma coming down from Philly, my mom's been cleaning like there's no tomorrow, which I don't get since Grandma's almost blind."

"She wants to stay on her mother-in-law's good side. There's nothing wrong with that."

"There is when she's driving me crazy. I even bailed on a tennis lesson to help her wipe down individual blinds."

"You should get her a maid service for Christmas, like the kind that deep cleans top to bottom."

Betsy laughed. "You're right. That's a better idea than the canvas prints I bought her last year."

"You and your sister in matching puffy Easter dresses? Come on, your mom cried for hours over how cute that was."

"Yeah, well, I spent an hour cleaning the frame with a toothpick yesterday, so I'm less than attached to it at the moment. Now I'm heading out to pick up some last-minute things at the grocery store."

"This close to Christmas? Yikes. I'm sorry I'm not there to help you."

"That's okay. You just enjoy your *chambers* while I find a maid service."

"Call me if you have time when something good happens. Otherwise, I'll see you when you get home."

"Real quick, how is Blitz? Does he miss me?"

Betsy aimed her camera at the dog, who lay sprawled on the floor. "Of course not. He likes me more than you."

"I can live with that. Tell him I love him."

"I will. Merry Christmas."

"As they say here, *Happy* Christmas."

Scarlett hung up with Betsy, still conflicted about talking to Greyson. She truly felt it was the right thing to do, but she also didn't want to upset him. The more she thought about it, though, the more she felt she needed to say something. If she wanted to have a truly honest relationship with him, she had to speak her mind. She agreed with his mother. He was leaving his people with a ruler who wasn't ready. Maybe if Scarlett explained to him about his father being sick, it would make a difference. It definitely wasn't her place to say something about his health, but if it meant Greyson ensuring his people were taken care of, then that was what she had to do. The ends justified the means, right?

She revisited her thoughts about what a future with Greyson as the king of Aldora would mean. There would be two options. They could either split up, living separate lives, or she could follow him to Aldora. Long distance with a literal ocean between them just wasn't in the cards.

Her bed and breakfast dream would also be put on hold if she stood beside Greyson. Was that something she was willing to give up? It wasn't something she was ready to think about yet. She was getting way ahead of herself. Greyson hadn't proposed; they weren't getting married. There wasn't a mad, whirlwind love affair in the works, although she certainly felt the winds.

Scarlett flopped on the bed, then stared up at the canopy. She didn't have any reason to think she'd be queen. But if Greyson asked her to stand by his side for a few years to allow Harrison time to learn and grow, she couldn't help but think of the tiara. She looked like a queen, but it was more than that. Scarlett respected Philipa, and with the queen's help, Scarlett would put her dream on hold if Greyson asked her to.

Her phone rang again. Thinking it was Betsy calling her back, she answered without looking at the caller ID. "Miss me already?"

"As a matter of fact, I do."

Scarlett sat up, heart pounding. "Mama?"

"Of course it's me, Scarlett."

"I didn't think I'd hear from you."

"I might be a stubborn woman, but I'm not too hard-headed to tell my only daughter when I'm in the wrong."

Scarlett had never in her entire life heard her mother say she'd been wrong about anything. "Then I'm glad you called."

"I couldn't let Christmas go by with us fighting. I've been so focused on keeping you close and making sure you had the future I built for you that I chased you away." There was a watery feel to her voice, like she spoke through tears.

"You didn't chase me away. I wanted to meet Greyson's family."

"And how's that going, sugar? Are they being nice to you? Did you bring your good coat?"

"Yes, Mama. Yes to all of that." Scarlett smiled. Not talking for days had killed her.

"Then tell me everything. I'm so behind in your life."

Scarlett opened her mouth, but then shut it. While she

trusted Betsy to keep the secret of Greyson's family, she knew her mama wouldn't be able to keep things to herself. At the first mention of someone else's daughter getting married or snagging a fabulous job, she'd lay it all out on the table, just to prove her daughter was better than theirs.

"There's not much to tell," Scarlett said. "So far, we had a nice dinner with just the family. Tonight, I'll be meeting some of their old friends."

"That's good to hear. I'm hoping...will you bring him to dinner when y'all get back to Savannah? I think I'd like to get to know him."

"Of course. That's all I wanted since I met him."

"Perfect. Maybe buy him a good coat to wear. It's such a lovely gift, and it makes a good impression."

"How about this, Mama? Why don't you pick out a lovely coat for him, then give it to him for Christmas? Then, he'll have the one you like the most."

"I think that's a great idea. I have to go but be good, sugar."

"Always. Love you and Dad."

"I'll tell him."

CHAPTER FOURTEEN

S CARLETT WAS FACEDOWN on her bed, half stirring from a dream, when she heard a rapping at her door. She groaned, glancing at the time on her phone. It was seven, and she was hoping to sleep for at least a bit longer. But she rolled out of bed, then trudged to the door. She reorganized her face to a pleasant expression before opening the door.

"Hello, ma'am," a maid said, curtseying.

"Oh, hello. Is everything all right? The queen told me I could have breakfast in my room, then I could get ready for the evening at my own pace."

"Yes, that's still true. But the queen wanted me to bring you this for dinner tonight."

The maid handed an ornate box to Scarlett, then turned away, leaving her and the heavy oak box in the open doorway. Scarlett kicked the door shut with her foot as she took the box to her bed. She assumed it held the jewels she'd picked out the night before with the queen. Philipa had said she wanted the jewelry cleaned and would send it after the royal jeweler tended to the pieces.

When Scarlett opened the box, though, tears filled her eyes. She was staring at the family tiara from the night before, nestled in a velvet bed of Montgomery family burgundy. The diamonds sparked, the pearls gleamed, and the note read beside it read—*Rules are Meant to be Broken for Those who are Worthy*—in perfect cursive upon royal notepaper.

"Those who are worthy," Scarlett repeated out loud, as if she needed to hear it again. Philipa approved of her. She truly did. Scarlett went over to the mirror, then placed the crown on her head, the weight resonating within her. She understood Greyson's torn love for the crown, and its physical and metaphorical weight.

The night before, the queen had told her when hosting a dinner, things were not simple. Hosts couldn't just be ready at four, when the guests would begin to arrive for the receiving line. They had to be there by three to greet them. And they had to be down and in their places by two forty-five in order to ready themselves, which meant Scarlett needed to be ready by two thirty so she could find Greyson and have him escort her there, as was expected.

Scarlett took the crown off, then carefully placed it back in the box. That was when she noticed two other black boxes accompanying it, tucked snugly alongside the tiara's holder. One was little and square, the other a long rectangle. She went to the square first, finding a pair of diamond studs. Immediately, Scarlett took out her normal pearls, placing them in her portable jewelry box, then slid in the diamonds. They weren't the original ornate ones she had picked the night before, but it showed Philipa was genius. They were beautiful, but still subdued. They wouldn't distract from the crown, but they would enhance the beauty.

In the other was a diamond pendant on a platinum chain. The single stone was easily four carats, maybe even five. It was a princess cut, but not adorned by any additional designs or frills. It was just the solitaire. With her gown, the tiara, and the jewelry, Scarlett was going to feel like royalty. Now, she just had to make sure the rest of her matched the illusion.

GREYSON FINISHED PINNING his last medal on his military uniform. He couldn't help but feel like a fraud since he hadn't earned those medals. He'd never been to war. But they were symbolic of the wars Aldora had won, the peace they maintained, and the life the Montgomery family sought to ensure among their people. As he looked down, he sighed, relieved this life was soon going to be a memory. It was the last time he'd wear the uniform. After he abdicated, he would gift it to Harrison, as it was meant for the crown prince.

Greyson finished tying his shoes, then left the room, ready to find Scarlett. When he thought about her, all he wanted to do was curl up on her couch in Savannah with her and Blitz to watch a movie. And if he were honest, he was craving some of her fried chicken. The cooks in the castle were amazing, but they didn't hold a candle to the good Southern cooking like Scarlett happily made for him.

When he reached her door, he knocked gently, "Scarlett, are you ready?"

"Just one minute," she called.

He was dying to see her. She was a natural beauty, one of the things he'd initially been drawn to. Who wouldn't be? And he loved seeing her out with Blitz in her workout clothes with her hair in a plait. But at the same time, there was something to be said about women in ball gowns. The elegance, grace, and sophistication they possessed must be engrained within them. Scarlett oozed poise and sophistication by nature. With the added element of a ball gown, Greyson was excited to stand in front of his family, friends, and the dignitaries at the party and say, *this is the woman who makes me happy.*

When the door opened, he felt all the breath leave his body. Scarlett's dark blue dress was the most beautiful gown he'd ever seen in his life. The brilliant shade made her eyes pop, and the sparking skirts made her look as if she walked in the night sky.

She would easily be the most beautiful person in the room. But he hardly had time to take it in as something else took his entire focus. The Montgomery family tiara was firmly upon her head. He had to blink to see if he was merely imagining the addition. When he opened his mouth to talk, nothing came out.

Scarlett brought her fingers to her head as if reading his mind. "Is it all right? If you don't like it, I can take it off. I mean, I know we're not married and I'm not suggesting *you're* suggesting we should be, but your mother just thought I'd like to wear it. And I've never worn a crown except at beauty pageants, which I don't count because they definitely don't have the history this crown has. Well, is it a crown or a tiara or—"

"Scarlett, you look beautiful," he said. Seeing her in the tiara gave him a serious case of mixed emotions that battled to get to the forefront of his heart. On one hand, she was made for finery and deserved everything wonderful that came with being a royal. But on the other, he loved the girl with the ponytail who sat cross-legged in her living room before the lit Christmas tree.

A smile slowly spread across her face. "So it isn't too much?"

"This tiara looks as if it was made for you, as does this gorgeous gown. I am truly honored to escort you tonight."

"Thank you."

"Ready to go?"

"Oh, yes, I am." Scarlett took his arm, allowing him to lead her down the long corridor. "Greyson," she said they strode though the darkened and silent halls. "I have to say you look quite handsome in your uniform. I'm actually a little taken aback. I know you're a very handsome man, but this? It's something else."

"I'll be giving the suit to Harrison by the end of the holiday. Take your fill of it." Greyson let go of her arm, then did a dramatically slow turn. "This is the crown prince's suit."

"Well, then I'm glad I got to see it. And maybe it won't be the last time," she teased, reaching out to poke one of the medals on his chest.

"Trust me, it will be."

SCARLETT THOUGHT SHE should feel more nervous as they neared the starting point of the evening. But as she leaned on Greyson, enjoying the look of him in the perfectly tailored uniform with the burgundy sash and a chest full of medals, she was the most confident she had ever felt in her life. Trimmed in gold rope with the Montgomery lion on his chest, he seemed to hold himself differently as well. It was as if the ornamental sword on his hip or the signet ring on his hand had transformed him. He looked the part of a perfect royal, her own Prince Charming, right from the storybooks of her youth.

The receiving room was, as Greyson explained, a lesser version of the throne room. Empty save for a small couch on either side of the chamber, the gold-embellished walls and ceilings loomed around her, a series of windows adding to the light cast by the three massive chandeliers above. She hadn't actually seen the throne room, but she couldn't imagine it could be any grander.

She scanned the room, noting the king and queen were not in attendance. However, Harrison was sitting on one of the couches, speaking animatedly with a young woman Scarlett had never seen before.

"Who is that?" she whispered to Greyson as they stood in the doorway, wondering if she'd forgotten a family member or some young member of Parliament.

"Gina. She and Harrison are friends…well, in a manner of speaking."

"In a manner of speaking? Care to share with the class what that means?"

"It means they are in love with each other but like to pretend they're just friends. She's the one I mentioned to you back in Savannah when you tried to connect Harrison and Betsy."

She smiled. "Ah, I know what you mean. I know people like that. It usually takes a big push for them to see it."

"They've been friends for a long time—even attended and graduated university together. Her father is in Parliament, so he will be in attendance with the rest of the guests. But Gina is usually Harrison's date for occasions such as this. He's afraid Mother will try setting him up with a bride if Gina isn't there to play interference."

"So then why aren't they a couple?"

He shrugged. "Your guess is as good as mine."

"Well, she's gorgeous, so I just may have to have a talk with your brother."

"Please let me be present for that. Maybe you could knock some sense into him."

The quasi-couple walked over to Greyson and Scarlett, allowing her to inspect Harrison's potential girlfriend. Gina's light brown hair was piled on her head in an elaborate bun that made Scarlett a little insecure about her simple half-updo. The other women's dress was black with off-the-shoulder sleeves and a sweetheart neckline. If Harrison didn't make a move, it wouldn't be long before Gina found a "best friend" to escort her to events.

"Scarlett, you're looking lovely, as always. Greyson, you're looking...well, like an older, less handsome version of myself," Harrison said with a grin as he fiddled with his own decorative sword. His uniform was like the diet version of Greyson's. "Scarlett, this is my friend, Gina. Gina, this is the woman who has taken my brother's heart and the reason he's gaining weight."

Scarlett wagged her finger at Harrison. "Hey, mister, with that attitude, I'm not going to introduce you to some good ol' Southern cooking."

"As I said, the woman who has taken my brother's heart and is a wonderfully giving human being."

Scarlett shook hands with Gina, happy she wasn't wearing long gloves. She'd debated wearing them but despised them from cotillion, so she'd decided to risk it.

"Hello, Scarlett," Gina greeted in a polished British accent. "It's so nice to meet you. I love your gown. Those flowers are just stunning."

"I was just going to say that to you, Gina. You glitter with every step. You're sure to have every man's eye tonight." Scarlett watched Harrison fiddle with the button at his neck, then he excused himself, claiming he needed a mirror to deal with it. "Greyson…" Scarlett said. "Why don't you go help him before he chokes himself and you have no one to take the throne?"

"We definitely wouldn't want that." Greyson moved over to Harrison. They began having a profoundly serious conversation involving several hand gestures. Though neither touched Harrison's top button.

Gina's hazel eyes drifted upward. "Is that the Montgomery tiara?"

"Yes, it is. The queen sent it for me to wear."

237

"Wow, she must like you. Is this your first formal dinner?"

"To this standard it is. But I've heard it's not yours."

Gina laughed. "Hardly, but I'm pleased to be here, as always. I studied international diplomacy. Events such as these are where the real diplomacy happens. Deals are always being discussed, proposed, and secretly agreed upon at things like this."

"That makes perfect sense. Back in Georgia, most of the best contracts and business alliances are made at parties...although never at a castle."

They continued to talk for a little while, until the king and queen arrived. The king was in a military uniform, much like those his sons wore. But the queen was in a floor-length silk gown in a dove gray that flowed around her ankles. The modest bodice, which was the same hue of the shirt, had cap sleeves with a sheer, intricately beaded design covering it. Scarlett would've bet her inheritance that each of those beads had been placed by hand and the dress had been custom made. The queen was radiant beneath her simple diamond tiara, and it was as if the years had been rolled off her.

When her husband took her hand, gave it a slight kiss, and helped her sit on one of the couches, Scarlett smiled. Those two were in love. It wasn't an act. She wasn't sure why she felt such conviction, but there was this feeling inside that screamed it was the kind of relationship she hoped she could continue to build with Greyson.

Then she remembered the fear and devastation in the

woman's eyes from the night before when she'd talked about her husband's illness. She watched the queen. Philipa reached a hand out to her husband. For a few moments, they sat like that, looking at each other and whispering under their breath. It was beautiful.

"Scarlett," Greyson said, causing her to jump. "Sorry, are you well?"

"Yes, I was just thinking."

"Give me a few seconds of your time, then feel free to go back to your thoughts."

"I think I can spare a few seconds. But my watch didn't go with this outfit, so I'm timing you in my head."

"Fair enough. The dinner doesn't officially begin for another two hours, but I'd like to tell you how the event will proceed. We will all line up against that wall." He motioned to the one lined with windows overlooking the castle's grand gate. "It shall be Gina, Harrison, you, me, my mother, and then my father. When the guests have arrived, they'll enter on the left, then go down to the grand dining room on the right."

"Do we have to do anything?"

"Not really. Don't worry about curtsying for this part, as they'll only be bowing and curtsying to me. They will speak to my parents after, then be escorted into the ballroom by a valet. But when we're at the ball with more time to spare, you will need to curtsy to anyone I introduce as a lord, lady, duke, or duchess."

"Oh, all right. Easy enough to remember."

"Do I have any time left?"

"A few more seconds."

"Have I mentioned just how ridiculously beautiful you look tonight? You said Gina was going to be attracting the attention, but it's *you* the people won't be able to take their eyes off."

Scarlett smiled. "You just earned a full minute of my time."

"Ah, compliments are the way into your world?"

"They don't hurt."

"Then I'll be sure to give them all night. Has anyone told you that you have the most delicate pinky finger? I am serious. You could be a pinky ring model. Truly, I should be your agent. We could make millions."

Scarlett rolled her eyes, giving Greyson a little shove. "You're ridiculous. I can't take you anywhere."

Greyson laughed, offering his arm to Scarlett. "Let's just greet my parents, then, as soon as the holidays are over, you can take me home with you to Georgia."

The queen, ignoring Greyson entirely, went right to Scarlett. She brushed a finger over the curve of her cheek, giving her a small smile. "Scarlett, my dear, you look perfect in that tiara. I fear I'm going to cry. It's like I have a daughter."

"Philipa, I cannot thank you enough for letting me wear it tonight. I never thought I would feel this magical."

"That's what balls are all about." Then she turned to Greyson, smiled, and placed a hand on his face. "And you...such the handsome man. Don't you two just make a lovely couple? I want a professional shot of you and Scarlett tonight. No running away from the camera like every other year."

"Mother, having Scarlett by my side is something I will need documented, or no one will believe I got someone like her to actually tolerate my presence."

IT WASN'T LONG before people began arriving. It was funny to Scarlett. People strived to be late to parties in America in order to seem fashionable. But in Aldora, there was a line to arrive early. The difference in cultures amused her.

As they stood there in the perfectly straight line, Greyson proved to be a wonderful guide. As each person made their way through the receiving room, he would quietly explain each was, some fun facts about them, and their impact on the country. Scarlett knew she'd never remember who they all were, but she was grateful to have Greyson. He actually did know them all, and she was sure he could help her remember them if they ran into each other at the dinner.

But by the time they greeted everyone who passed through the room, there was a kink in her neck from nodding and she felt the weight of the tiara. It was much heavier than it appeared, and no one ever gave thought to how much the metal and jewels weighed. She thought to the queen's golden coronation crown, which Scarlett had seen in the jewelry room. It was four times the size of the one she wore, boasting massive rubies and emeralds. Now that one would have definitely given her a headache.

"Now it's time to be announced," Greyson explained as

Harrison and Gina stepped up to the door to the dining room. "They'll go first, then us, then my parents."

"Wow, so much formality."

"It goes by rank. Next year, I suppose we'll be down there with the guests."

Scarlett smiled. He had hinted they would be in Aldora again, but with him as a non-royal. While the thought of him stepping down began to nag at her once again, she ignored it to stay in the moment. She had time aplenty to speak with him yet.

Suddenly, the doors opened. A booming voice called out, "Announcing His Royal Highness, Prince Harrison Christian Alexander Montgomery and the honorable Miss Eugenia Violetta Ainsworth." And Harrison and Gina stepped through the threshold.

"Eugenia?" Scarlett asked in a hushed tone as she and Greyson took their place on deck.

"Don't mention it. She despises being called Eugenia."

"Noted."

"Announcing His Royal Highness, Crown Prince Greyson Charles Rudolf Leopold Montgomery and Miss Scarlett Calhoun," the bodiless voice called out.

She took a breath as they made their way into the bright lights of the dining room. Everything was dipped in gold and marble, the crystals threatening to bring the ten chandeliers overhead crashing to the floor. On the ceiling were paintings of clouds, cherubs, and birds, all done with the same care as any fresco in Florence.

There were touches of Christmas everywhere she looked,

starting with the massive twenty-foot tree, which was glowing merrily against the far wall, the vibrant red-and-gold ribbons in perfect coordination with the tablecloth. And when she and Greyson came to their seats on one side of a table set for at least fifty, she saw at each place was a nameplate of gold edged in glass sprigs of holly she knew she wanted to keep.

"All stand at attention for His Royal Majesty, King Leopold, and Her Royal Majesty, Queen Philipa of Aldora, long may they reign!"

The crowd was silent as the royal couple stepped though the room. And when they each stood on either end of the table, everyone sat, save for the king.

"Ladies and gentlemen," he began, "Once again, I welcome you all into my home to share in this Christmas season with my family. After all, family is the center of Christmas. Although we do not all share the bonds of blood and birth, we all share the birthright and the love of Aldora. Year after year, I greet my constant friends and subjects and guests who decide to grace me with the gift of their companionship. Let us end this season with good cheer, better company, and a fine celebration. Happy Christmas."

"Happy Christmas," the crowd replied in jolly unison.

"Hello, Grey," a soft voice said from beside Scarlett.

She turned and saw a lovely redhead. She was about to say hello when Greyson spoke first. "Hello, Arielle."

"Happy Christmas," Arielle replied with a smile. "It's wonderful to see you again. I slipped in through the other entrance to skip the receiving line."

"I see." His tone wasn't cold, but it definitely lacked the warmth he used when speaking to anyone else.

Scarlett thought it a little funny her name was Arielle and her hair was the same color as the Disney princess, but kept her mouth shut as the *Little Mermaid* wannabe glared in Scarlett's direction. "Grey, is this some distant cousin of yours I hadn't had a chance to meet? She's wearing the Montgomery family tiara, so she must be some manner of relation."

"No," Greyson said curtly. "Arielle, this is my girlfriend, Scarlett Calhoun. Scarlett, this is Lady Arielle Tinley, the daughter of the Duke of Rachburg."

"Nice to meet you," Scarlett said cheerily.

Arielle laughed, one of those fake-sounding, high-pitched tones. "Goodness, Grey, an *American*? How perfectly common."

Scarlett tried to keep her face a perfectly composed mask, but the façade began to slip as she stumbled to try to think why this person was being so nasty. She had just curtseyed to someone who thought so little of her. She looked to Greyson, whose eyes blazed with unsaid fury.

"Good evening, Arielle, and Happy Christmas." He peered around Scarlett to Arielle's nameplate. "I see you've mistakenly sat where Lord Grimsby is meant to, and I know he'll be coming in late. Do see to it you find your proper place before my mother notices and throws a fit. You know how she is."

Arielle's face turned the same color of her hair, but she didn't reply. She stood and shook out her skirts, then went to an empty seat down the line.

"I apologize for her behavior," Greyson murmured when Arielle was gone. "Her treatment of you was terrible."

"It's okay. It's just...is that how people talk about me behind my back?" she whispered, wracking her brain to think of any other time someone had seemed rude since her arrival in Aldora, but nothing sprang to mind. "I'm not ashamed of being American or not being a royal, but the way she said it was just so hurtful."

He took her hand beneath the tablecloth and squeezed. "Pay her no mind. To be honest, she and I were involved for a time, before I realized she was far more interested in the tiara you're wearing than me."

"She's your ex-girlfriend? That explains everything. I'd be bitter if I lost you, too."

"And it's exactly that attitude that drew me to you. You never cared I was just a construction worker. You were more than happy to come home with me, expecting to stay in a small house with simple people, just to spend the holiday with me. Just as you could have had a hundred American businessmen and still chose me, be firm in the knowledge I could have had a hundred noblewomen and still would have always chosen you—will always choose you."

As GREYSON WATCHED Scarlett speak with nobles and dignitaries throughout dinner, he thought she completed just about everything in his life. She could move between worlds, being the caring girlfriend of Greyson the construction worker and then becoming the gorgeous woman on Prince Greyson's arm. And she did it all so well. It must have been second nature to her, like she knew exactly what he needed without him having to ask. He couldn't image anyone being a true partner in everything the way she was to him.

And after dessert as everyone rose to mingle, he pulled her to her feet. "There's something I want you to see. Follow me." He took her out to the hall to a set of burgundy drapes, hidden behind a marble pillar.

She looked up. "Lovely curtain. Is it velvet?"

"Don't toy with me. Just follow me and try not to jostle the fabric too much as you enter. I don't wish to be followed."

"Oh, so secretive."

"It is. It's a royal secret." Greyson pulled the drape back slightly, revealing a portion of the paneled wall. It was just like any other in the room, a warm cream with gold edges, but at the same time, it was so much more. He pressed the wall gently and it popped open, revealing a darkened spiral staircase.

"Wow, a hidden door."

"Follow me."

Hand in hand, they crept into the small space. The door shut behind them, and all was silent. There wasn't any light, nor any trace of the events just a wall away. He held tightly to Scarlett's hand as they climbed the stairs until he reached up and felt the trap door above him. He pushed it open, coughing slightly as years of dust was disturbed.

"Where are we?" Scarlett asked.

He reached into the stairwell, then lifted her into the hidden alcove. It was a small room with bare rafters, sporting a railing on one side and a large window on the other. He could hear music and voices again, swelling around them, but it was the view he wanted to show her.

"This is my favorite place to visit during these sorts of events. Come see." He stepped over the bare wooden floor to the railing. "Look down." The entire ballroom was in plain view, three stories below them. They had the perfect view of the darkened ballroom, half decorated already for the Christmas Eve party. "Now come to this side."

The other end revealed a sliver of the dining room. As a child, he had adored sneaking up for a moment alone to enjoy the party without all eyes being turned to him. It had become his refuge, and he hadn't even shared it with Harrison.

"Can they see us?" she asked.

He shook his head. "The ceiling is made in such a way that this is hidden from all angles. I presume the architect made it for spying. That way, someone could watch the royal proceedings in secrecy."

"I wish I had my camera," she whispered. "Can we come back during the ball? I'd love to see the ballroom all decorated from above."

"Wait, look out the window. I think you'll like that view even better."

She did as he instructed, and her mouth split into a grin. The windows gave them the perfect, bird's-eye view of the village, which was all lit up with Christmas lights. It was good bit away, but it was like when he was in a plane that was getting ready to land, with the city below the wing, stretched out for him to view from the small window. She had wanted to see the village as it was decorated at night, but he hadn't had the time to take her. This was the next best thing.

"Greyson, this is amazing. Thank you for showing it to me."

"Harrison doesn't even know about it."

"Then why share it with me?"

"Because…because I care for you, Scarlett. I've let you into my life in a way no one else ever has. Just look down there. Everything is so far away, but you're a constant for me now. I'm happy with viewing the royal life from afar like this as long as you are with me."

"I think it's an amazing sight from any angle," she said as she leaned over the railing.

He placed a hand on her waist. "Be careful. The wood up here is old, and I can't promise your safety."

She took a step back and turned, poking one of his medals. "What's the good of all these if you can't even save me?"

"Honestly? They aren't good for anything. They're merely symbolic in nature, and I'll be glad to be rid of them."

"Is that what you want?"

"Is that not what I've been saying to you all this time?" Greyson was confused. It was like she was constantly forgetting their conversations and the fact he had been prepping to abdicate had slipped her mind.

She bit her lip, then took a deep breath. "Won't

you…would you consider…staying on as crown prince, at least for a little while?"

"What?" A chill rolled down his spine at her words. He couldn't believe she was suggesting he stay on in Aldora.

"Not forever. Just until Harrison is a little older, a few years?"

"Harrison will make a fine crown prince."

"Maybe when he's grown a bit. Your country needs you, Greyson."

He scowled, feeling the magic of his secret place melt away. "My country needs a ruler who has a true heart for kingship. I am not that man."

"But you are," she said, placing a palm on his chest, just above his racing heart. "You were born for this. You're meant to be the next king, at least until Harrison can handle the weight."

"Scarlett, where is this coming from?" He felt he already knew the answer. His prayer was he'd be wrong and his deepest fears *weren't* coming true. She couldn't have been chasing a tiara. There was no chance he'd read her wrong. It'd break his heart, and he feared he'd never be able to love again.

"I'm…I'm just worried about you, and I hate to do it now, but I needed to tell you before you did something rash. Your mama said your dad was sick and—"

"He's *not* sick. I can't believe my mother would use that as leverage to get you on her side."

"I'm not on a side. I just want to make sure you're not abandoning the country in its time of need."

The hidden alcove seemed to spin as he felt anger toward her for the first time since she had entered his life. Was that what she thought of him—that he would just leave like his country didn't matter? He loved his country, which was why he wanted to abdicate. Harrison would make a better king. "Scarlett, I am always thinking of my country. It comes first. Harrison's more than capable of ruling. He's been trained for the task, just as I have."

"Not as well trained as you. And he doesn't have the relationships you have. He can't even figure out he's in love with his best friend. How do you expect him to make important decisions?"

"How would you know a thing like that? You've only even known about this country's existence for a few days."

"Your mama told me," she admitted softly. "She's worried Aldora will fall apart without you. She asked me to speak with you, to beg you, to consider ruling for a couple of years. A couple of years won't ruin your dreams."

He took a deep breath. He hated speaking out of anger. Always tried to sort out his words before he said something he regretted. But this time, he couldn't calm himself. He couldn't right the spinning in his mind, the pain forcing its way from his chest, nor the disappointment ringing in his ears. She didn't know what she was saying. "You're naïve if you think it would only be a few years. Every time I'd try to abdicate, she would try this same game. It'll never end, and my dreams will be long forgotten. What's worse, I won't be the leader my country deserves."

"I think you should still consider a couple of years. Maybe sign a three-year commitment or something. I'll come here. I'll help remind you who you are."

Greyson didn't know how to respond. He thought he'd warned Scarlett about what she was stepping into and stressed the importance of presenting a united front as the team they were. He'd thought they were partners. He'd thought she understood how important following one's heart was. But he'd thought wrong. "So that's it, you want to be a princess?"

"What? No, that's not the issue. I don't care about the title."

"Says the woman in the tiara," he spat with a little more malice than he had within him.

Her eyes sparkled, and he knew she was close to tears. "Greyson, this was just a little gesture from your mama to make me feel welcome." Her voice was soft, almost a whisper, her hands touching the tiara. Was it a possessive thing? She could keep it. Without his title, the tiara was just any other piece of jewelry.

"Or to convince you to have this conversation with me."

"I am not being manipulated."

"I think we should return to the party," he said, his voice sounding even emptier than his heart felt.

"Greyson, let's—"

"Here, I'll help you down." He stretched out his hand, and she silently took it.

The short walk down to the main level was quiet, save for the creaking of the metal stairs beneath their feet. His mind raced as he tried to think of what poisonous lies his

251

mother had fed Scarlett. A week ago, she would have never told him to abandon his dreams. It was like the castle and tiara were draining away what had drawn him to her in the first place. It was like Arielle all over again. But this time, his heart was mixed up in the mess.

THE REST OF the evening went by uneventfully. There were desserts, mulled cider, and plenty of conversations. But Greyson didn't say another word to Scarlett.

Around ten, she had just about enough of the night. Her feet hurt from standing around, her neck hurt from the tiara, and her heart hurt most of all. She placed a hand on Greyson's arm, and he turned to her. But it wasn't Greyson—it was his royal front. Staring into his eyes, she didn't even recognize him. "Greyson, I'm not feeling well. I think I'd like to head to my room."

He nodded, then took a sip from his glass. "All right, I'll fetch a valet to escort you to your chambers."

She leaned in close and whispered, "I would prefer you walk with me. I think we need to clarify a few things."

"I will not abandon my station here. I need to stay. I'm sure you agree." She wouldn't call his tone overtly sarcastic, but it certainly delivered a crystal-clear message. He was displeased with her for sticking her nose in royal business.

Scarlett squared her shoulders, then stood. She wasn't going to wait for a valet. Instead, she'd escort herself, because she was a strong and independent woman who not only didn't need a man but also wasn't manipulated by their mothers. She turned on her heel, then walked out of the ballroom. As she rounded the corner, she took her shoes off. While not particularly ladylike, she couldn't take the pinching anymore and thought it better to just walk barefoot to her room.

Behind her closed door, she allowed herself a moment to wallow and shed a few tears of frustration. But then she took a breath, slipped out of her dress, and climbed into the bathtub. The lavender soap soothed her to the point of relaxation, allowing her to think more about how she would fix the mess she had unknowingly created.

CHAPTER FIFTEEN

S CARLETT AWOKE EARLY the next day. She wanted to be dressed and ready when Greyson came to pick her up for the parade. Well, *if* he did. She wasn't sure if he'd send a valet or just leave her to her own devices to get down to the foyer. She didn't want to wait to find a maid for breakfast either, so Scarlett put her robe and slippers on, then went off to find the kitchen.

She had an idea where it could be, so she turned toward the ballroom. It was safe to assume the staff wouldn't have lugged all the food and drink through the entire castle to bring it to the ball. So she wandered the surrounding halls until she smelled something delicious.

When she walked into the massive kitchen, her eyes about flew out of her head. There was Harrison, in a pair of sweatpants and a baggy football jersey, standing over the stove and cooking. He must have heard her come in, because he looked over his shoulder and smiled.

"Does your mama know you know how to cook?" she asked. "I hear that's frowned upon when you're royal."

"Oh, it's definitely frowned upon, but I've always fancied myself a bit of a rebel."

"Your brother almost burned down my apartment the

first time he tried to cook," Scarlett said, laughing at the memory.

"Yes, well, I don't think that's his gift."

"What do you think it is?" Scarlett sat at the large kitchen table, watching as he popped two halves of an English muffin into a toaster.

"The wood. Obviously, I'm sure you've seen it."

"I have. It's beautiful."

"But also, I think Greyson's skill is with people. He has this ability to make them fawn over him."

"Is that not you?"

He froze for a moment before continuing to cook. "Eh. I'm okay. I prefer to watch from the outside. But I'll figure it out. I have to, right?"

"So there's no changing his mind?"

"No, I suppose not. Could you change his mind?"

"I don't think so. We got in a bit of a row about it last night."

"Would you like some eggs?" Harrison asked, smoothly changing the topic. "Then you can decide if you like his woodwork over my eggs benedict. Though, fair warning, I'm quite the chef."

"Sounds great."

Harrison turned back to the stove and continued with his cooking. "I am a particularly gifted man, so I can talk and cook at the same time. Listen, up until a few months ago, Greyson wanted to rule."

"So what happened?"

"I'm not sure. I think the best way to explain it is to say

it's like bridal cold feet. It was like one day he woke up and simply changed his mind."

"What about you?" she began, wondering if she was overstepping again. "Are you ready to rule?"

"Yes, I suppose." He began assembling their food with every care for detail. "Between you and me, Greyson would've been rubbish. He cares too much about the trivial things, innit? I'm the big-picture type of lad. To be honest, I never thought I'd get the chance. Now that I do, I want to be ready."

"What do you mean?"

"Well, you know, without offing Greyson, I'd always be *the spare*. And hit men are notoriously unreliable, so I'd probably just have to outlive the sorry sack. That is, unless you had children together, then I'd have to outlive them, too."

"Oh, wow, Harrison, I think you're moving a little fast. It's just not like—"

"I know. But I see the way he is with you. He's different. Happy."

After a pause, she asked, "And your mother, do you think she played me?"

"She definitely played you. But she has years more experience in politics than you, so I wouldn't feel bad."

But Scarlett did feel bad, downright terrible even, for allowing herself to be swayed after being specially warned about the queen. Scarlett thought herself pretty savvy when it came to catching on to manipulation and guilt trips, but the Southern mamas she was used to were no match for a ruler.

Smiling at Harrison, Scarlett accepted the plate of eggs. She ate them, praising his cooking abilities, and nodding when he spoke. But nothing else he chatted about was sinking in. She was too busy thinking about what Harrison had said. It was his dream to rule and Greyson's to leave. Instead of trusting Greyson, the man she knew, she'd trusted a woman in politics Scarlett had been warned about. Rookie move. She was manipulated, and, frankly, embarrassed as well. She owed Greyson quite the apology.

"Would you mind taking me to Greyson's room?" she asked Harrison when they finished eating. "I would just like to see him before the parade, but I don't know if I can find it by myself."

"I would, but I can't. He's overseeing the task of getting the horses ready for the parade. But I'll be happy to take you down to the carriage when you're ready. Gina will be tagging along with me. I'm sure she would enjoy your company, so she doesn't have to suffer through mine."

"Thank you, that would be great."

Scarlett insisted on doing the dishes. She ignored Harrison's complaints she was a guest, hip-bumping him out of the way. When everything was washed, she excused herself and agreed to meet Harrison downstairs in two hours, ready for the parade.

"And Scarlett," he said to her as she walked out of the kitchen. "That tiara, though clearly made for you, can still be worn by someone who isn't queen. Even by someone who has made a few mistakes in her day."

For someone who came off as a young Hugh Grant, with

the cheeky wit to match, Greyson's little brother was surprisingly wise. Perhaps he would make a fantastic king after all. "Thanks Harrison."

Once back in her rooms, Scarlett opened the garment bag that had magically appeared by care of a maid. She felt awful as she stared at the green-and-black plaid coatdress. She had picked it under the careful eye of the queen, and now the shopping trip Scarlett thought she would always hold dear was tainted by lies and made her hate the outfit. But what choice did she have? It was the only thing socially acceptable for her to wear.

As she slipped it on over her fleece-lined tights and slip, the once-soft wool fabric now felt itchy and uncomfortable. The perfect flare of the skirt that highlighted her nipped-in waist now looked frumpy. And the tiny black buttons with the *fleur de lis* design now appeared cheap. It was funny how much emotion clothes held. Before, when she'd wanted to impress the queen, the dress had been elegant and refined. Now, it mocked her naivety.

Scarlett reluctantly curled her hair, then attached her green velvet hat just off to the side of her head as she had seen the royals do in the magazines back in Georgia. It had a matching looped knot on the side that tied in the middle. Philipa said all Aldorian women wore hats at events outside the castle. So, Scarlett would follow the social order that was expected. But she did add red lipstick instead of the pale pink matte the queen had recommended. Scarlett's own version of rebellion. "Time to take a page out of Harrison's book."

GREYSON STROKED HIS horse, whispering soothing words to him. He would be pulling the carriage holding Greyson and Scarlett, and Greyson didn't want the horse to sense his agitation. He wasn't ready to talk to her again. It was too soon, and he was still shaken. But he was trying to bring his spirits up. The parade was his favorite part of the holidays. He tossed candy to children, shook hands with the people, and loved watching the performers who went alongside the royal carriages. It was magical.

He heard voices and looked up. Harrison and Gina were off to their own carriage, but Scarlett stood still as a statue at the base of the stone path that led to the stables, shifting from one foot to the other and fidgeting with the handle of her handbag. Like the night before, his breath and his words caught in his throat as he took her in. Scarlett was lovely. The coatdress was in his favorite deep shade of green. It brought out the roses in her cheeks and the bright red of her lipstick. Perfect red and green for the holiday. And then he remembered the conversation from the night before and how she'd joined forces with his mother. *Princess Syndrome* had struck another victim.

"Hi, Greyson," she said softly, stepping closer. "You look handsome. I like that coat. Maybe you can bring it back with you to the States. I know it doesn't get this cold in Georgia, but—"

"I like my leather jacket, thank you," he said with a little more coldness than he'd meant. "You're lovely as ever."

"I like your leather jacket as well. It's nice to have different looks, right?"

"Right. Well, we need to get going. The parade will be starting soon." He opened the polished black carriage door for her, then grabbed the matching faux fur blanket off the seat. When she had settled herself in place, he held it up to her. "We wouldn't want you getting cold."

"Thank you, that's very considerate."

Greyson sat next to her, then told the driver to go. The horses began to trot slowly. Eventually, they joined the line setting up for the parade. While he wished things between them weren't so frosty, he couldn't bring himself to talk to her or bridge the mere foot between them.

"Greyson, before we start moving, I just want to say...last night, I seriously overstepped. You were right. I never should've doubted you. I think I just got caught up in all of this," she said, waving her hand around the air. "I talked to Harrison. He helped me see, despite your warning, I did get played by your mama. And I don't need to be a princess. And the tiara, it was heavy. Personally, I wasn't a fan."

He wanted so desperately for her words to be true, to have the girl who'd fallen for him as a construction worker back. He was searching her face, trying to see the woman who'd captured him to the very soul. And with tears starting to come down her face, he felt like he found her. She'd admitted she was wrong, which was more than Arielle had done. He'd been harsh and quick, and it was possible he too had been caught up in all of it.

"Scarlett," he began slowly. "Maybe I'm partially to

blame here. I threw you into this circus, not even telling you about my home until we were practically on the plane. I should've warned you in advance. I just don't want to fight with you. This is one of my favorite Aldorian traditions and I'd love to share it with you."

Scarlett visibly relaxed, placing a hand on his arm. "I never should've gotten involved in your family matters. You're right… I just got here and I had no business butting in. I don't know this country. I mean, Betsy told me to stay out of it, and I just should've listened—"

"Wait, what?"

"I said you were right."

Greyson rubbed his forehead. He couldn't believe what she'd just said. "Why does Betsy know about this?"

"Because I told her."

"Didn't I ask you to keep all of this a secret?" he asked, although he knew he had. He'd strictly made her promise to keep his confidence, to refrain from telling anyone about who he was until he could safely leave the castle firmly behind him. And as he gazed back at her, it felt as if Scarlett had just as quickly become a stranger. The woman he thought he knew who respected his word, respected his wishes, and listened when he spoke. This stranger—she ignored everything, as if it were nothing more than a gnat buzzing in her ear. He'd told her his mother played games. He'd told her not to talk to anyone. Yet, here she was, betraying him again. Maybe he didn't know Scarlett after all. But what he did know was their perfect bubble from Savannah was perfectly popped. He had his country to worry about now. "What if word gets out about my abdication before we have a chance to make a formal release? What if she tells others about my title? I didn't want any of that. My family, they have a plan for this. The country is delicate. What if they riot? This could cause grave consequences. We have to do it the right way. That's why I asked you to keep it quiet."

Her eyes were wide, her face growing pale. "It's just Betsy. She's not going to say anything."

"And how do I know that?"

Her brows rose. "Excuse me?"

"You heard what I said. I have met this woman twice, yet you've told her my family secrets." He didn't understand why she was defending her choice to blatantly throw away a promise. If she could brush off her earlier promises so easily, what about others? Like to be loyal, true, and to care in sickness and in health? Were those just words, too? Meaningless vows that sounded nice on the wedding video?

"I called my *best friend* and discussed a problem I was having. I have no doubt she can keep a secret because I asked her not to say anything. I trust her."

"I don't think you understand. It wasn't your problem to discuss with anyone. You knew that. I asked you not to, yet you disregarded my wishes again." He couldn't stop the rage from building in his chest, heating his face. "Is this what a future with you would be like? When I make a request, you'll instead do what you think it best, say whatever you want, despite what I've said and asked?"

"Greyson, she's my best friend," she said in a small voice.

"I tell her everything."

"So, that means you and I, will what—have nothing that's just between us?"

"What do you want me to say?"

"Nothing. I want you to say nothing." Greyson opened the carriage door, then stepped out onto the cobblestones. "I'll be walking alongside the carriages today. I think I need some air."

"No," she shouted, catching his—and everyone else's—attention around them. "You just ride in the carriage. I'm going to my room. I don't think I can fake a smile this long."

Greyson watched her stalk back inside. He should go after her. He should talk to her. But he couldn't bring himself to do it. Everything was ruined. It didn't matter how he felt toward her. He should've waited until he'd abdicated to bring her home to meet his family. Then, he'd know she wasn't trying to win his throne.

So, instead of making some grand gesture and trying to work this out, he climbed in his carriage and put on his royal smile, ignoring Harrison's worried glances. Greyson wasn't sure what there was to work out. It all seemed pretty clear to him.

He'd finish the parade, then head to the stables. One of the pens looked a little loose, and he could use a way to blow off some steam. Nothing did that better than a hammer. Though, at this moment, it seemed like Scarlett was the one with the hammer...and she was aiming straight for his heart. He'd trusted her blindly, and now he was paying for that leap of faith. Had she ever respected him? Would she respect him back in Georgia when he left the throne behind? Or worse, would he respect her at all after this?

SCARLETT HAD STAYED in her room the rest of the afternoon, wearing her own clothes and sitting by the window. The only person she saw was a maid who brought her a light lunch. And even then, the maid didn't say anything. It was a quiet day, but outside, there was nothing but din. She had the perfect view of the road, so she saw the royal carriages appear just as the sun began to set. She could see Greyson, all by himself, leave his seat and begin toward the stable. Harrison ran up to him and placed a hand on his shoulder, but he shook it off and stalked inside.

Even from three floors up and through a thick pane of snow-dusted glass, she knew he was still angry...and rightly so. She'd been so focused on making the royal family love her that she'd forgotten Greyson's feelings. But she'd apologized for that. She thought they could've moved on.

On the other hand, the way he'd blown up over her talking to Betsy was ridiculous. Just like he trusted her enough to bringing her to Aldora to meet his family, he should have trusted in her word that Betsy wasn't about to go run off to the tabloids. It wasn't like Scarlett had told her mother or some stranger at the airport. She'd told the one person she trusted more than anyone.

She watched the drive below slowly empty as the royal family came inside after the parade finished and all the staff dispersed, but she didn't see Greyson. By her clock's standards, they were supposed to be congregating downstairs in something called the *family sitting room* for dinner. While she knew she could find her way there somehow, she didn't feel right barging in when her one tie to the country was so angry.

But just as she turned away from the window, there was a sharp knock on the door. She hopped from the gilded chair, then sped through the sitting room. Scarlett knew it had to be Greyson there to make up. It warmed her to think there was a chance to salvage their trip after all.

"Good evening, madam." It was one of the valets in a pressed burgundy suit. "I was told to give you this and inform you that your dinner will be served to you shortly."

"Okay, I'll be done in a few minutes."

"I apologize for the confusion, ma'am, but your dinner will be served up here."

"And the family?" she asked, wondering if something had happened to postpone the meal. "Is everything all right?" Were they doing damage control for the abdication? Had she actually caused a problem by telling Betsy? Scarlett felt a wash of guilt rush over her. She truly felt like she'd been making the right decision by talking to her friend. Now, she wasn't so sure.

"They have eaten."

Scarlett's heart began to race. Had she been banned from dinner with Greyson? Was he so mad at her? What if he was, and it wasn't about damage control? The guilt quickly changed to fear. What if, once again, she'd screwed things up? Her greatest fear. "Well, maybe I can join them for dessert."

"I apologize, but that will not be possible," he said, handing her the envelope.

Scarlett took the envelope from his hand. It wasn't sealed. When she opened it, she saw it held one first-class ticket back to Savannah in her name. But it wasn't for the day after New Year like she'd expected. It was for tomorrow. Was she being banished for her mistake? She could go to Philipa, Harrison maybe, to explain she meant no harm. Promise them she could be trusted. And then, when they were back in Savannah, she and Greyson could fix things. She had to fix things. She and Greyson couldn't leave Aldora like this. "Is there any chance I can speak to anyone about this? I don't think Greyson and I need to leave so soon."

The valet cleared his throat. "No, madam, you are instructed to return to Savannah alone."

CHAPTER SIXTEEN

GREYSON WATCHED THE town car depart from the library window. The early morning light made the small courtyard glow, and he could see the footman load Scarlett's luggage into the boot. Then he saw her. For the briefest of moments, right before she entered the backseat, she had turned and looked up at the castle. He couldn't say if she was searching for him, or merely mourning the royal life she had lost.

When the car was gone, he sat heavily in one of the leather wingback chairs upholstered in a dark green. He knew he'd made the right decision in sending her away, but it didn't make it hurt any less. He had taken the coward's way out by sending a valet to do his dirty work, but he knew if he were the one who'd handed her that plane ticket, one look into those blue eyes would have broken him.

Then he thought about Savannah. While a big city by some standards, it was small enough he had run into her not once but twice without meaning to in the span of a week. Moving flats and trying his hand at living in another state was probably his best bet, but he had signed a lease and had a decent job with men he liked. And on his construction worker pay, he couldn't afford to move.

"Greyson, what's going on?"

He looked up, seeing Harrison leaning against the doorframe. "I was awakened by the sound of two maids gossiping outside my rooms. Why did Scarlett just leave on Christmas Eve of all days?"

"It's complicated."

"Try me. I'm going to be king. I hear there are complicated issues I'll have to sort out." He stepped in, then closed the library door.

"I'd rather not discuss it at present."

"That line isn't going to work on anyone. Mother already pitched a fit last night because you told us Scarlett was feeling ill and wouldn't be joining us for dinner, and now she's leaving. Unless she's on her way to hospital, I think it's best you come clean."

"We needn't discuss her again," Greyson said, his words edged in frost.

Harrison crossed to the other chair and sat. "And why's that?"

"Because she's gone and she's not coming back. She and I have decided to part ways."

Harrison's brows rose. "Why ever would you do such a foolish thing?"

"Why ever would you care?" Greyson spat back, despising his only brother wasn't instantly on his side. "You've only just met her. You've known her for a few days."

"And I've known you for the entire duration of my life, *brother*, and I think I know you well enough to tell when you're holding things back. Scarlett was good for you. Why did you let her leave?"

"I *asked* her to leave."

"Is that because you had some flash of idiocy? Should we summon the doctor?"

"Because I didn't want to go through what I did with Arielle with Scarlett," he confessed. "Scarlett proved to me that she wasn't particularly keen on my stepping down and allowing you to take over. It seemed she rather liked wearing the crown."

Harrison snorted with a roll of his eyes. "Everyone likes wearing the crown. Even you enjoy wearing the crown. Doesn't seem reason to toss her."

"She and I have parted ways, and that's that."

"Over a simple misunderstanding?"

"You don't know it's a misunderstanding."

"What I do know is you brought a lovely woman home for Christmas. She and you seem to be a perfect couple, and she managed to spend a day with Mother without pulling her own hair out. Now, have you given it some thought that our dear mother may have had something to do with this?"

"Of course I have," Greyson admitted. "I can almost certainly guarantee that's what happened. I warned Scarlett something like this would happen. I asked her to stay by my side, respect me, and she chose to go clear to the other side."

"Grey," Harrison said, placing an arm on his shoulder. "Go speak to her. Rush to the airport—do one of those grand gestures in the movies Gran used to make us watch."

"And then what? Continue the relationship always wondering if she is disappointed in me? Knowing she'd rather have the crown? What if she is one of the Americans simply looking for a title?" Greyson said, rising from his seat. "What was between Scarlett and me was just so, between *us*. You'd do well to remember where *your* loyalties lie, because *she* certainly didn't. I asked her to keep this whole royal thing a secret, and she couldn't even do that."

"That wasn't fair of you. It's quite the secret."

"It doesn't matter. She agreed," he insisted stubbornly.

"How could you be so brilliant in every aspect of your life, yet this hopeless when it comes to love?"

"Because, brother, women are hopeless."

"No, Greyson, it's you who is hopeless. As am I, I suppose." Harrison's voice was flat, devoid of any emotion.

"What's going on?"

"Nothing. I just…I have a lot on my mind."

"You know another way to sort things out? Discussing them with your wildly helpful brother."

"Do we have some other sibling I don't know about?"

"Don't joke, Harrison. What's the matter?"

"I don't know how to tell you this, so I'll just come out with it. I can't rule. I've been fooling myself, but I'm not you."

Greyson started. Out of everything Harrison could have said, that surprised him the most. "What're you saying? You've said multiple times you're ready. This is just cold feet."

"And Grey, how is that different from what you're doing? You've always wanted to be king."

Greyson didn't have an answer. He stared at his feet, trying to find one, searching for some brotherly advice. Trying desperately to tell him it'd be okay. But, as he began to open his mouth, everything he wanted to say could be used for his own circumstance. How could he tell his brother it'd be different when he was ruling? That it was okay he was nervous now because at the end of the day, ruling was in his blood. That he'd been training for this since he was born. That he was a natural.

He leaned against the desk across from Harrison, studying his younger brother. Instead of seeing the future ruler, Greyson saw the pudge of baby fat still in Harrison's cheeks. Greyson saw stress lines by his brother's eyes. He saw a kid. It'd be irresponsible to expect Harrison to take control of everything.

"Grey," Harrison said. "You had a fit, I get it. But I think it's time for you to return home and take your place as king. The role was never meant for the spare, and I don't have your way with people. More than that, I think you'll regret giving it up. And I'm not saying this for Mother's benefit. I'm saying this because I legitimately think it. You're my best mate, always have been, and I know I'm nowhere near up for the job like you."

"You truly think I can do this?"

"I always have."

Greyson nodded, feeling some of the weight slip off his shoulders. He didn't know how or why, but Harrison calling him out on his fears and asserting Greyson could take on the crown put everything he had felt the past few months into perspective. "But Harrison, I can't do what I want to do and rule."

"Why? You're in charge. If you want to meet with the people and fix roofs, go do that. Believe it or not, you don't have to be the monarch Father is."

"I guess I just…"

"I know. It's a lot of responsibility. But on the bright side, while I'm not meant to rule, I have been by your side since I was born, and I'm not just going to leave it because you put on a bigger crown than me. I'm here to help you. Don't you think two Montgomerys are better than one?"

"Of course I do."

"Then think about it, Grey."

And Greyson did. True, he'd left because he'd been scared. He'd wanted to find who he was. He'd wanted to live his own life. But Harrison was right—Greyson could still do that. He could be his own ruler. His own man. Greyson had been a fool, a selfish one who'd hurt people in his attempt to find himself when he already had a true and firm identity. He wouldn't have to give up his passion to sit on the throne. He could bring Aldora to a new age. Turn it into something to be proud of. "You promise you won't leave me to join the circus or some other crazy idea?"

"No, if the circus has an act for me, I'm gone. But bar that, I'll be by your side the whole time."

"Done." And he was surprised at just how easy—how right—this decision felt after months of convincing himself he wanted nothing to do with being king.

Then they sat there, reminiscing about their childhood, discussing the various times they'd narrowly escaped trouble, the times Greyson had taken the fall for Harrison with their mother, and the jaunts they'd taken over the years. And then the joy ended as the queen waltzed dramatically in to the room.

"Well, I've already gone through the trouble of having the royal jeweler resize the coronation crown, so I suppose there's no going back now, is there?" Philipa asked as she threw her arms in the air, falling into a seat next to Harrison.

Greyson smiled at his mother as he stood. He kneeled beside the chair, taking her hands. "I was going to tell you I've officially decided to take the throne, but if the royal jeweler is unable to resize the crown, then I guess Harrison will just have to do."

Her eyes widened. "Greyson Charles Rudolf Leopold Montgomery, don't you play with my heart. I've been feeling faint this morning."

"Mother, I would never play with your emotions. I thought…I thought I had no choice but to step down, but if you can forgive me, I'd like to formerly accept the throne tonight." He'd said it to someone other than Harrison. There would be no going back now.

"Oh, my boy, of course I can forgive you. We must speak, though. Harrison, would you give us the room?"

"Sure. Now that he's agreeing to take the throne, I'm quite certain you won't murder him in a fit of rage and emotions."

"Why must everything be difficult with you, Harrison?"

"I suppose it is because I take after you, Mother. Dramatics and all."

"I wanted to apologize," she said when Harrison left. "I rather liked Scarlett. She would have made a beautiful queen by your side. True, she wasn't royal, but there was good breeding there."

His chest tightened as he dropped back into his seat. He was sick to death of being reminded about Scarlett, and she'd only been gone from the castle an hour. "Mother, enough."

"Greyson, I just want to see you happy. Scarlett agreed you'd have made a wonderful king. That's why she spoke to you about it. Yes, I pushed her, but I genuinely think she had your best wishes at heart."

"I made such a mess of it all, and I just don't know if I can trust her after all this. She went against my wishes repeatedly."

"Yes, and I go against your father's daily. You don't want a woman who only does what you say, when you say it. You want one with her own mind. Scarlett has manners, beauty, and opinions, but she isn't perfect. Neither are you, my sweet boy."

Her words filled him with guilt. To him, Scarlett *was* perfect. His own insecurities and fear had spoiled everything, not that his mother had helped. "That all may be true, but I did not exactly leave her in the best way."

"Aldora may not be the most technically savvy place in the world, but we do have telephones. Call her before the plane takes off. Tell her you overreacted, and you were a fool for sending her away. Or she's too good for you... That you're going to rule a country, and you'd like her by your side...if you do want her by your side."

Greyson did, more than anything. He didn't care if she was beside him in his flat in Georgia or if she sat on the throne next to his. He loved her dearly, yet he had pushed her away just because she'd sought the help of a friend. The weight of the crown and all that went with it had been too heavy for him to carry, and he'd punished Scarlett for seeking help in bearing the load. He was a hypocrite. But more than that, he was desperate. Desperate to get her back. He'd promise to apologize every day if she'd just take him back. He'd get her pastries from the bakery every morning. Take Blitzen on runs every night. He'd do whatever he needed to if it meant he'd get her back. "I did overreact, didn't I? However, I am not sure if I'm ready for marriage…or even if she would be. We've only just met."

"And if you don't bring her back, you'll never have the chance to know. Though, if I'm being honest, I don't think you would have brought her home to meet us if you weren't at least considering she was the girl for you."

He laughed lowly. "How do you know I didn't bring her home to irritate you?"

She smiled. "Because you aren't Harrison."

"That's true." Greyson laughed with her, but it wasn't a real one. It didn't come from his belly, squint up his eyes, or take him over. Instead, fear was rampant inside him. He could admit he'd made a mistake—he could beg her to come back—but that didn't mean she would. What would his life be like without her? How could he love another, knowing how he cared for Scarlett? Every other woman would feel like second best. Greyson, a scared little boy, sitting where a man previously had, looked up to his mother—not the queen, but his mum. "Do you truly think she'd give me another chance?"

"You won't know until you ask. But Greyson, I think that girl loves you, too."

He pulled his phone from his pocket, hurriedly unlocking it. His thumb hovered over the call button, the screen showing Scarlett's number.

Greyson took a deep breath. He'd do it. He'd reach out. Do what he needed to in order to get her to trust him again. How could he have let his insecurities affect his relationship? He called her. But as soon as it connected, he heard her voice mail.

Swallowing the lump in his throat, he hung up on the disembodied voice and then looked up the number for the Aldorian airport next. But when the man on the other end said the plane had already taken off, he lost all hope.

"She's gone," he whispered.

"You can always ring her later when the plane lands."

"By then, she'll decide she hates me…and then there's the announcement this evening and the coronation… I don't know what to do."

"She met you as a non-royal, a construction worker, then knew you as a prince." Taking his hand, she held it tightly. "And when you go to her as a king with a country behind you and a future before you that you ask her to share in, I believe Scarlett will forgive you."

CHAPTER SEVENTEEN

G REYSON COULDN'T THINK about anything but Scarlett. As he oversaw the pressing of his suit for the Christmas Eve ball and later dressed, all he could see was Scarlett's stricken face as she'd climbed into the car.

He needed to focus on the night's events, as it would be the end of his life as he knew it and the beginning of his destiny. Greyson left his chambers for the appointed room beside the ballroom, where they would then make their grand entrances. Harrison would enter, then him, and then his parents, and when everyone was firmly in the holiday spirit, his father would make the announcement.

While he wasn't particularly keen on attending a massive party in the same ballroom he had promised to show to Scarlett from their hidden alcove, Greyson knew he could handle it. And as soon as he was announced and he stepped down the massive stairs to the throng of people, he slipped through them and took a seat against the far wall. Half hidden by a massive Christmas tree, he was content to watch the party and be alone with his thoughts.

He'd been contemplating his mother's words that it was never too late. If he trusted his instincts, he had to go see Scarlett face to face. As soon as he could get away, he'd take the royal plane to Savannah. He'd beg on his knees for her to forgive him. He'd promise to never let his mother put a wedge between them. And he'd promise never to dismiss her so quickly again.

If she didn't allow him back into her life, then he'd go from there. However, he had to try. But the very idea of it was making him bounce inside, and he didn't know how he was going to wait. He'd find someone to call and make the arrangements at once so he could leave as soon as the ball ended. With any luck, he'd be by her side in Savannah soon.

Then, the trumpeters began a long and overdone introduction. People had been using the herald for the usual introductions, but the trumpets were saved for the royals' grand entrances. Greyson crept out of the shadows to see who'd been invited. He thought he knew the guest list, and there was no one who warranted the brass. It had all been executed too quickly for their prince cousins in England to arrive or any other royal heads of state.

But then he laid eyes on the only person who deserved such fanfare.

SCARLETT STOOD ON the stairs, listening to the trumpeters bellowing out a greeting. When she had made the decision to stay in Aldora and had watched the plane to Georgia take off without her, she hadn't had a plan. All she knew was she couldn't leave her heart in Aldora.

Even after she had gotten a cab to the castle, no one had been willing to let her in. She'd insisted the family knew who she was and had begged to speak to Harrison. They'd all brushed her off, some threatening to have the guards throw her out. It was by a stroke of sheer luck that word of her arrival had made its way to Harrison, just he'd been leaving his rooms to go down to the ball. With his word, she had been allowed entry and her presence wasn't told to Greyson.

Now, as part of her hastily cooked plan, she scanned the ballroom, the beautiful dresses, the elegant linens, the tuxes, the trees, and the chandeliers, but she wasn't looking at their beauty. This time, she was searching for one man standing among them.

She was dressed for her missed flight in a pair of jeans and a cardigan. Her hair was in a loose ponytail, and she wasn't wearing any makeup. She wanted to prove to Greyson that none of the finery mattered to her. She didn't need to be a queen, and she definitely didn't need him to be a king. She just needed *him*.

Finally, she saw him pushing through the silent, staring crowd, then he was running in her direction. Scarlett wanted to rush down the stairs, but kept to a slower pace, nervous about what would happen when he saw her. She was taking a risk. What if he was embarrassed by her? What if he yelled at her to leave or called for the guards? What if he didn't want to see her at all?

"Scarlett, what are you doing here?" Greyson asked breathlessly as he reached her. His gray eyes scanned her face as if he couldn't decide if she was real.

"I'm apologizing. I don't care about the title. If you want to give it up, then that's your choice and I never should have questioned you. I just...I was doing it...I mean, it was coming from a good place. I promise. I never should have—"

"No, I never should have asked you to leave. We should have spoken of it, and I cannot believe I did that to you." Greyson wrapped his arms around Scarlett's waist, then pulled her tightly to his chest.

She melted in his arms, grateful to feel peace for the first time in twenty-four hours. Not only was he not angry with her, but he also regretted his actions. It was the best possible scenario. She'd been so afraid she'd lost him forever, but here he was, holding her tight, keeping her safe in his arms, grateful she'd snuck into the palace and kind of illegally crashed the palace ball.

"I want a life with you, darling," he continued. "I want to learn how to cook, take Blitz for walks, and figure out how to have a proper picnic. I want to get to know Betsy more because if you love her, she must be amazing. Maybe we can even find a duke or something for her to marry. I don't know. But I do know I want to spend several days, weeks, months, or years convincing your mother I am worthy of you."

Tears welled, and she blinked them away. Her heart was fit to burst at his declaration. Just when she thought he couldn't be more perfect. He didn't even hate her mama. He wanted to make it work, not just with her, but with everyone in his life. Maybe she could make it work. Maybe he was the man she could make it work with. And that thought sent her soaring high with such elation she was afraid her feet would float off the ground "Then let's go home. Back to Savannah.

We'll leave the crowns here."

He slowly shook his head. "I can't do that. When I make my announcement, you'll know why."

For a moment, her stomach flipped. Was he refusing to come with her? Was he going to send her away again? "What do you mean?"

Greyson didn't answer her. He raised his hand to silence the last of the whispers. "My dear friends and family, I stand before you as your humble servant. From birth, I have been extraordinarily lucky in being able to live in Aldora and know its history and people. We are a small nation, but a proud one who is growing in the world's esteem every day. And now the most important woman in my life is here—" he paused and took Scarlett's hand, "—I can now announce that on the New Year, I shall be crowned king."

The cheers and applause were deafening, and Scarlett thought she would faint. She had come all the way to the castle to fetch her construction worker, but she'd ended up side by side with a future king.

His father then began his own speech on the other side of the room. From his stage, he went on about how proud he was of Aldora and how, while it pained him to step down, he knew his son was perfect. But as it continued, Scarlett couldn't concentrate. She was too focused on Greyson.

"What are you doing?" she asked. "I thought—"

"You were right, Scarlett. I couldn't give up the crown when I have so much to give to my people. My only regret is it took me sending you away to see it. I tried to contact you, to bring you back, but the flight took off before I had a chance. After the announcement, I'd planned to go straight to Georgia to beg for another chance."

She clung to his jacket, almost afraid if she let go, he would disappear. "I couldn't leave."

"And I'm grateful. I'll never let you out my sight again. Not that I would want to, since you look so beautiful. I'm quite jealous of how comfortable you must be."

"I just want you to know I don't need any of the royal package to be happy. Yes, the crowns and the jewels are all lovely, but I am just as happy in jeans and a T-shirt." Scarlett needed him to know. She couldn't let him walk away thinking she'd come back to force him to be king. She wanted him as he was—*needed* him as he was. And now that he'd forgiven her, and her him, she wanted to start her regular life with him.

He cupped her cheek, his thumb wiping away a stray tear. "I know that. I always knew that, deep down. I was just being ridiculous."

"Then you forgive me?" she dared ask.

He smiled down at her, his arm tightening around her middle. "There's nothing to forgive. Besides, I shouldn't have forced silence on you. If you trust Betsy, then I do. It was wrong of me to expect you to carry the weight of my secret alone when I refused to do the same."

Tears welled up in Scarlett's eyes as all the drama just passed over them like a rapidly moving storm cloud.

"What I need to know now, Scarlett, is do you forgive me?"

"Of course, Greyson."

"I love you."

"And I love you." She stood on her toes to kiss him, but a familiar voice cut in.

"Scarlett," Harrison boomed. "I am thrilled to see you. I had no idea you were coming."

"Of course, Prince Harrison." She bobbed in a dramatic curtsy, her hands holding the hem of an imaginary gown.

"You helped her into the castle, didn't you?" Greyson asked.

Harrison shrugged. "Little bit, yes. You two just needed a push, and I was feeling particularly violent. Now, I hate to be a stick in the mud, as you look lovely and I do appreciate the point you were trying to make here, but before Mother has an absolute panic attack, Gina has a few dresses upstairs if you'd like to slip into something a little, well, dressy?"

As if on cue, Gina appeared at his side in a whirl of vivid red silk. The neckline was plunging, the sleeves skimming her arms just below her shoulders. Her smiling mouth was painted in the same shade as the full skirts, and she tucked a brown curl behind her ear. "Scarlett, marvelous to see you."

"Hi, Gina."

However, a hand took her forearm and turned her around. It was the queen. "My dear Scarlett, it is lovely to see you. But please, allow me to take care of you personally. We have some catching up to do, and I think some serious apologies are in order."

"I'll come with you, Your Majesty," Gina said, taking Scarlett's arm on her other side. "And Scarlett, please, call me your fairy godmother. I always travel with lots of options, and we appear to be of comparable size. Now, if you boys will excuse us, I need to get Cinderella ready for the ball."

GREYSON COULDN'T CONTAIN himself as he paced the length of hall beside the ballroom. He couldn't just stand downstairs and wait for her. He had enough of waiting, and he never wanted to make another grand entrance without her at his side. He hadn't lost her. And she wanted Greyson and not just the crown prince. The jeans had been a perfect move. Greyson was sure she'd been significantly mortified at the idea of entering a ball dressed as so, but he'd thought it was just the thing. If he were honest with himself, she'd look just as beautiful in the dress as she had when he'd seen her on the staircase, with the light shining bright behind her and the air of confidence she'd felt being just who she was. It was breathtaking.

But when Scarlett entered in a ball gown, he quickly realized how naïve he was and just how much he'd underestimated her beauty. She was dressed in a gown of brilliant cobalt blue that made her eyes even more luminous than ever. The hem swept the floor as she walked toward him, flashing the toes of her golden shoes. Her hair was wavy and loose around her bare shoulders, held away from her face by a gold headband marked with gems. A band of the same kind rounded her waist and she toyed with one of the off-the-shoulder straps, flashing a golden cuff.

"Scarlett, you look…you look…well, you don't look like a princess at all." He circled her, scrunching his nose. "No, you look every bit like a queen." He offered her his arm. "Now, please, allow me to escort you into the ball. I'm quite eager to make everyone jealous as I expertly lead you through the dance floor."

"Then we can't disappoint. Game face on," Scarlett said as she smiled big, pushed her shoulders back, and raised her chin slightly.

His chest filled with pride as they returned to ball, without the bellowing horns and fanfare that usually accompanied his arrival. But even without the ordeal, the guests still turned to watch them descend the staircase. He couldn't blame him, as Scarlett was an absolute vision.

As soon as their feet hit the floor, they whirled into a waltz, intermingling with the other dancers. Just as before, they were perfectly in sync, each step coming in tune. And although they were in a room packed with people, it was as if there were no one else in the world. Now that Scarlett was in his arms, he was never going to let her leave.

CHAPTER EIGHTEEN

S CARLETT SAT IN one of the deep red wood pews of the throne room, then turned to look over at the doors behind them. It seemed as though everyone in the kingdom sat or stood waiting for the royal family to arrive.

The room was festooned in gold and burgundy, the colors draping from the arched ceilings and falling to either side of the set of thrones at the head. It was evening, the traditional time of a coronation in Aldora. Gina had explained the king was always crowned on the night of the New Year, symbolically beginning a fresh era just as the clock struck midnight.

All the guests had eaten a late dinner at the castle, then enjoyed the traditional twelve desserts of Aldora before assembling in the throne room. The royals were absent for all of it. In fact, she hadn't seen Greyson for two days. He had told her there were some secret pre-coronation things he needed to take care of.

But at least Gina was always there. She'd loaned Scarlett another gown for the event, a buttery-soft champagne number with a V-neckline, a shimmering overlay, and a train that fell behind her like waves when she walked. The queen had loaned her a pair of rather flashy diamond earrings and even offered a tiara to match, but Scarlett hadn't wanted any more attention on her. It was Greyson's night.

When the doors opened and the trumpeters announced the entrance of the royal family, everyone stood. Scarlett's heart hammered madly as the king and queen passed, both wearing crowns of gold and ermine capes befitting their status. Then Harrison followed, looking a little more serious than usual in a military-style suit he'd told Scarlett itched like mad and made him feel like a boy playing dress-up.

Then Greyson appeared, and an unseen choir began a low melody in Latin that sent a chill down her spine. He walked slower than the others, taking his time as he strolled the length of the pews. But as he came beside Scarlett, he smiled for just a moment before stepping beside his parents and brother. Then the guests all sat as one.

"Today, I end my reign as King of Aldora to pass our land to my son, Prince Greyson, of my own free will and with all powers invested in me by our blood and birthright." The king nodded, and a line of footmen appeared. With some ceremony, they removed the cloaks and crowns, bearing them back down the hall and out the doors. Then the royals left and sat in the first row of pews opposite Scarlett, save for Greyson.

The doors swung open and a party strode in, headed by a tall man in a black suit who looked to be not a day over a hundred. Even more footmen, each carrying either a crown, a sword, or a robe followed him, and he joined Greyson on the platform. Greyson kneeled before him, his head down.

"Greyson Charles Rudolf Leopold Montgomery," the tall

man bellowed, "are you of pure mind and pure spirit?"

"I am," Greyson replied.

"And do you come this day with a heart for service for your country?"

"I do."

"Will you serve Aldora faithfully and with mercy, justice, and the utmost wisdom of your birthright?"

"I will."

"With your promises, I cover thee with the mantle of your birthright so you may always know the love and weight of your nation." A footman held out the ermine-trimmed cloak, and the speaker spread the red robe over Greyson's shoulders. "And in your hands, I pass to thee the symbol of your strength so you may always protect your people." The sword came next. "And now I place the crown upon your head, the final icon of your position, and ask you to stand, King Greyson of Aldora!"

Greyson rose to his feet, turning to face the cheering crowd. Scarlett wiped away stray tears, as did many others. He looked out among his people until his gaze settled on her. He spoke with a smile. "I promise you, people of Aldora, I will be a fair king and a just one. I will do my utmost to bring honor to our nation, but there is one thing I must do before I truly feel able to rule." He allowed everyone to titter for only a moment before he said, "Scarlett, please join me."

She sat there, stunned, until Gina gave her a small shove. She half stumbled into the walkway, then straightened as she walked toward him. He looked so imposing with his crown and sword, but his smile melted her heart. When she stood beside him, he dropped to one knee, making all the assembled guests gasp. She almost wanted him to rise as she gazed down at the lavers of red velvet and ermine that pooled on the floor.

"My darling Scarlett." He held something that glittered in the candlelight. It was *her* mother's ring. "Our time has been brief, but it has also been the most meaningful time of my life. You helped to show me not only who I was, but also who I can become. In this moment, I am sure of everything in my life, especially who I wish to share it with. Scarlett, will you marry me? Will you not only be the queen of my heart, but also the queen of Aldora?"

She opened her mouth to reply, but only a small sob escaped at first. "Really? You want to marry me? How in the world did you get my mama's ring?"

"That secret pre-coronation errand I had to complete? It was actually a trip to Savannah. I spoke with your parents, and I brought them back with me."

"You did?" She gazed over the faces of the crowd, spotting who she was searching for. Tucked among the hundreds of guests were her parents and Betsy, all dressed for the occasion and grinning like crazy. Scarlett turned back to Greyson, still dizzy with the reality that a king kneeled before her. "I can't believe you did that."

"For you, I would do anything. Marry me, Scarlett."

"Yes," she cried, trying to control her emotions as he slid the ring on her finger. The rose gold held a large diamond surrounded by a cadenza halo, each peak of gently pointed arches surrounding yet another small diamond, making the entire thing sparkle more than any royal tiara. "Of course I'll marry you, Greyson!"

Beaming, he rose to his feet and wound his arms around her waist. He picked her up, twirling her as she laughed aloud, before setting her on her feet and kissing her. The feeling of the moment encompassing her, Scarlett welcomed the warmth of being so utterly loved.

It was then the clock struck midnight, fireworks exploding outside the wall of windows overlooking the mountaintops. Flakes of gold like falling snow drifted from the ceiling, surrounding them all on a glittering storm of merriment. The people cheered as Scarlett and Greyson kissed again, and she decided once and for all that she *did* believe in fairy tales.

EPILOGUE

Four Months Later

SCARLETT SAT AT the desk she'd taken over, planning her first big charity event for the orphanage in town. Blitz laid curled at her feet, quite enjoying his role as the crowned puppy of Aldora. She was working on some of the particulars for the dinner when Greyson walked into the room.

"Aren't you just stunning?"

"Don't tease," she said, brushing the hair from her face. She had been at a meeting with the wedding planner late into the night, and she knew she probably looked as tired as she felt.

"I mean it. Just seeing you takes my breath away."

She smiled, knowing how he felt. In truth, just looking at him did the same thing. She was distracted whenever he was around. This dinner was never going to get planned at this rate, let alone their wedding.

"I see you're hard at work, and I respect that, but you and I have some plans this afternoon."

"It wasn't on the itinerary for the day," she said, glancing at her planner. "What's going on? Is there a meeting? Will I have time to change?"

"Like I said before, you're beautiful."

"Actually, you said I was stunning. Beautiful is good, but stunning is a much better word."

"Well, allow me to make it up to you. We're going on an excursion. You're going to need jeans, boots, and your riding jacket."

"Are you going to tell me anything else? Like where we're going?"

"No. Just get dressed."

Scarlett did as she was told. When she found Greyson, he was sitting astride his motorcycle before the castle steps, waiting for her. She pulled on her pink helmet and climbed on, wrapping her arms around his middle. They drove off through winding roads without the guards, without anything. Just the two of them.

But they didn't go far, just a few miles toward the mountains. She knew it was still part of the royal estate, but she hadn't ventured that far back. And as he brought the bike to a stop and they climbed off, she couldn't imagine what the surprise was.

"I'm not particularly good at waiting. What's going on?" she asked.

The corners of his lips curled into a smile. "It's a secret."

"And I hate secrets."

"Too bad, because, as you know, I'm fantastic at setting up some pretty memorable ones."

"That's the understatement of the century," she said with a small laugh as he took her hand in his.

The day was warm, the spring flowers in full bloom. Dots of red, white, pink, and blue littered the grass and crept over the hills. Their scent washed over her, and she tilted her face up to bask in the sunlight as they walked. The view was beautiful and the silence a stark but welcome change to the castle, but she didn't understand what the surprise was.

"Greyson, what are we doing here?"

"You came to Aldora with me and left a few dreams behind. How can I call myself the man for you if I were to jeopardize your dreams just to make sure mine happened?"

"What dream?"

"See for yourself."

Greyson took a set of papers from the inner pocket of his jacket, then handed them to her. On the first page was a drawing of the Victorian house she loved so much. Then she flipped to the second. "It's the blueprints for my bed and breakfast."

"It is, and I'm going to build it here."

"You are?"

"Yes. But there's more. I've been planning with Betsy...and her visa will come through any day now. She'll be living here with us as a guest and your formal companion."

"But the house—"

"Will be yours to do with what you please. It could be a guesthouse for important dignitaries, or just your family. Or it could be for us. It'll be done by Christmas, by the wedding even."

"Could we live here?" she asked, hoping against all hope she could have her own corner of Savannah in Aldora. "I assumed we'd have to stay in the castle."

"Darling, when you're the queen, you'll make the rules. Besides, we'll only be in the backyard."

"Some backyard."

Laughing, he drew her close. "So, what do you say?

"I don't know what to say," she said honestly. With Greyson, life was one beautiful surprise after another. She'd given up on that dream, forcing herself to become the perfect queen of Aldora. But with Greyson, it seemed she could have both. She knew people said it was possible to have more than one dream come true, but she'd never imagined herself that lucky. That was until she'd met the one man who was more than eager to ensure all of her dreams came true.

"Say you're happy. Say it'll do, even if it isn't the house in Savannah. Say I haven't overstepped my bounds. Say you'll be the happiest wife a man could ask for."

"You know, I would have stayed here and married you without the promise of the house, Greyson."

"But it'll certainly help, won't it?"

She giggled, leaning her head on his shoulder. "I can't believe I'll be missus...are you still a Montgomery?"

"Yes, Scarlett. You'll be Her Royal Highness Scarlett Montgomery, Queen of Aldora."

"Royal Highness?" She looked up at him. "That's a lot to take in."

"Your mum was exceedingly fond of the idea when I went to Savannah to ask for their blessing."

"That's why she gave you the ring, huh?"

"It didn't hurt. So, are you ready to head to back to the castle?"

She shook her head and sat in the grass, pulling Greyson down with her. "Not just yet. I want to sit here in the flowers, imagining just what this place will look like." Then she laid back, the leaves and petals tickling her cheeks. Greyson lay beside her and interlaced their fingers, his thumb running over the back of her hand.

Scarlett laid there, visualizing what was to come, thinking about how her dreams had changed. She'd wanted to run the bed and breakfast to show people warm hospitality, thinking it was the best job for her skills. But now, with the prospect of being a queen laying in front of her, she was terrified. Her heart pounded in her chest. "Greyson, do you think I'll be a good queen?"

"Scarlett, I have no doubt you'll be one of the best queens Aldora has ever seen. You've basically been trained for this your entire life. You know how to entertain, you're ridiculously intelligent, you'll look beautiful in the crown, and you bring out the best in me. After all, you saw the king in me before I did. What more could I ask for than a queen who believes in me?"

"Will the people accept an American? I mean, I know your mother was a non-royal, so I'm not worried about that, but—"

"But nothing. Yes, you're an American. You'll learn the country. You have the former crown's support and my support. The people will take our lead."

"And if they don't?"

"Blitz will win them over for you."

Scarlett laughed, a calm settling over her. She was excited

for it all to start, but she didn't exactly know where. But she'd figure it out. For now, she was debating which way she wanted their bedroom to face in order to get just the right amount of sun through the yellow lace curtains she intended to hang.

Their bedroom. Scarlett turned her head to look at Greyson, everything coming into perspective. She could handle anything as long as he was by her side. And just think, she'd almost lost him. As the sun's warmth spread through her, mixing with the heat that came from being loved, Scarlett was grateful she hadn't been royally abandoned.

THE END

If you enjoyed this book, please leave a review at your favorite online retailer!

Even if it's just a sentence or two it makes all the difference.

Thanks for reading *Royally Abandoned* by Sarah Fischer and Kelsey McKnight!

Discover your next romance at TulePublishing.com.

TULE
PUBLISHING

More books by Sarah Fischer and Kelsey McKnight

Cupid Clause

Available now at your favorite online retailer!

If you enjoyed *Royally Abandoned*, you'll love Kelsey McKnight's

The What Happens series

Book 1: *What Happens in the Highlands*

Book 2: *What Happens in the Ruins*

Book 3: *What Happens in the Castle*

Available now at your favorite online retailer!

ABOUT SARAH FISCHER

Sarah Fischer works hard fighting the good fight in personnel security. She graduated with a degree in criminal justice and married the calm to her crazy. Then Sarah had a health scare and needed heart surgery. While recovering, she finally had the time to write the stories playing out in her mind.

Her college romantic suspense series, Elton Hall Chronicles, is now available in its entirety on Amazon. First Semester, Second Snowfall, and Third Wheel remind you what you loved about college, show you what you missed, and make you yearn for what could have been. Sarah also has a contemporary short story in the Craving Bad anthology.

In her spare time, you'll find her with a book in her hand, at the movies, or watching just one more episode of reality tv.

ABOUT KELSEY MCKNIGHT

From Scottish lairds to billionaire businessmen, Kelsey McKnight will ignite your soul, no matter what century it lives in.

Kelsey is a university-educated historian from southern New Jersey. She has married her great loves of romance, history, and literature to create her own tales of dashing heroes, sultry bad boys, and lovable heroines who have their own stories to tell. They will take you through the ballrooms of Victorian London, to the hills of the Scottish Highlands, and into New York City penthouses, all at the flip of a page.

When she's not writing, Kelsey can be found reading, drinking too much coffee, spending time with her family, and working for two separate nonprofit organizations.

Thank you for reading

Royally Abandoned

If you enjoyed this book, you can find more from all our great authors at TulePublishing.com, or from your favorite online retailer.

TULE
PUBLISHING

CPSIA information can be obtained
at www.ICGtesting.com
Printed in the USA
BVHW030028021019
559923BV00013B/12/P